LOVE LIFE

Also by Ray Kluun

Help, I Got My Wife Pregnant
The Widower

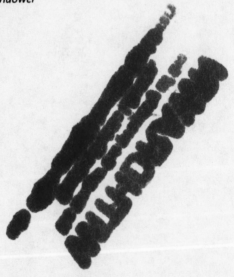

Ray Kluun

LOVE LIFE

Translated from the Dutch
by Shaun Whiteside

 ST. MARTIN'S GRIFFIN ☈ NEW YORK

LOVE LIFE. Copyright © 2003 by Ray Kluun. Translation copyright © 2007 by Macmillan. All rights reserved. Printed in the United States of America. No part of this book may be used or reproduced in any manner whatsoever without written permission except in the case of brief quotations embodied in critical articles or reviews. For information, address St. Martin's Press, 175 Fifth Avenue, New York, N.Y. 10010.

www.stmartins.com

Library of Congress Cataloging-in-Publication Data

Kluun, Ray, 1964–
    [Komt een vrouw bij de dokter. English]
    Love life / Ray Kluun ; translated from the Dutch by Shaun Whiteside.—1st U.S. ed.
        p. cm.
    ISBN-13: 978-0-312-36681-0
    ISBN-10: 0-312-36681-7
    1. Breast—Cancer—Patients—Fiction. 2. Breast—Cancer—Patients—Family relationships—Fiction. I. Whiteside, Shaun. II. Title.

PT5882.21.L88 K6513 2007
833'.92—dc22

2007013422

First published in 2003 as *Komt Een Vrouw Bij De Dokter* by Uitgeverij Podium, Amsterdam

First U.S. Edition: August 2007

10 9 8 7 6 5 4 3 2 1

I dedicate this book to Juut and Naat

Wrample [wraempel] (n.), lit: *written sample*:
a fragment of music or text inserted into a passage of
writing. Cf. *wrample* (v.), *wrampling*. Variant on what is
known in music called hip-hop and house as a *sample*;
a fragment of music previously recorded by a third party,
which is used as a component of a new piece of music.

Mono'phobia [< Gr] (n.), morbid fear of a (sexually)
monogamous life, leading to a compulsive need for
infidelity.

Yesterday, all my troubles seemed so far away . . .

The Beatles, from 'Yesterday' (*Help*, 1965)

Contents

Part One

DAN & CARMEN

What the hell am I doing here, I don't belong here . . .

Radiohead, from 'Creep' (*Pablo Honey*, 1993)

One

The average journey time's coming down nicely, I think to myself as I walk through the revolving door of the Sint Lucas Hospital for the third time in as many days. This time we're to go to the first floor, Room 105, it says on Carmen's appointment card. The corridor where we're supposed to be is full of people. Just as we're about to ensconce ourselves in their midst, an elderly man, wearing a conspicuous toupee, points to the door with his walking-stick.

'You have to go in there first, and tell them you're here.'

We nod and nervously enter Room 105. *Dr W.H.F. Scheltema, internal specialist,* it says on the little board by the door. The room inside is the actual waiting-room – the corridor is really for the overflow, I can see now. When we come in, the average age plummets by a few decades. We get intense and compassionate looks from the other patients. Hospitals have their hierarchies too. We're clearly new here, we're the waiting-room tourists, and we don't belong here. But the cancer in Carmen's breast has other ideas.

A sixty-year-old woman in a hospital wheelchair, clutching in her bony hand the same plastic-covered appointment card as Carmen, looks us up and down brazenly. When I notice, I try to assume an air of superiority – my wife and I are young,

3

beautiful and healthy, which is more than I can say about you, you leathery heap of old wrinkles. Don't even imagine for a moment we're staying here, we'll be out of this cancer joint like a shot – but my body language won't play ball, betraying my insecurity. It's like walking into a small-town bar and realizing from the mocking glances how much you look like an overdressed Amsterdammer. I wish I hadn't picked the baggy red shirt with snakeskin laces this morning. Carmen isn't comfortable either. Reality check: from now on we really do belong here.

There's a reception desk in Room 105 as well. The nurse sitting behind it seems to read our minds. She quickly asks if we wouldn't prefer to sit in the little adjoining room. Just in time, because I can see out of the corner of my eye Carmen's welling up again. What a relief not to have to cram in among the walking corpses in the waiting-room or the corridor.

'It must have been a terrible blow, the day before yesterday,' says the nurse when she comes back with the coffee. I figure out straight away that the Carmen van Diepen case has come up at the departmental meeting. She looks at Carmen. Then at me. I try to hold myself together. A nurse I've only just met doesn't need to see how pathetic I feel.

Men who pursue a multitude of women fit neatly into two categories. Some seek their own subjective and unending dream of a woman in all women. Others are prompted by a desire to possess the endless variety of the objective female world.

Milan Kundera, from *The Unbearable Lightness of Being* (1984)

Two

I'm a hedonist with serious monophobia. The hedonist in me was bowled over by Carmen and clicked with her immediately. But from the start she's been rather less happy with my panicky angst about monogamy. At first she was sort of sympathetic to it and found my infidelity-filled relationships funny and saw it more as a challenge than a warning.

Until just a year later – we weren't living together – when it came out that I'd screwed Sharon, the receptionist at BBDvW&R/Bernilvy, the advertising agency where I worked at the time. She knew for sure, then, I'd never be faithful or even attempt to be. Years later she told me that after the Sharon episode she was on the point of dumping me, but realized she loved me too much. Instead she turned a blind eye to my infidelities and treated them like a character defect that couldn't be helped. One guy picks his nose, another plays away. Something like that. It gave her emotional protection against the idea that her husband was 'frequently sticking his dick into other women'.

Nevertheless, down the years she still threatened to leave me if I ever did anything like *that* again. She wanted to be sure I'd keep my future escapades secret from her, at the very least. And it worked.

For the next seven years we were the happiest couple in the western hemisphere and its environs.

Until three weeks ago, when Carmen rang me as Frank and I struggled to stay awake while the product manager of the Holland Casino wittered on.

It's the end of the world as we know it . . .

REM, from 'It's the End of the World as We Know It
(And I Feel Fine)' (*Document*, 1987)

Three

The people who go to casinos are Chinamen, creeps and women in viscose dresses. Not once have I seen an attractive woman in a casino. Dreadful.

So, of course, when the product manager of the Holland Casino rang us up and said that he just possibly wanted to become a client of the MIU Creative & Strategic Marketing Agency, I told him I was crazy about casinos.

▶ We, that is, Frank and I, make our living from **MIU.** People who have actually learned a craft make things. And then there are people who sell things. Less respectable, but pretty useful none the less. Frank and I don't sell things. We sell hours. And we don't even make them ourselves. The bulk of the brainwork at MIU is done by six boys and girls in their twenties, all highly strung types like Frank and I once were before we started working for ourselves. So Frank and I assemble the ideas produced by our clever twenty-year-olds, put them in a report, get our secretary Maud – a shockingly gorgeous creature – to put a pretty cover on it and present our ideas to our clients, with great aplomb. They react with terrific enthusiasm, compliment us extravagantly and then proceed to do nothing whatsoever about it. After which we start on the next lucrative report for the same client. That's how our business model works.

The Holland Casino would be good for a few hundred hours a year, we reckoned. So next morning we're sitting in the casino on the Maw Euwe-Plein in Amsterdam. The product manager wanted us to 'come and take a little look at one of his emporia'. Emporia. That's right, 'emporia'. That's the kind of word our clients use. I can't do anything about it. They probably talk about getting their 'heads around the table for a good old chinwag'.

Frank asks the questions he knows always go down well with clients, the product manager makes an attempt at the world record for information overload, and I pretend to listen. This is something I've elevated to an art form. The client thinks I'm meditating deeply about his marketing problem. The truth is I'm thinking about sex, clubbing or Ajax. Sometimes I haven't the faintest idea what a client just said, but it doesn't matter too much. Dreamy absent-mindedness combined with a frown and long, mystifying silences are prerequisites in my line of business. They even keep your hourly rates up. Just as long as I can stay awake, it'll work out, Frank always says.

I'm having a lot of trouble staying awake today. I've already yawned unmistakably, twice, to Frank's great irritation. Just as my eyelids are threatening to droop, my mobile rings. Relieved, I excuse myself and fish my phone out of my pocket. CARMEN MOB.

'Hi, lovey,' I say, turning away from the table.

My lovey's crying.

'Carm, what's up?' I ask, shocked. Frank glances at me, worried. The product manager prattles happily on. I make a 'don't worry' gesture to Frank and walk away from the table.

'I'm at the hospital. It's not good news,' she sobs.

The hospital. I'd forgotten she had to go there today. Two

days ago, when she asked me if I could see anything wrong with her nipple, which felt inflamed, I tried to persuade her it was just her period. Or maybe a scratchy bit in her bra. Nothing serious. Just like six months ago, another false alarm. I said she should go and see Dr Wolters if she was worried about it, and put her mind at rest.

I'm hopeless at dealing with bad news, and immediately try to convince myself and everyone else that everything's going to turn out just fine. Like I'm ashamed, or something, that things are sometimes irrefutably, inescapably and inevitably bloody awful. It has happened to me before, when my dad asked how NAC Breda had done and I had to tell him they'd lost 1–0 to Veendam. I felt like I'd tricked him into an own goal. Giving or getting bad news ruins your day.

'Listen, Carm, tell me calmly what they said,' I say into the phone, carefully avoiding the word 'doctor' because Frank's nearby.

'He didn't know exactly. He thought my nipple looked strange, and said he didn't entirely trust it.'

'Hmm...' I say – an oddly pessimistic remark for me. Carmen takes that as a sign she should really start panicking.

'I told you my breast felt hot!' she yells, her voice breaking. 'Damn it, I knew it wasn't good!'

'Calm down, darling, we don't really know yet,' I venture. 'Do you want me to come and join you?'

She thinks for a moment. 'No. There's nothing you can do. They're going to take blood samples, and I have to give some urine, and they'll let me know a date for an exploratory operation, like last time, remember?' She sounds a little calmer now. Talking about practical matters helps you suppress your emotions. 'It'd be brilliant if you could pick up

Luna from the crèche. And I'm not going to Brokers. I can't handle turning up there with a long face. I hope I'll be out of here before six. What'll we do about food?'

▶ Brokers, in full, is **Advertising Brokers.** It's Carmen's company. She hit on the idea when I was working for BBDvW&R/Bernilvy, the Real Madrid of the advertising world, as we called ourselves. Carmen used to get incredibly annoyed with that cliquey little world. 'Full of inflated egos that think themselves superior to their clients, their colleagues and God,' she used to say. 'Playing at being creative, when what they really want to do is drive a big fat car and earn great wads of money.' She thought it might be amusing to stir things up a bit. At one of Bernilvy's receptions she furtively asked one of our clients (B&A Central) why they didn't sell the rights to their commercials and adverts to non-competitive companies in other countries. 'A kind of brokerage of ideas, like you get with books, films and TV programmes,' she said. The client thought it was a brilliant idea, and the following day he presented it to Ramon, Bernilvy's director. For the sake of a quiet life, Ramon grudgingly agreed. Carmen set herself up. Within six months she had sold the rights for B&A Central's commercials to companies in South Africa, Malaysia and Chile. The advertising world screamed fit to bust. They thought it was vulgar, vulgar, vulgar. A cattle market. Carmen stood her ground. She'd hit pay dirt. And suddenly everyone wanted to become a client of Advertising Brokers. The advertising agencies had seen the light. Unexpectly, thanks to Carmen, they were earning about four or five times as much from their creative ideas. And their clients, who had been paying them – through gritted teeth – hourly rates far beyond what they would have paid at, say, Amsterdam's most exclusive 'men's club' (the Yab Yum), swiftly saw cash-guzzling ad campaigns bringing in the money. And all of this just because Carmen saw an opportunity to sell the ads to some company in Farawayistan. Within two years, Carmen had twenty people working for her, and clients all over the world. She enjoys her self-made career, and sometimes, if she feels like it – it has to be a nice place – she flies off to see one of her clients somewhere in the world and enjoys herself hugely. 'What a laugh, eh?' she says each time she gets a new client.

I couldn't help laughing. We never make a fuss about food. We're the sort of couple who only remember at the last minute in the evening that we have to eat something, and are genuinely gobsmacked to discover there's nothing in the house, apart from a drawer full of baby-food for Luna. Our friends tease us over how much of our weekly spend goes on Domino's Pizza, the Chinese takeaway and the corner shop.

'We'll sort out something about food. Make sure you get away soon so I can hug you. And perhaps in the end everything'll turn out for the best,' I say as airily as I can, and hang up. But my back is drenched with sweat. Something tells me that our life here has just taken a knock. I stare straight ahead. There must be something positive about all this. Later on we'll calmly set everything out in a list. Look for the upside. Something we can use to comfort Carmen, sitting there on her own in that bloody awful hospital.

Then I take a deep breath and walk back to the table where Frank is sitting with the product manager, who has just started drekking on about the problems involved in turning first-time visitors into regular customers.

You were fucking happy, but it all came to an end.

Jan Wolkers, *Turks Fruit* (1973)

Four

I park my Chevrolet Blazer opposite our house on Amstelveen-seweg, on the edge of the Amsterdamse Bos, the city forest.

I hate the Amsterdamse Bos, I hate Amstelveenseweg and I hate our house. For five years we lived in the city centre, in a first-floor flat in the Vondelstraat. Within two months of Luna's birth Carmen wanted out. She was fed up to the back teeth continually hoisting an oh-so-hip three-wheeler buggy up the stairs, having just driven around for twenty minutes looking for a parking space. And then, after the time we'd just settled down with a picnic basket and a couple of bottles of rosé on a rug in the Vondelpark, and discovered Carmen – 'No, you go and get them, Dan' – had forgotten the nappies, she launched an intensive campaign in favour of Amstelveen. A house with its own garden. In the end it turned out to be a house on Amstelveenseweg.

▶ Our **house** is number 872. It's a typical little pre-war house, beautifully renovated by the previous owners. The façade is painted black, and it has a green wooden pointed roof with white edges. The estate agent called the roof 'picturesque'. What do you mean picturesque, I thought, this isn't fucking Zaandam, it's hardly a conservation area. But Carmen's pressure to relocate grew more intense by the day, and, heck, I was reassured that at least we weren't going to end up in a dreary suburb like Het Gooi or Almere. So now we're still living in Amsterdam, but the 'feel' is seriously Amstelveen. I've felt out of place here since the get-go. The moment I drive on to the A10 viaduct out of the city I feel like I'm on safari. 'Look, a zebra,' I said the first time we went to view the house. Carmen wasn't terribly amused. No trams, but there's a bus that goes past the house. You get the idea. But hey, it's good enough for a couple of years, until MIU and Advertising Brokers mature into goldmines and we can afford a ground-floor apartment in the centre of Amsterdam, so till then, the zebra it is.

I can see by the black Beetle parked about fifty yards further along that Carmen's home already. I carry Luna out of the car, run to the front door, take a deep breath and stick the key in the lock. My nerves are more on edge than they've been since 1995, when Ajax had to defend their 1–0 lead over AC Milan in the closing minutes of the match.*

► **Luna** is my little ray of sunshine. We share a birthday. When she was born I knew immediately all my friends were guaranteed to come to my sixtieth birthday party. They won't want to miss my daughter's gorgeous, firm-bodied young girlfriends running round the place.

It seems like a perfectly normal evening. The moment Luna sees Carmen she grins, her face almost splitting in two. Carmen calls her usual drawn-out 'LUUUNAAA!', pulls a silly face, imitates Luna's waddling trot and squats down to hug her. Luna replies with an intensely happy 'MAMAAA!' This evening the scene touches me even more than usual.

---

* Champions League Fina, 24 May 1995, Wenen, Ernst Happel Stadium. 1–0 (Kluivert). Van der Sar, Reiziger, Blind, F. De Boer, Rijkaard, Seedorf (Kanu), Litmanen (Kluivert), Davids, Finidi, R. De Boer, Overmars.

'Hi, my love,' I say as Carmen gets to her feet, and I kiss her on the mouth. We hug and she immediately starts crying. Bye-bye normal evening. I hold her very tightly and look over her shoulder into the void. I tell her everything will turn out fine in the end, just as it did six months ago. It's the best I've managed to come up with since this afternoon.

■

She gets into bed and I press her to me. We start to kiss. I can tell by her movements she's aroused. Without a word, I move my head towards the bottom of the bed. When she comes, she presses her dripping crotch to my face. 'Do me, now!' she whispers. We fuck hard. She senses that I'm about to come, says with yearning eyes, 'Come on, fill me up,' and with a few last hard thrusts I come, biting my lip to avoid waking Luna in the next room.

> ▶ When **Carmen** undresses in the bedroom, I look at her breasts. The first time I saw her naked, I gaped, open-mouthed, at her body. I stammered that I'd never been to bed with a body like it. She laughed and said that in Rosa's Cantina, earlier that evening, she'd noticed that I couldn't take my eyes off the canyon in her low-cut black T-shirt. After Luna's birth her breasts dropped a little, but I find them no less beautiful for that. Carmen can still turn me on just by getting undressed and revealing her fantastic tits. It's a feast every evening. Life with Carmen is always a feast for both body and soul.

Immediately after my orgasm she starts crying again.
'Come on, my darling,' I whisper. I kiss her hair and stay inside her for a few minutes.
'It's your birthday next week,' she says later when I've turned the light out. 'It might be my last time celebrating it.'

One typical mark of regret,
is that it always comes too late,
and never on time...

Extince, from 'On the Dance Floor'
(*Binnenlandse funk*, 1998)

Five

By half past three I still haven't got to sleep. I can't bear the idea of having to tell our friends and family bad news again. It's like we cheated them six months ago when we said it was a false alarm. Now we'll be suspended in uncertainty again, until the biopsy. That's happening Friday week. Ten days away. Ten fucking days waiting for an exploratory operation. They can't do it any sooner, Dr Wolters told Carmen, and ten days won't make much difference anyway, he assured us. When I got annoyed about it this evening, Carmen got snappy with me again. 'What the hell was I supposed to say, Dan? That we'll do the biopsy ourselves?' I kept my trap shut after that.

Dr Wolters. It's been six months, and I only saw him then for perhaps half an hour altogether, but I can see his face clearly before me. Roughly fifty-five, distinguished grey hair, side parting, round glasses, white jacket. Six months ago the nightmare lasted less than a week. It started with a visit by Carmen to our family doctor, Dr Bakker. He recommended we have the breast examined in hospital, just to be on the safe side. We were terrified. In the Sint Lucas Hospital we found our way to Dr Wolters. He took a look and decided Carmen should have a biopsy. That terrified us even more. Not that we knew what a biopsy was, but if you go and have something done in a hospital you've never heard of, it's bad news by definition.

Lying in the twilight of our bedroom the evening before the biopsy, I had tried not to let Carmen notice that, inside, I was howling. Earlier that evening I had seen in her eyes that she was frightened to death. And I really understood that. Because cancer kills you.

Then Wolters's words shot through me: 'The cells are restless, we don't know exactly what it is, but whatever it is it isn't *malignant*.' I remember he'd hardly said the words before we were on our feet. How relieved we were, how keen to get away, away, away from the hospital, back to our happy life, which we could go on living long and cheerfully, just as we had planned. With time on our side, and plans for a hundred thousand years.* Once outside, we collapsed into each other's arms. We were happy like we'd just had a healthy baby. I jubilantly phoned Carmen's mum, Thomas and Anne, Frank and Maud to tell them that nothing was wrong. Carmen was *healthy*.

Not malignant. Shouldn't we have grilled Wolters about not-knowing-precisely-what-it-was? Shouldn't we have insisted on getting a second opinion from another hospital? Isn't it our fault, in the end? Didn't we simply allow ourselves to be fobbed off? That Carmen was happy and relieved is

---

* Wrample from 'Een dag, zo mooi' by Tröckener Kecks (*Andere plaats, andere tijd*, 1992).

understandable enough, but shouldn't *I* have pushed for answers, shouldn't *I* have insisted he continue his investigations until he fucking well *knew* exactly what was going on? I'm the dickhead here, not Wolters. *I*'m her husband, after all. Shouldn't I be protecting her?

Perhaps it could all have been prevented, the words go crashing through my head.

It won't happen this time. If he assures us that everything's OK next week, I'm going to haul him over his desk by the lapels of his white coat. I can assure *him* of that.

A smile, that is merely parodic ...

Rita Hovink, from 'Laat me alleen' (*Een rondje van Rita*, 1976)

Six

Oncology is the name of the department of the Sint Lucas Hospital where the biopsy is being done, I see on the board above the swing door. Oncology. I know the word vaguely, but had no idea it had anything to do with cancer. It sounds so innocent. More like a science that busies itself investigating why the mammoth died out, something like that.

> ▶ **The Sint Lucas Hospital.** There are people who find the big Europarking car park the most depressing building in Amsterdam. Others go for the Nederlandsche Bank. Or the high-rises in the Bijlmer district. I invite them to visit the Sint Lucas. I come out in a rash the minute I see it stretched along the A10.

Luna is waving Elmo around in the air – she got him for her birthday last week. Carmen is sitting on the edge of the bed. She has just been weighed and had a blood sample taken. The black bag in which she put her washing things, slippers, a Persian silk nightshirt – which I didn't know she had – and a copy of *Marie Claire* is lying on the bed. I sit down next to her, still wearing my jacket, and pick up the two little leaflets that we've just been given – a green one, *Living with Cancer*, and a blue one, *Breast Cancer*. On the cover of both is a logo that I recognize from collection tins – The Queen Wilhelmina

Fund. I start flicking through the blue leaflet, the way you read the guide to Duty Free on a plane to get yourself in the mood. *Who is this brochure for?* it says at the top of the first page. I read that Carmen and I belong to the target group for this leaflet. I don't like belonging to a target group, certainly not the one for this leaflet. On the contents page I see the chapter titles, *What is cancer?*, *Prosthetic breasts* and *Conquering pain*. And why are we reading this oh-so-enjoyable material, actually? Isn't it just an exploratory operation? Couldn't we just temporarily act like everything is going to come right, like the retracted nipple on the inflamed breast – which has, over the past few days, been growing visibly redder and larger, even to my unpractised eye – might be caused by, I don't know, hormones or something?

By now it's nine o'clock, and a nurse comes in. She's carrying a folder with Carmen's name on it.

'You really *do* belong here,' I say, with a nod towards the dossier.

Carmen laughs. A little.

'The biopsy's scheduled for twelve o'clock,' says the nurse.

The nurse is about fifty. She does her best to make the routine chat as impersonal as possible. Once she even lays her hand on Carmen's knee. Carmen is friendly, just like she always is to everyone. I feel extremely weird, and what I really want to do is get back to the crèche with Luna, then back to MIU as soon as possible. No idea what I'd get up to on a day like this, as soon as I can get away from this fucking hospital. Make as normal a day of it as possible, I suppose.

Carmen notices. 'You go on, I'll manage. And the coffee's much better at MIU.' She laughs.

'When your wife's come round from the anaesthetic we'll give you a call,' says the sister.

Luna and I hug Carmen and I whisper that I love her. I blow her a kiss from the doorway. Luna waves.

Carmen does her best to smile.

I hide my tears behind a painted smile...

The Isley Brothers, from 'I Hide My Tears Behind a Painted Smile' (*Soul on the Rocks*, 1967)

Seven

At ten o'clock I open the front door of our office. It's in the Olympic Stadium. From the moment we got the key I've felt more at home here than I do at home. Part of my youth belongs in that stadium. As a sixteen-year-old kid from Breda, I found the riotous Amsterdam of the early 80s unbelievably amazing. As often as I could, I took the train to Amsterdam on Sunday so that on Monday morning I could tell everybody at school about the riots at Ajax (or 'Ojox', as we called it) and the trashing of the number nine to De Meer or the number sixteen to Olympisch on the way to the game. Though I was careful to stay out of it myself because, just like years before, on the NAC terrace, I was actually crapping myself with terror. But then my schoolmates didn't need to know that.

▶ Frank loves beauty and I love Ajax. That's why **our office** – right under section TT, where the F side always stood when Ajax played in the Olympic Stadium – is a compromise. I insisted on a photograph seven metres by one-and-a-half covering the whole length of the side wall. In it you'll see the players coming out on to the field before the last Champions' League match in the stadium,*

---

* Ajax–Panathinaikos, 3 April 1996, 0–1. Van der Sar, F. De Boer, Blind, Reiziger, Bogarde, R. De Boer, Litmanen, Davids, Finidi, Kanu, Overmars. At the away match Ajax won easily, 0–3.

surrounded by a sea of banners and red smoke. MIU's office looks like my bedroom when I was fifteen, only ten times the size. And many, many more times cooler. That's the influence of Frank and the designer, an English poof with ludicrously hip glasses. The designer didn't think my football fetish fitted in with the space in its entirety. I said that was tough, and his creative concept was fine as long as he kept his hands off that photograph. I have very strong principles where football's concerned. He sullenly agreed, but wanted carte blanche for the rest of the office in compensation. 'Fine by me,' I said. And it was. He insisted there had to be three coloured Plexiglas screens, two metres wide by one-and-a-half metres high, in the open space of the office – a red one, a yellow one and a blue one. He also insisted on pink fluorescent lamps shining from behind the bookcases, one five-metre-high wall being painted apple green, and another being covered with Persian felt cushions. All very colourful, I suppose. And completely irresponsible in budgetary terms. Frank told me not to harp on about it, hadn't I had my way with the Ajax photograph?

Since then, the poof and Frank haven't let the grass grow under their feet. In the few weeks we've been here, Frank has chucklingly announced the arrival of journalists from *Het Parool*, three international magazines all to do with marketing and advertising, a journal devoted to important buildings, two trips by groups of architects (including one from Denmark with a woman so gorgeous I decided to stop nagging about budget excesses from now on, what's done is done) *and* a new client. It's not all that hard, having your own marketing business.

'Hi,' I say as I come in. Everyone's already in. I first make my way to the coffee machine in the little kitchen, out of sight of everyone. The rest of our office in the stadium is so open plan you can't even give your nose a good old poke without everybody gawping. The coffee machine is Frank's acquisition, so the coffee's a legitimate expense. After you press the button it takes half a minute before your cup fills up. Today it can't take long enough as far as I'm concerned. When my cup's full, I stay there for a bit. I summon all my courage and walk past Maud's office. I avoid her eyes.

Frank gives me a probing look when I sit down.

'Well – so – she's in the hospital,' I try to say as laconically as possible. Maud has come in, too. And I feel the others' eyes on my back.

'Yup. OK? We'll see how it goes, won't we?' I say and switch on my PC. I can hardly hold back the tears. Maud lays a hand on my shoulder. I lay my hand on hers and look out through the window. If only I was a child. Then I could convince myself that everything miserable will stop dead if you just don't talk about it.

It ought to be easy ought to be simple enough,
man meets a woman and they fall in love,
but the house is haunted and the ride gets rough ...

Bruce Springsteen, from 'Tunnel of Love' (*Tunnel of Love*, 1992)

Eight

At five in the afternoon I get a call from Carmen. I've just got in the car to drive to the crèche. I don't even need to ask how she is. I can already hear it in her voice.

'The doctor just left ... It's all terrible, Dan.'

'I'm on my way. I'll just pick up Luna, and then I'll be there.'

I don't dare ask anything else.

■

Heart pounding, I walk down the corridor of the Oncology Department with Luna in my arms. I walk into the room where I left Carmen this morning. She's dressed again, sitting on the bed with a crumpled paper tissue in her hand, staring out of the window. Her eyes are red and swollen. Beside her are another two paper tissues, in the same state. She sees us come in and puts her hand to her lips. Without a word I run over to her and hug her. She presses her head against my shoulder and starts crying uncontrollably. I still don't have the courage to ask any questions. I can't ask a single thing. I can't get a word out. Luna hasn't made a sound since we came into the hospital room.

24

Carmen kisses Luna, and actually manages to force a smile.

'Hi, my lovey,' she says, stroking Luna's head.

I clear my throat. 'Tell me,' I say. There's no getting out of it.

'Cancer. A very dangerous form. Diffuse, they called it. Not a lump, but an inflammatory form, and it's already spread through my whole breast.'

Boom.

'Do they know for sure?' It's all I can come up with.

She nods, blowing her nose in the tissue, which now really can't absorb any more moisture.

'It's called mastitis carcinothingumibob' – I nod as though I understand – 'If you like, you can even call in on Dr Wolters, he said. He's a few doors down.'

Wolters. That name. We've kept it deadly quiet all week. Questions from Thomas and Anne and Carmen's mother – whether he might have made a terrible mistake six months ago – were swiftly brushed aside. Maybe even then it was already there, and even then it was too late, was our answer. End of subject. Just the thought that Carmen could die because of a medical blunder.

Wolters is sitting behind his desk. I recognize him immediately from six months ago. He doesn't recognize me. I knock on his open door.

'Hello?' he says with a frown.

'Hi,' I say curtly, just so that he doesn't forget it's all his fault. 'I'm Carmen van Diepen's husband.'

'Oh, sorry, hello, Mr van Diepen,' says Wolters, jumping up from his chair to shake my hand. 'Take a seat.'

'I'll stay standing. My wife's waiting for me.'

'Fine. You've come for the results of the biopsy, I assume.'

No, for the result of the NAC–Ajax game, come on.

'Yes.'

'Hmm. It didn't look particularly good.'

'No. I understand that,' I say with a cynicism that he probably doesn't even notice. 'Can you explain to me exactly what the problem is?'

Wolters tells me why it's particularly bad this time. I only half listen to what he's saying and understand even less. I ask him what degree of certainty there is.

'A considerable degree . . . We still have to investigate, but it looks like mastitis carcinomatosa. There's nothing more we can do at the moment.'

I nod. Wolters shakes my hand.

'Now, be brave, both of you, and go to Dr Scheltema tomorrow. She's the internist and she'll be able to tell you everything about what's about to happen. OK?'

I nod again. And I don't knock him over his desk. More to the point: I say nothing. Nothing. I keep my mouth tight shut. If a client tries to stick his fingers into one of my strategies, I'm liable to chop them off, and now that this clodhopper has fucked up our lives because of an error six months ago, I behave like a footballer from a Limburg club playing his first ever away game in the ArenA.

■

Carmen has Luna on her lap, and is looking out over the almost empty hospital car park when I come back into her room.

'Can you come with me, or do you still have things to do here?' I ask.

'I think I'm ready,' says Carmen. She looks around the

room, searching for her black bag. I walk silently to the table with her jacket draped over it and help her into it, which I never normally do. It's an attempt to give myself the feeling of doing something useful.

'Not so far back,' says Carmen, when I hold her jacket open behind her. 'I can't move my arms back so well because of the wound in my breast.'

'Oh. Sorry. Come on, Luna, let's go,' I say and pick her up from the bed. She's still strikingly calm.

Carmen sticks her head through the doorway of the nurse's room and says, 'Byeee!' The nurse, the same one from this morning, quickly pushes aside her plate of hot food, gets up from her chair, grips Carmen's hand with both hands and wishes us strength.

'Are you going to manage this evening?'

'Definitely,' I say stoutly, and give her a reassuring nod.

The three of us walk to the lift. We don't say a word.

The times are tough, just getting tougher,
I've seen enough, don't wanna see any more,
turn out the light and block the door,
come on and cover me . . .

Bruce Springsteen, from 'Cover Me' (*Born in the USA*, 1985)

Nine

When I get home I ring Frank and tell him Carmen's got breast cancer.

'Christ almighty' is Frank's concise appraisal of the situation.

Carmen rings Anne. She tells her what's going on. Within an hour she and Thomas are standing on the doorstep. She hugs me for a long time and then, still wearing her jacket, runs to the sitting-room and hugs Carmen tightly. Carmen immediately starts crying again.

Thomas gives me a clumsy bear hug. 'This is really shit, mate,' he mumbles. He runs in and barely dares to look at Carmen. He stands and stares at the ground, shoulders slumped and hands in his pockets. He's still wearing his suit and tie.

> ▶ **Thomas** comes from Breda-Noord as well, and I've known him since primary school. 'We liked the same music, we liked the same clothes, we liked the same bands,'* sings Bruce, and that's how it

---

* Wrample from 'Bobby Jean' (*Born in the USA*, 1985).

was with Thomas and me too. When we were twelve we went to see NAC together, when we were sixteen we went together to see punk bands at the Paradiso, and when we were eighteen we went on the pull at De Suykerkist in Breda on Saturday evenings. Thomas was incredibly popular there. I had spots and bottle-thick glasses and had to make do with Thomas's leftovers.

After middle school we both went to business college in Amsterdam, where we met Frank. Thomas scraped through his degree with dripping armpits and sweat between his buttocks. Thomas wasn't, and isn't, super-intelligent. He became a sales rep for a company that sells salt for the roads. His clients are council officials and the Water Board. Thomas is close friends with them, and I think it's because, like them, he enjoys jokes about Belgians, blacks, blondes and women who go to the doctor, and because he also wears pastel-coloured button-down overshirts from Kreymborg. Thomas and I often speak on the phone. We don't see each other as often as we used to. Apart from the carnival in Breda he's not so keen on going out boozing. He'd rather stay at home at the weekend with a nice bit of cheese and a nice glass of wine and a movie full of guns and tits and helicopters. The decline in his appetite for boozing is connected in some way with the fact that he started going bald a few years ago, and his belly began to assume awe-inspiring dimensions. 'Damn it, Danny, we don't all age at the same rate – I'm just milk and you're just wine,' he once said to me when he worked out that his decreasing popularity among 'the females' was beginning to assume structural forms. Pragmatic by nature, Thomas took action. And when a nice young trainee came skipping into his company's offices, six years ago now, he took her out for dinner and after that he never let her go.

▶ That trainee was **Anne.** Thomas and Anne really were meant for one another. Anne is averse to everything that's trendy (meaning: from Amsterdam), she too is wild about children, cheese and wine, and just like Thomas she looks like she's chronically pregnant. Since the birth of their children, Kimberley

(4), Lindsey (3) and Danny (1), Anne has silted up. Anne says she finds her family and housekeeping more important than her outward appearance. She wears leggings and T-shirts from Miss Etam. Carmen calls it a deliberate state of neglect. But Anne doesn't know that. Carmen would never hurt Anne. And rightly so. Because Anne has grown to be Carmen's best friend. They phone each other every day and when Carmen was terrified about the biopsy six months ago it was impossible to get Anne out of our house. Though it drove me round the bend that she was always there when I came home from work, I had to admit Anne knows the meaning of friendship. Carmen and Anne are now far closer than Thomas and I. Carmen tells Anne everything. I don't do the same with Thomas. At least not since I discovered he passes on everything I do (and he would like to do) to Anne. Before you know, it would get back to Carmen and of course we couldn't have that. Honesty is an over-estimated virtue. Anne thinks differently. But it's easy for her to talk. You wouldn't necessarily describe her outward appearance as an invitation to sexual intercourse.* Anne couldn't be unfaithful if she wanted to.

Anne is sensible. She advises us to write down all the questions we want to ask the doctor tomorrow. We decide that's a good plan. The four of us consider all the things we want to know. I do the writing.

It works. We temporarily reduce the cancer to a neutral object we can analyse critically and almost objectively. Carmen hasn't cried for an hour.

Thomas and Anne leave at half past nine. I phone Frank and Carmen goes on to the internet. When I've hung up, she asks me if I remember the ordinary name for her form of breast cancer.

---

*   Wrample from De Avonden by Gerard Reve (1947).

'Wolters didn't tell me. He did give me the Latin name, though, mastitis carcinosomethingorother—'

'Carcinomatosa, that's it.' She looks at the screen. 'Inflammatory Breast Cancer ... which means that it's the kind of cancer that – if you're too late – enters your blood cells. That's right, isn't it?'

'Well – I think so, yes,' I reply carefully.

'Well, that's pretty shitty, then, because it means that' – her voice breaks – 'that my chances of living for more than another five years are less than forty per cent.'

Forty per cent. 'How can you be so sure that it's the same one?' I react irritably. 'Are you sure you've read it right?'

'Yes, I'm not bloody retarded, Dan!' she shrieks. 'It says here! Or doesn't it?'

I don't look at the screen, but press the off button on the iMac.

'OK. Bedtime.'

Perplexed, she looks at the black screen, then at me, with a deadly expression. Then she starts sobbing incredibly hard.

'Christ alive, if that bastard had seen it back then, then perhaps it mightn't have been too late!'

I grab her by the arm and drag her upstairs.

After a crying fit that seems like it'll never end, she falls asleep in my arms. I'm wide awake and don't know if I can face the morning. The moment when I wake up and realize that it wasn't a dream, but that it's really true.

Carmen has cancer.

It's raining harder than I can bear...

Bløf, from 'Harder dan ik hebben kan' (*Boven*, 1999)

Ten

Dr Scheltema shakes us by the hand, gestures to us to take a seat and sits back down behind her desk.

She's going through a file, an old-fashioned brown thing from one of those hanging units. I peer over at it and see that it's the same one that the nurse had the day before yesterday. It contains X-rays (of Carmen, I assume) and I see a long hand-written report (by Dr Wolters?) and a drawing of a breast, with a little arrow and an illegible text next to it. Scheltema reads the file as though we aren't there. It's terribly quiet in her office.

> ▶ **Dr Scheltema** isn't the kind of person who makes you think, 'I bet she's a bit of a laugh.' Grey hair, loads of pens in her breast pocket, science-geek face. Dr Scheltema and I don't click. I caught that from the expression on her face when she clocked my shit-brown leather 70s jacket as I walked into her office.

I grip Carmen's hand. She winks at me and makes a Mr Bean-style nodding-off motion as Scheltema still, after half a minute and no word, peers into the file, leafing forwards, leafing backwards and forwards once more. I glance away from Carmen so as not to burst out laughing, because I have this strange feeling it wouldn't strengthen the bond between me and the doctor. I take another look round the office. Hanging behind her desk is a framed copy of an Impressionist painting (don't ask me who by, I'm from Breda-Noord and I'm pretty impressed that I know it is an Impressionist painting), and on the wall by the door there's a little rack of pamphlets in which, among new titles like *Eating Well with Cancer*, *Cancer and Sexuality* and *Conquering Pain with Cancer*, I spot the by now familiar blue pamphlet, *Breast Cancer*.

Dr Scheltema looks up from the file.

'How have things been over the past few days?' she begins.

'Not great,' Carmen says with classic understatement.

'No, I can imagine,' says the doctor. 'It is awful for you that things went so badly earlier. It was, well, er – unusually careless.'

'Yes, because it's too late now, isn't it?' Carmen mutters.

'Now listen, you mustn't think that way,' says Scheltema. 'There are still lots of things we can try. There's no point looking back, we've got to look at what we *can* do.'

Dumbstruck by her what's-done-is-done attitude towards her colleague's blunder, I glance at Carmen. She has a resigned look about her. I restrain myself too.

'So what I've got is "inflammatory breast cancer", is that right?' asks Carmen.

'The official name is mastitis carcinomatosa, but yes, inflammatory is the term – and, um, how do you know that exactly?'

'I looked it up on the internet yesterday.'

'Ah, now, you want to be careful with that,' says Scheltema tetchily.

You bet, I think, because it's a nuisance for you. I chuckle to myself, and unlike yesterday, when I was furious with

Carmen convincing herself things were as bad as they could possibly be from the dozens of sites devoted to every imaginable form of breast cancer, now I'm proud of her because she already knows enough to make the doctor uncomfortable.

'And is it true that only forty per cent of women diagnosed as having this form of cancer survive the first five years?' Carmen goes on.

'I'm afraid it's even less than that,' says Scheltema frostily, in a clear attempt to discourage the reading of this kind of website once and for all, 'because you're still young, which means that the cells divide quicker than they do in older people. The tumour in your left breast now measures thirteen centimetres by four, and it's probably grown in a few months.'

Thirteen centimetres by four? A courgette is thirteen by four! And it can do that in a few months? Well, yes, I suppose it can. Surely even Dr Wolters can't have missed something that big.

'Can it be removed?' Carmen asks. 'I'd lose my breast if I had to, you know.'

I can't believe what I'm hearing. Without blinking an eye she's saying that her pride, her trademark, is going to be amp—

Scheltema shakes her head.

'It would be difficult to operate at this point,' she says. 'The tumour's too big. We can't see precisely where the cells have spread. If we do cut into it, there's the danger that the tumour will enter the scar tissue of the amputated breast, and then we'll be even worse off. Operating isn't a possibility until we know for sure that the tumour in your breast has shrunk.'

She says it like we should be delighted about it.

34

'Another thing we sometimes use to attack a tumour is hormone treatment' – *yes, hormone treatment! I read something about that, I remember* – 'but that's not going to work either. We've seen in your blood that your oestrogen receptors are negative. Your tumour cells wouldn't react to hormones. But the really difficult thing is that the biopsy showed' – *OK, get on with it* – 'that the tumour is diffuse, which means that it's probably in the blood vessels already, and then you know, well . . .'

No, I don't know, because I did arts subjects at school and, crazy as it may sound, until recently I went whole days without thinking about cancer, even once. Because Carmen also has an expression on her face that suggests that she doesn't know either, Scheltema goes on like one of the newsreaders on children's TV explaining why grown-ups make wars.

'Look, it's like this. Blood cells travel through your whole body. And that means that your cancer cells are doing that as well. The tumour markers in your blood haven't reached alarming levels yet, but it's still likely that cells are already spreading through your body.'

Carmen and I spend a long time looking at each other in silence. I rub her hand with my thumb. Scheltema falls silent too. For a moment.

'If we do nothing now, I'm worried that you've only got a few months left. A year at the most.'

The remark is nothing more than a logical consequence of all the previous information, but it still comes like a sledge-hammer blow. It's finally been said. So that's how it is. *A woman goes to the doctor and hears that she's only got a few months to live.* Carmen starts trembling, brings her hand to her lips and begins to cry, her shoulders shaking. My stomach clenches. I throw one arm around her and hold her hand tight with my other hand.

'It's a bit of a blow, isn't it?' Scheltema observes perceptively. We don't reply. We sit with our arms around each other. Carmen crying, me stunned.

'What now?' I ask after a while.

'I'd advise you to start chemotherapy as soon as possible,' Scheltema resumes the conversation, visibly relieved to be able to return to technical matters. 'This week if possible.'

Chemotherapy. It took a few minutes, but it gradually sank in. Chemotherapy. Read: bald. Read: fatally ill. Read: we - know - very - well - that - it - doesn't - help - a - single - bit - but - we've-got-to-do-something.

Scheltema goes on: 'Chemotherapy actually affects your whole body, so it has the best chance of getting to grips with the cancer.'

'And what about radiotherapy?' I ask. Carmen also looks up for a moment. Yes, radiotherapy, they often do that too, I see her thinking hopefully. For some reason radiotherapy sounds less awful than chemotherapy.

Scheltema shakes her head. Stupid question.

'Radiotherapy only has a local effect. On the breast, that is. And we have to try to get the cancer out of the body, so chemotherapy really is the best thing,' she says, clearly irritated because she'd just explained all that.

'Can you tell us a bit more about this chemotherapy?' I hear myself asking, as though I'm inquiring about the sat-nav system in the new Audi A4.

Scheltema perks up. She looks like a child delighted to be asked to talk about her favourite game. We get a crash course in chemotherapy. The principle is simple. Your body gets an enormous wallop from the chemo, and the purpose of that is to give the cancer cells an even bigger wallop. The cancer cells lose their bearings, they go thrashing about in all directions, like a soccer team without a midfielder. They can even grow through bones, Scheltema says admiringly, getting a little carried away with her enthusiasm. But for that reason they're also more vulnerable to attack than the healthy cells in the body. Unfortunately, all healthy cells that divide quickly are duped as well. 'For example, your hair, Mrs van Diepen, you're going to be suffering hair loss.'

Scheltema is getting nicely into her stride now. 'I think a course of CAF treatment would be the best for you. CAF, that's cyclophosphamide, adriamycin and 5flu' – we nod like we have a clue what she's talking about – 'and a medication that counteracts the vomiting and nausea caused by the chemotherapy' – we nod again. 'Even with this, some people do throw up a lot for a few days. But you'll get medication for that, which you can take after each treatment if necessary' – we gradually slip into a state of emotional stupor – 'so most people tend to eat less. Of course the combination of nausea and the lack of taste doesn't encourage your desire to eat – and there's also a chance of diarrhoea. If that lasts more than two days, you must contact us' – as though she's talking about a leaking washing machine – 'and the mucous membranes in your mouth may also become inflamed, and your periods may become irregular or stop altogether. Finally, you must take care that you don't develop a fever. If that happens you must call us, even if it's the middle of the night.'

I don't want to hear any more, I don't want to hear anything any more. Carmen has gone numb at the words 'hair' and 'loss'. But Scheltema carries on regardless.

'Right, so then the cancer cells in your body may not be responsive to the CAF. But the chance of that is only twenty-five per cent.'

'And then?'

'Then we'll try a different treatment.'

'Oh.'

'But we're not working on that assumption.'

'No.'

'The other thing I have for you is this,' she says, and takes a little yellow pamphlet from her desk drawer. 'If you want you can make use of the psychotherapist here at the Sint Lucas. She specializes in counselling patients with cancer.'

Carmen glances at the pamphlet for a moment and says, yes, we'll probably do that. On top of everything else. Well, if we're welcoming cancer into our lives, let's have the full works.

I look at our little list of prepared questions. Scheltema sees and glances at her watch. I spot another question that won't lighten the mood.

'Wouldn't it be better for my wife to be treated in the Antoni van Leeuwenhoek Hospital? Don't they specialize in cancer treatment?'

Scheltema reacts like Louis van Gaal at a press conference.

'That makes no sense at all. We discuss all our patients with the Antoni van Leeuwenhoek. We talk to each other every week, and discuss all our cases.'

I look at Carmen. She nods hastily that it's OK. She doesn't want to have a row with the doctor who's going to be treating her. I decide not to force the issue. I look at our list again. There's a nice one coming up.

'Last question. Isn't America a bit further ahead than Europe in terms of cancer treatment?'

Scheltema looks at me as though I'm a schoolboy who's dared to look up teacher's skirt.

'I'm sorry, hm – it's not that I doubt your expertise,' I add quickly – in fact of course I do, but I don't want to say anything that's going to get me thrown out of class – 'but we want what's best for my wife, you understand?'

Scheltema doesn't understand me at all; I can see it in her face, which shows she's getting seriously riled. She gives a sigh, and starts talking in a frosty voice.

'We read all available information about cancer, and all the medical research that's published, Mr van Diepen. If something is discovered in Chicago or Los Angeles, then we know it too, the same day. And since the arrival of the internet, everything's completely open. Anyone can look at it. Your wife has discovered that already . . .'

Oh, how I hate that mocking tone, the arrogance that Scheltema displays, given that she knows all about the 'unusually careless' mistake that her colleague made in the same hospital.

'Anything else?'

Yes, three slices of roast beef, bitch.

I look at Carmen, who is shaking her head. She wants to get away. Questions that were relevant yesterday are now just a boring extension of the hospital visit.

'No. That's it,' I say.

We get to our feet and put our jackets on.

'You'll let me know if you want to start the chemo treatment. I would do it, though,' says Dr Scheltema as she shakes Carmen's hand, now sweet as pie.

'Yes – fine. We'll call you tomorrow.'

'And goodbye to you too,' she says, cool again. I actually get a handshake.

'Thanks for your time. See you soon,' I say.

As we walk down the corridor, I grip Carmen's hand and don't look at anybody. In the corridor, waiting for their appointment, I feel the other patients' eyes boring into my back. It's like walking along a terrace with a gorgeous bird wearing too short a skirt – you know everyone's looking, but you act like you don't care. Carmen isn't wearing too short a skirt today, but she's got red eyes and she's holding a hanky. I have my arm around her, my eyes fixed firmly on the end of the corridor. People must be nudging one another, nodding in our direction, whispering to one another. Oh, God, that woman, still so young, so nice-looking. She must have just heard she's got cancer. And look at that boy with her, how sad. I can feel their pity, their thirst for sensation. Shame Luna isn't here today. It would have made the whole picture even prettier for them.

I don't believe in magic, but for you I will,
darlin' for you, I'm counting on a miracle . . .

Bruce Springsteen, from 'Countin' on a Miracle' (*The Rising*, 2002)

Eleven

Carmen reads out what it says in the pamphlet Dr Scheltema has given us. The psychotherapist follows the Carl Simonton method. According to the pamphlet, he is 'a pioneer in the field of techniques of cancer treatment in which not only the body but also the mind has an important role to play'.

'He'll be a nephew of Emile Ratelband,* then,' I say sarcastically.

Half an hour later we leave the bookshop with two of Dr Simonton's books.

■

When we've put Luna to bed, and taken the phone, which never seems to stop ringing this evening, off the hook, we each pick up one of Dr Simonton's books. Carmen opens *The Healing Journey*. I begin reading *Getting Well Again*.

'Some people may be concerned that we are offering "false hope", that by suggesting people can influence the course of their disease we are raising unrealistic expectations. But in our

---

* Dutch motivational guru.

opinion hope, in such a situation, is a much healthier attitude than despair,' I read.

A moment later *The Healing Journey* goes flying across the sitting room.

'Christ almighty, I'm sitting here reading about cancer! I SO DON'T WANT TO READ ABOUT CANCER!' screams Carmen. 'IT'S NOT FAIR, IT CAN'T BE TRUE, IT'S NOT POSSIBLE!'

I couldn't agree more with her perceptive analysis, but all I can do is hold my bellowing, shivering little Carmen tight, stroke her, kiss her and whisper, 'Calm down, my love, come on, come on . . .'

It's the evening before the Queen's official birthday. While the whole city is out there getting hammered, at number 872 Amstelveenseweg two little scraps of misery are holding one another tight.

Then I want to dance, dance, dance,
dance on the volcano . . .

De Dijk, from 'Dansen op de vulkaan'
(*Wakker in een vreemde wereld*, 1987)

Twelve

At a quarter past nine the bell rings and Frank's at the door. I nearly keel over with surprise, because when he isn't working Frank doesn't really consider the day to have begun before about lunchtime.

▶ **Frank** is a lazy, egocentric snob and he's my best friend. Unlike Thomas, Frank knows everything about me. We work together all day. He knows how I think, what I like in my sandwiches, he knows that at BBDvW&R/Bernilvy I screwed not only Sharon, but also Lisa, Cindy and Dianne, and that when Carmen and I hadn't been going out that long I went on doing it regularly with Maud and – because over the years he's shared loads of hotel rooms and flats with me – what sort of noise I make when I come.

Frank's libido is precisely the opposite of mine. When I hadn't known him for very long, I thought he must be furtively getting his rocks off in brothels, but now I know he just isn't that interested in screwing. That still holds true now. Very, very occasionally a woman will chat *him* up, and then he'll have sex. To my knowledge that's happened three times in the fifteen years I've known him. And I think I've figured out how it's happened. Frank puts himself at the centre of the universe, and it suits him just fine. He doesn't need anything else. No wife, no family, nothing. The only thing Frank spends money on is Frank. And

Frank spends incredible amounts of money. Shed-loads. Always carefully, though. Frank has style, and he wants everyone to know it. Frank goes to the right exhibitions, to the restaurants that matter. And he has the newest Pradas before they even reach the shops (and he never passes up the opportunity to mention them casually over lunch at MIU). Most of his money goes on sensible gear for his penthouse on Bolemgracht. The penthouse is the size of a dance hall, and everything in it is expensive. The kitchen alone cost more than all the furniture in our house on Amstelveenseweg. Not that Frank often goes into the kitchen because Frank can't cook. And Frank can't iron. Or wash clothes, do the shopping or change a bicycle tyre. What's more, Frank has no housekeeper, no driving licence and no idea how he would get hold of such earthly things. His father sometimes comes over from Breda and does all the chores in his penthouse. His mother cleans up and does his washing. Twice a week he comes to eat at our place, and he takes it perfectly for granted that he can always come with us if we go anywhere in the car. He always comes with us because there's one thing he brings in return. Frank is a Friend.

'Surely I can't leave you alone on Koninginnedag?'* Unlike Thomas, Frank isn't embarrassed to hug and kiss me. When Frank and I come back to the office after a holiday, when we have our birthdays and when we've won some new business, we always hug each other. I like that. It makes me think of the sort of friendship you only normally come across in Bruce Springsteen songs and beer commercials. The mood chez Danny & Carmen has just lifted. Carmen is happily surprised and Luna crows with pleasure. She's wild about Frank, and Frank is wild about her.

When we're sitting at the kitchen table, and Frank has gladly accepted Carmen's invitation to join us for a croissant,

---

*   'Queen's Day', a Dutch national holiday.

he asks us how we are. Carmen tells him the whole story, with occasional interventions from me. Each time she starts finding it difficult, he lays his hand on her arm. Frank listens attentively to our account of all the things we found out yesterday. Dr Scheltema's explanation, the chemotherapy, how we felt when we walked down the corridor and out of the hospital.

I'm getting quieter by the moment. A few minutes ago I got up and went to the toilet when I didn't actually need to, and now I'm completely at a loss. Fortunately I catch a sickly whiff of shit.

'I'm going upstairs to change her nappy.'

I pick her up and take her upstairs. My eyes filled with tears, I wipe Luna's bottom clean and put a new nappy on. Luna observes me, amazed, from the chest of drawers. 'Oh, my darling ... My dear little darling ...' I close the poppers of her romper suit. I lift her up, take her firmly in my arms and, as the tears run down my face, I stare out of the window. I still can't get my head round it. We're thirty-five, we've got a darling of a daughter, we've each got a business, we're living a cool life, we have as many friends as we could possibly want, we do whatever we like, and now we're sitting here on Koninginnedag spending half the morning talking about nothing but cancer.

When I let Frank out (he asks if we really don't fancy going with him today – Carmen won't yield), I feel even more agitated. Carmen had previously told me this morning she didn't want to spend the afternoon surrounded by a yelling crowd. I understand, of course, but the prospect of spending a whole afternoon sitting grieving nearly drives me out of my mind. Denying Danny a party is even worse than snatching

Luna's dummy away from her. Now, especially. I want to get out, I want to get pissed, I want to party, I want to do anything except go on talking about cancer.

I sigh demonstratively as I sit back down at the kitchen table.

'You could make less of a show of the fact that you're bored,' Carmen snaps at me. 'I can't do anything about the fact that I've got cancer.'

'No, neither can I,' I say furiously.

I want to run, I want to hide,
I want to tear down the walls, that hold me inside . . .

U2, from 'Where the Streets Have No Name'
(*The Joshua Tree*, 1987)

Thirteen

An hour later I can't bear it any longer. Carmen is sitting there flicking through *World of Interiors*, and I know she doesn't appreciate what she's reading.

'Damn it all, what are we doing at home for Christ's sake?' I shout suddenly.

She looks at me, on the point of tears. Oh no, just what I need, the umpteenth crying jag over the last twenty-four hours. I force myself to calm down, scamper over to her and hold her tightly. 'Darling, I think it would really be better for us to go out and do something. This is getting us nowhere. Let's at least take Luna to the Vondelpark.'

She wipes away her tears. 'OK . . . Yes, maybe that'd be better.'

■

On Koninginnedag the Vondelpark is full of children from South Amsterdam, the posh part of the city. Even the talents on display are very South Amsterdam. Two little boys who sound like they might sing in a children's choir are selling homemade orange tart. I never made a tart as a child, and I can't imagine any of my friends from Breda-Noord did either. A child with a face far too serious for her age – 'If I had a child like that, I'd opt for a post-natal abortion,' says Carmen – is reciting poems. Who brings up children to do things like that? Poetry's like pomp-rock, like the 4–3–3 formation in football, like eating Chinese food – apart from my old Dutch teacher and the reviewer in *Het Parool* I don't know anyone who still reads poetry. Carmen and I are getting increasingly fed up with the children declaiming, scraping away at violins, juggling and generally being irritating, under the watchful eye of their proud parents. A little girl in an orange dress, with her hair in a ponytail, lets us hear what she's learned at her violin lessons. 'I'd rather Luna went to jail than to violin lessons,' I whisper in Carmen's ear. She snorts. The mother of the child with the orange dress doesn't think we're funny.

'That was nice, wasn't it?' I ask as we walk down the street, Luna on my shoulders, down Cornelis Schuystraat to the bus stop on De Lairessestraat.

Carmen kisses me on the cheek and winks.

That lovely summer is gone now,
that summer that began in May,
you thought it would never come to an end,
but before you know it summer is long gone again ...

Gerard Cox, from 'Het is weer voorbij die mooie zomer'
(*Het beste van Gerard Cox*, 1973)

Fourteen

Within three months, both summer and chemotherapy are over. And Carmen is bald. In the car on the way to the hospital for Carmen's first course of therapy I suddenly realized all the things I could safely forget this summer. Sunday trips to the seaside at Bloemendaal? No, Carmen's hardly going to fancy that if she's lost her hair. And we can forget our plan to go to New York for Ascension Day if the chemo's taken root in her body. Football in the park on Tuesday evening? Forget it. I have to be at home to feed Luna and put her to bed, because Carmen will be lying upstairs puking. Of course I could always call Frank or Maud and ask them to come round and then go and play football on my own ...

And I haven't even considered life after the summer, after the chemo. I can't even begin to guess what's going to happen over the coming months – I don't dare look beyond that. It's like Ajax–Juventus in the ArenA in the last days of Louis van

Gaal's trainership. 0–2 at half time and we still had another three halves to go.*

As we're driving on the ring-road it starts to drizzle. Fine. As far as I'm concerned it can freeze this summer. I turn off the radio. Edwin Evers, the DJ, is too bubbly for me this morning. I hit the CD button. Michael Stipe sings that we mustn't let go when the day is long, that we mustn't let go when we think we've had too much of this life, when everything is wrong. We both sit there in silence. Carmen listens too. She wipes away a tear. I grip her leg firmly. *No, no, no, you're not alone. Hold on. Hold on.* Carmen lays her hand on my hand. *Hold on. Hold on.*† 'Uff,' Carmen sighs when the song's over.

∎

We walk past Scheltema's office to the end of the corridor. Blood sample first. Can't remember what it was for, something to do with white blood cells. Or red ones. Carmen has a needle stuck into her, is given a piece of cotton wool to put on the puncture and then we go back into the corridor. Waiting. One thing I've learned spending a few weeks in hospitals is that waiting is the most natural thing in the world. The appointment time they give you is really just a preparatory stage. After a quarter of an hour I've already read the copy of *De Volkskrant* I bought in the hospital shop. I saw a moment ago that there was a *Voetbal International* among the

---

* 9 April 1997. 1–2. Van der Sar, Melchiot, Blind, F. De Boer, Musampa, Scholten, Litmanen, Witschge, Babangida, R. De Boer, Overmars. 0–1 Amoruso, 0–2 Vieri, 1–2 Litmanen. And it's downhill after that (Lombardo, Vieri, Amoruso, Zidane).

† From 'Everybody Hurts' by REM (*Automatic for the People*, 1992).

women's magazines, the *Stories* and *Margriets* in the corridor but I already know the score of the Holland–Argentina match in last year's World Cup. Finally we're called in to see Scheltema. She's even seems to be quite cheerful this time.

'So, we're going to tackle it today, aren't we?' she says, like an Akela with her cub-troop at the foot of a hill in the Ardennes.

Carmen's blood is fine. The therapy can continue. We're to go to the chemo room on the third floor, she says.

■

I've never done it before, but something tells me watching chemotherapy isn't going to be a picnic. I promised Carmen I'd go with her every time. She was relieved and said she thought it was nice of me to want to do that. Well, yeah, 'Want to?' I thought. The only thing I want less is for Carmen to go alone. I can't imagine anybody really *wanting* to go along to chemotherapy.

I'm not wrong. Most of the partners of the chemo patients are at home, at work, or wherever, but wherever they are they aren't in the chemo room.

When we walk in there, a new world opens up in front of us. This isn't an ordinary hospital room, far from it, somebody's made a determined effort to make the place look really cosy. Next to the window there's a table with two coffeepots, a stack of coffee cups and a plate of gingerbread slices on it. Half of them are buttered, half of them bald, to stick with the chemo theme. There are two empty round tables with tablecloths. Standing on one of them is a little plant (don't ask me what kind of plant), which has withered. Low chairs surround both tables. Everything has been done to create the feeling of

51

an ordinary room in an ordinary house. A shame, then, the patients spoil the tone somewhat. They have huge plasters on their hands, from which transparent tubes emerge to rise to a kind of hatstand on wheels, with pouches of red fluid and clear fluid hanging from them. The fluid drips down through the tubes, I see now, and disappears under the plaster, and after that, I fear, into the body. It doesn't look healthy, and it certainly doesn't look pleasant.

Three of the four patients have a hatstand like that. One man, a jovial character with big, faded tattoos, has no hatstand, which means he, like me, isn't a patient, or so I assume. He must belong to the elderly, fat woman who's sitting next to him and whose hand he's holding tightly. His wife does have a hatstand with pouches of fluid. And very thin hair, dyed dark red. You can see her scalp through it. On the low chair next to her is a man of about fifty, who's as bald as Collina, the Italian referee. This man too has strange, bulging eyes. He too is linked up to a hatstand. Now that I look at him closely, I see it isn't his eyes that make him look so weird, but the absence of eyebrows and lashes.

The third hatstand belongs to a hip young guy wearing a Gatsby cap. I'd say he's about twenty. He was here last week, too, I remember, in the corridor outside Dr Scheltema's office. He was with his girlfriend that time, a small girl, Italian-looking, black curly hair to her shoulders. Gorgeous little thing, she was. I remember feeling glad we weren't the only young people with cancer. So where's the girlfriend today? I expect she's left him because he has cancer of the balls or something. And if she hasn't left him then she's even more of a cow, because where is she while her boyfriend's getting his chemo? No, I'm not as bad a friend as that, I note smugly.

'Good morning, I'm Janine,' says a cross-eyed nurse.

'Hi, I'm Carmen,' says Carmen sympathetically.

'Hi – Dan,' I say coolly, shaking Janine's hand.

The cross-eyed nurse gestures towards an awkward-looking girl of about twenty, who's also wearing a white jacket: 'And this is Yolanda, our trainee.'

Trainee? *Trainee?* Some twenty-year-old tart is going to get the chance to sit in on our chemo-baptism, which I feel in my bones isn't going to pass without tears, as part of her *training*? And then doubtless tonight in the pub she'll tell her little student girlfriends, 'There was this woman in chemo today, lovely-looking girl, couldn't have been more than thirty-five, Carmen or something her name was, very friendly, with her friend, an arrogant dickhead, he didn't say a word, so this woman and her friend, right, it was their first time, and then the woman started crying, and I had to look after her … Look, do you want another beer? And how's your training going, by the way, you said you were due for a reappraisal?'

Bitch.

Boss-eyed Janine tells us Carmen's chemo stuff's already been ordered from the hospital pharmacy, and it shouldn't take too long because there aren't too many people in today. Sometimes they can have eight patients at the same time, and then it's incredibly boring because the pharmacy doesn't finish preparing the last medication until around noon.

I don't fully understand, but I do grasp there are going to be some changes this summer. In three months' time we'll know how early we have to get here if we want to be seen to quickly, the way I know exactly what time in the evening I have to get to Paradiso without having to spend too long in the queue but without finding myself standing in an empty club.

The phone rings. Janine picks it up.

'Mrs van Diepen's chemo cure is ready,' she says to the trainee after putting the phone down. 'Will you go and get it?'

She nods and leaves the room.

'She's a good girl,' Janine says, bending towards us slightly, 'and you can't always say that about trainees.'

'Yes,' says Carmen with a smile, 'I know.'

'Have you got trainees too?'

Carmen and Janine chat cheerfully on about the ins and outs of having trainees. Once again Carmen surprises me with her ability to have friendly, spontaneous, carefree conversations. I know she's incredibly nervous, that she sees the chemo cure as a huge mountain she has to climb, but she still manages to listen with interest to the story of Janine's former trainee.

I don't. I don't mean to be rude on purpose, but every time I walk into the hospital it happens of its own accord. There's nothing I can do about it. I hate cancer and I hate what it's doing to our life. I hate my new status as the husband of a cancer patient. I'm furious, frustrated and powerless. I'm angry with Dr Wolters, with Dr Scheltema, with the nurses, with the trainee, with the other patients, with the man who built this godforsaken, depressing Sint Lucas Hospital, with the guy in the car at the lights this morning who didn't notice they'd been green for ages, with Janine who's so friendly that with the best will in the world I can't see her as a cow.

And I'm angry with myself for being so angry. I'm angry I can't resign myself, I can't accept Carmen has cancer, I'm her husband, for better or for worse. Yeah, I've come here with

54

Carmen today and, of course, I was proud of myself yesterday when I heard Carmen saying to her mother and Anne on the phone that she thought it was lovely of me to go with her to chemo. And of course I say the two of us are going to deal cancer the death blow, we're not going to let it get the better of us. OF COURSE I know all that! What else am I supposed to do? Am I supposed to tell Carmen I'm only giving her cuddles, comforting words, kisses on her cheek and the top of her head, and thumb stroking her palm when we walk together down the corridor because I'm deliberately forcing myself to be nice? Out of a notion of duty: thou shalt be nice to thy wife who hath cancer. It's my sense of honour, my sense of 'that's-what-you're-supposed-to-do' that's making me nice. But it doesn't happen all by itself. I have to drag the love all the way up from my toes.

The trainee comes in with a massive Tupperware box, its lid fixed on with two iron clips.

'That was quick,' Janine calls cheerfully. 'I'll just call a doctor to apply the drip.'

The doctor is a shy young man in a white jacket.

'This lady needs to be fixed up with a drip, Frans,' says Janine, pointing to Carmen.

Frans the doctor shakes Carmen's hand and blushes. A bit of a change from all those old wrinklies, eh? Luckily for Frans, Carmen's wearing a loose sweater, or else his glasses would steam up. When I see other men finding Carmen attractive, it makes me as proud as a dog with seven dicks, and I always demonstrate this in a typical Dannian manner by looking at the person in question as coolly as I can. You like this beautiful woman you're looking at, you mug? Dream on! And then I almost explode with pride at being Carmen's husband.

I start out of my daydream when Carmen starts crying because Frans, who's getting more and more nervous, says he has to do it all over again. He failed to get the ludicrously fat needle – half a centimetre in diameter, I see with a terrified glance – into the right vein. I glare at Frans, but he doesn't notice because he and Janine are too busy staunching the blood pouring out of Carmen's hand.

Frans's second attempt seems to be successful. I conclude as much from the encouraging way he says, 'That looks better,' as he gently pats Carmen on the hand.

'Yes, it worked,' Janine says immediately, with relief. She grips Carmen's left hand and strokes it while I – scarcely able to hold back my tears – sit on Carmen's other side and press her head to my chest, so she doesn't have to look at all the poking around that's going on in her hand.

'Sorry that took so long. Your veins aren't easy to find,' Frans says apologetically. He shakes Carmen clumsily by the left hand, mumbles 'Goodbye' without looking at us and then makes his getaway as quickly as he can.

Janine asks if we want to go and sit with the others, who don't seem to have been embarrassed by Carmen's crying fit – cancer patients get used to anything – at one of the long tables, or if we'd rather take a seat in the adjacent room. I look at Carmen, who's wiping away the last tears from her cheek with the hand that hasn't got a tube sticking out of it.

'No, let's go and sit at the other table, with those people over there. It's a bit more sociable.' She laughs.

I'm not sure it's all that sociable. I'm aware I'm slightly ashamed in front of the others. The boy with the Great Gatsby cap, the man with no eyebrows, the woman with the white sweater and her jovial husband have all had a detailed view of me kissing Carmen dozens of times on the top of the head. And they can't have missed seeing it took all my strength to control myself. Comforting a person devotedly is like dropping your trousers. You're showing your most intimate side. But Carmen's probably right. Let's join everybody else. We're going to have to get used to it. If it doesn't go the way it's supposed to, then it'll have to go the way it goes.*

I walk to the table near the window, the one with the tea on it. Carmen comes and stands next to me, and waits till I've poured. I have a sense she doesn't want to go and sit on her own among her fellow cancer patients.

'It isn't easy, is it?' says the fat woman with the white sweater and the thin hair. The red fluid dribbles through the tube into her hand.

'No,' says Carmen.

'I expect this is the first time you've had chemo?'

'Yes.'

'Don't worry, you'll get used to it.'

'I hope so . . .'

'But of course it's never much fun.'

'Christ, it's like going to the tax office,' her husband says cheerfully, in a strong Amsterdam accent.

'As long as they look after us better than they look after the plants,' says the fat woman, nodding towards the miserable-looking plant. Laughter. Carmen joins in, so I do too. I look at her and decide I'm going to make the best of it today. One of the little boxes, I think it's the one attached to Gatsby-cap guy, starts beeping.

'Has someone put something in the microwave?' I say,

---

*   Saying by Richard Krajicek.

trying to get as close as possible to the fat woman's husband's sense of humour.

'Yes, I did! A potato croquette and a cheese soufflé!' he crows, coming to my support.

There's more laughter, and Carmen joins in. The trainee runs over to the boy with the cap and sticks one of the other little tubes into the machine. I see two of the three pouches on his hatstand are already empty.

Carmen and I go and sit at the empty table. The chairs at the other table are all occupied. Shame. Just when it was getting nice.

Carmen gets a hatstand of her own, luckily from Janine. Cross-eyed she might be, but I'd sooner have her than the trainee any time. God knows what kind of mistakes a child like that could make. On the top of the stand Janine hangs two pouches of transparent fluid ('One against vomiting, we'll start with that at the same time') and a pouch of red misery ('That's the adriamycine'). The red stuff looks just as I imagined. Scary. Poisonous. It doesn't smell of anything. So this is it. Chemo. This stuff hanging from the hatstand next to Carmen, that's about to pour into her body, that stuff that might attack the cancer, and will certainly make Carmen bald.

The little tube in Carmen's hand is screwed on to the bigger transparent tube, which leads to a little box with tiny red digital numbers and arrows, about halfway up the hatstand. There's another transparent tube attached to one of the two pouches of clear fluid, and that one goes into the top of the machine with the red numbers. Janine says the salt solution goes through in twenty minutes, and presses a couple of buttons on the little box, which obligingly shows the number 20.

'It'll beep when it's ready, and then you have to call me if I happen not to see it.'

I know the procedure already, from cap-guy's hatstand.

'Cool – my very own chemo-car.' Carmen winks.

We start getting silly now.

'Christ, she really is cross-eyed, isn't she?' I whisper in Carmen's ear.

Carmen nods and bites her cheek to keep from laughing.

'Shall we call her Clarence?' I ask innocently.

Carmen chokes on a mouthful of tea and spits it out. Acting startled, I pretend to trip backwards over the wheels of her hatstand. With pretend irritation, I turn around, pull a Mr Bean face and threaten to hurl the thing across the room when Janine isn't looking.

'Please, Danny!' Carmen screams with laughter.

Janine smiles over at Carmen, pleased she's laughing. 'Sounds like you're feeling a bit better,' she says to Carmen, and winks at me. I blush, sensing she might have guessed my whispered joke was at her expense. And I realize that cross-eyed Janine would do anything in her power to make her patients' lives less miserable, even if it's only for a morning, for an hour, for a minute. And if being the butt of jokes helps her do that, then that's just how things have to be. I feel myself shrinking in comparison with cross-eyed Janine.

I go and sit next to Carmen. She kisses me and whispers in my ear that she loves me. I give her a loving look and feel very proud of us both. The Theatre of Laughter has allayed the first chemo-crisis.

Don't speak, don't tell me 'cause it hurts . . .

No Doubt, from 'Don't Speak' (*Tragic Kingdom*, 1995)

Fifteen

As I walk into MIU, Maud asks how things went this morning.

'Not too bad. We were even able to laugh about it.'

'That's good. And how's Carmen feeling now?'

'OK. She's been given a little mountain of anti-nausea pills.'

'Where is she now?'

'At home. Her mother's there.'

▶ **Maud** is my ex. We went out together during the 88/89 season. Maud was a model until she realized – a few years later than her agent did – that she was never really going to make it. She gave up modelling, and dieting. Her waist disappeared, her cup-size doubled, and Maud went to work in the hotel and catering industry. When MIU was looking for a secretary, I persuaded Frank to give her a chance. Maud is spontaneous and far from stupid, but it was her cup-size, which didn't escape even Frank's notice, that was the final resolving factor in MIU's decision-making process. Maud got the job.

In the early years of Carmen & Dan, Maud and I still used to meet up on the sly, but there came a time when she wanted to stop. She thought Carmen was far too nice. Now we sometimes swap kisses for old times' sake, and after last year's Christmas party things got a bit out of hand on the designer cushions in the lounge corner of our office (not quite what the Englishman had in mind), but it stopped there. Lately she's even started telling me off for my infidelities, something she never did when we were going out with each other. She once (for example) retouched Sharon's white skirt with a glass of rosé when she had greeted me a bit too physically in De Pilsvogel. Essentially I do agree with Maud's arguments about why I should stop being unfaithful now. According to Maud I'm putting the finest relationship in my life on the line. But following tried and tested Dan practices I leave it like this: we have a drink, we have a piss and everything's exactly as it was before. I remain monophobic.

Maud was devastated when she heard Carmen had breast cancer.

Meanwhile I've switched on my computer. I don't want to talk about cancer any more. 'Have Holland Casino rung yet to say if they agree with the estimate?'

Frank shakes his head.

Fine. That gives me the chance to give somebody a really good bollocking.

'Fucking hell, then phone them up! We don't want to wait for the tossers, do we? Phone the fucker up yourself! Christ alive, do I have to do everything myself in this fucking shit-hole?'

Frank lets the cannonade fly over his head.

At the same time I click on an email from Carmen that she sent about ten minutes ago, I see:

From: Carmenvandiepen@xs4all.nl
Sent: tuesday 4 may 1999 14.29
To: Dan@creativeandstrategicmarketingagencymiu.nl
Subject: Treasure –

Hi treasure,

I'm feeling a bit nauseous, but it's going reasonably well. I just
wanted to say that I'm so happy you're going with me, and I won't be
alone when I'm having my treatments.

xxx Carmen

PS: I love you, my treasure.

I get up quickly and, without looking at Frank, I walk to
the toilet. When I get there, out come the tears I've been
struggling to hold in all day.

After a few minutes I wipe them away, blow my nose,
splash my face with water a few times, check to see if I'm
looking reasonably normal – no – slam the toilet door like
I've been taking a good long shit, sigh once again and come
back in.

Eight colleagues act as if they haven't noticed a thing.

When I get older, losing my hair,
Many years from now,
Will you still be sending me a Valentine,
Birthday greetings, bottle of wine,
Will you still need me,
Will you still feed me,
When I'm sixty-four...

The Beatles, from 'When I'm Sixty-Four'
(*Sergeant Pepper's Lonely Hearts Club Band*, 1967)

Sixteen

Carmen's mother answers the phone. 'Hello?'

'Hi, Danny here. How's Carm getting along?'

'She threw up an awful lot this morning. She's sleeping now.'

'Fine. I'll go and pick up Luna from the crèche, and I'll stop off at the supermarket. What do you fancy?'

'Oh, anything, something ready-made or whatever.'

'Do you think Carmen's going to want anything?'

Carmen's mother laughs. 'An extra bucket?'

▶ **Carmen's mother** is an absolute treasure. She grew up in the Jordaan, the working-class bit of Amsterdam. She's pretty glamorous, in a down-to-earth sort of way. I don't know Carmen's father. He walked out ten years ago, after twenty-one years of marriage. Note on the kitchen table, that kind of thing. Carmen's mother couldn't believe her luck. Within a month she had a new boyfriend. Carmen thought she recognized him from when some work was being done on their house. (Nice anecdote about this: when Carmen's mother (then 54) introduced her new boyfriend (60) to Carmen (27), Carmen asked him: 'And what does your father do?') By now Bob the Builder is a thing of the past. A few months after he'd finished doing up the house Carmen's mother had just moved into, and made sure it was in perfect shape, she started having doubts about whether she really loved him enough. Exit Bob. Carmen's mother lives alone again now, in the magnificently renovated house in Purmerend. Every now and again she takes up with another jolly character, but not a single one has lasted more than a single Christmas dinner or a birthday party. 'My house won't need renovating for another ten years or so,' says Carmen's mother.

At the supermarket on the Groot Gelderlandplein I look at a man and a woman who must be in their eighties. They're walking arm in arm, shuffling along the wine shelf. He points with his stick to a red wine that's on special offer. His wife picks up the wine and puts it in the basket she's holding in her hand. He says something to her I don't catch. The elderly woman shrieks with laughter and pinches her husband's arm. I tighten my grip on Luna's hand, and look quickly in the other direction.

The elderly couple, still in love, fill me with jealousy. Carmen and I are never going to do that together.

Now all them things that seemed so important,
well, mister they vanished right into the air ...

Bruce Springsteen, from 'The River' (*The River*, 1980)

Seventeen

The anti-nausea medicines don't help. Carmen's been sick as a dog for two whole days.

From Thursday evening things start getting better. We even have a whole evening without one of the two of us crying.

On Friday Carmen goes back to Advertising Brokers. Daily life continues. Until the next chemo treatment, in about two weeks, we're trying to act like nothing's wrong, although we both know we're only pretending.

It isn't paradise any more.

In your head do you feel,
what you're not supposed to feel . . .

Oasis, from 'Sunday Morning Call'
(*Standing on the Shoulders of Giants*, 2000)

Eighteen

'Hi, I'm Gerda. So you've come along together? That's nice,'
says the psychotherapist as she shakes our hands and holds
on to them for a long time. I can see it already. Gerda's the
type who always goes and sits on the table even when there
are enough perfectly good chairs in the room.

'Yes, we thought it was a good idea,' Carmen answers.

I don't think it's a good idea at all. I think it's even worse
than the chemo. Not for a second did I ever think I'd end up
going to a psychotherapist.

Gerda's consulting room is a little den, two metres by
three. There are two low chairs – 'it makes talking a bit easier
than tall ones' – a pouffe, an old standard lamp and a long
table with a flat, old-fashioned cassette-recorder on it. A
Yoko, which looks like the very first one I ever had. The first
tape I recorded had, I think, 'I Love the Sound of Breaking
Glass' by Nick Lowe. Oh yes, and 'Psycho Killer' by Talking
Heads.

Gerda apologizes for the size of the room. 'Fortunately I
should soon be getting a different room, a bit bigger, with
windows that let the daylight in, but for the time being we

make do with what we've got. I haven't got any coffee. I don't care for it. I'd rather drink tea. Sugar?'

She pours the tea and goes to sit on the low chair beside the table. Carmen sits on the other chair and I sit on the pouffe.

'So,' Gerda begins the conversation in what I take to be a therapeutically responsible way.

'Yes,' says Carmen.

'So here we are then!'

'Yes. You could say so.'

You have to admit, Carmen is adapting wonderfully well to the level of the conversation. I'm not doing so well. I'm doing my best not to be too dull, but I suspect it's written all over my face that Gerda can get TB as far as I'm concerned. But Gerda's an old hand at this, and isn't even slightly perplexed by my barely concealed contempt. She remains irritatingly nice.

'Do you find it difficult sitting with a psychotherapist talking about an illness that might kill you? Do you think about that, now, while you're in the prime of life?'

Hey! Just hang on there a minute! Gerda knows exactly which buttons to press. Startled, I look at Carmen. Yup, here come the tears again. I hold her hand tightly and start to stroke it. In the few weeks Carmen's had cancer, I've stroked her hand more often than in the seven years that went before. Gerda doesn't say anything. I look at Carmen's hand in mine. I feel ill at ease, like I'm about to sit an exam to see if I think it awful enough my wife's got cancer and might die of it. Leaning towards Carmen, I feel the psychotherapist's eyes on my back, and am aware she's probably already made her judgement: he doesn't love her, because he hasn't shed a single tear.

'Let it out, Carmen,' Gerda says after a while.

Carmen says that over the past few weeks we've fallen from heaven and landed in hell. That everything was good, so nice, the three of us, we were happy, and then suddenly, smack, bang, wallop, it's all over.

'There's not a single minute in the day when I don't think about it,' she says to Gerda.

This is news to me, but obviously I don't let on to Gerda. As far as I'm concerned, whole hours pass without it coming into my head. For most of the day, from the moment I step into MIU in the morning, I don't think about it. I thought Carmen was the same. Take yesterday. It was like the kind of evening we had in the days before the cancer, Luna in bed, 'Will you put on some tea?', Carmen lying on the big sofa with *Elle*, me in front of the television, all's right with the world. Sure, I convulsively avoid any awkward subjects, and only ask emotionally innocuous questions. 'A syrup waffle or a slice of cake, darling?' 'Do you want a little glass of mineral water or a little glass of wine?' 'Shall we watch *The Sopranos* or the film on Canal Plus?'

'Is there anything you've done over the past few days that you've noticed calms you down?' asks Gerda.

Carmen has a think.

'When you play with Luna, or put her to bed, perhaps?' I suggest, in a bold attempt to reposition myself in Gerda's eyes from the-man-who-sheds-no-tears-over-his-wife to the constructively sympathetic, loving partner.

'No,' Carmen says, energetically shaking her head, 'that always reminds me I might never see my little darling growing up.'

The box of tissues on Gerda's table does overtime. Fuck,

how could I have said something so clumsy? My toes curl with shame. Back in your box, Danny.

'Although, now I come to think about it: last weekend, when I was doing a bit of work on the garden, I did calm down a bit,' says Carmen. Now it's Gerda's turn to make Carmen cry. Except Gerda does it on purpose, while I just put my foot in my mouth.

'But then you must be wondering if you'll see the plants coming up again next year . . .'

Oh, Christ almighty. Now Carmen's sluice gates are open all the way. Gerda says the thing we can't even think about: Carmen might not be around in a year's time. By saying yes to chemo we've hidden ourselves away from that disastrous scenario.

It's my turn now. Gerda is on a collision course.

'And you, Dan, be honest, aren't you thinking: what have I done to deserve this?'

A jolt.

Where Carmen, Frank, Maud, Thomas and Anne have failed, Gerda succeeds with the first remark she directs straight at me. Gerda hits the emotional nail right on the head. I haven't told anyone. I don't let anyone see it, but it's true. I feel the cancer has dealt me just as hard a blow as it has Carmen. She's got me bang to rights.

I lower my head, nod and feel my eyes moistening. Shit. Why now, at Gerda's first assault on *my* heart? Fuck, if only I'd faked a crying fit when it would have been good for the image. When I could have let Gerda see how much I love Carmen. Why do I crack up now, when Gerda starts rootling about in *my* feelings, why the hell do I get crying incontinence now, of all times? You can bet whatever you like Gerda thinks

I'm a selfish twat who pretends to think things are awful for his wife, but who's just been caught red-handed transgressing the unwritten rule of partners of cancer patients: thou shalt have no self-pity. With my head bowed and a tissue in my hand given to me by Carmen, I weep buckets.

'Do you feel guilty about thinking it's awful for you, too?' asks Gerda.

'Yeah – bit...' I sniff, deeply ashamed of myself. For weeks now I've had a little voice in my head nagging at me, telling me it doesn't count in the slightest that I'm reading Simonton's sodding books, that I have been going along to all the consultations with doctors and to the two chemo courses Carmen has had so far. The woman with the very thin hair wasn't there this time – holiday? cured? given up? dead? – so neither was her husband. And that boy was wearing his Gatsby cap again, but his girlfriend wasn't with him. It's as though the good things I'm doing are outweighed by my never-ending, impure need for self-gratification, for pleasure. Like a paedophile who struggles to contain himself for years and years, but still feels guilty all the time because of his dirty thoughts about children.

'You don't need to, Danny. It might even be worse for you than it is for me,' Carmen suddenly jumps in.

It takes a moment before I hear what she's saying. I look at her in surprise.

'Yes,' Carmen goes on, 'you're healthy, you've never asked for this, and here you are sitting with a wife who's weeping and grieving all the time and' – she sniffs and waits for a second – 'will soon have a bald head.'

I see she means it. She really does think it's terrible for me. *For me.*

Things can't get much crazier than this. After a few weeks of cancer our psycho-emotional-relational status is as follows:

1. Wife with cancer has guilt complex because she's doing this to her husband.
2. Husband with wife with cancer has guilt complex because he thinks he's feeling too much self-pity.

And then we howl for a little while longer, cosily, the two of us, arms around each other.

'OK,' says Gerda.

She says next time we'll go on with Simonton's meditation exercises. 'I think that'll do you good. In the exercises you learn to use your mind to fight the cancer.'

Carmen nods like she thinks it's the most normal thing in the world.

'We'll back it up with visualization techniques,' Gerda goes on.

I wisely keep my trap shut.

'But they also help you to be nice and calm.'

'Yeah, suits me,' Carmen nods.

I nod too. Though I didn't find Carmen all that calm when she was flinging Simonton's book across the sitting-room.

'If you're doing these exercises, I'll record them and you'll get the tape to take home with you,' says Gerda, pointing to the cassette recorder. 'Then you can do them at home, too, over the following week.'

'Well, hm – sounds good,' says Carmen.

'The other thing I want to ask both of you to do is to make a drawing' – *both of you, she says* – 'in which you try to visualize the tumour in your breast' – *my years of practice at listening to the most inane briefings and endless marketing crap*

71

from clients is about to pay off – 'You can join in, Dan, just imagine the tumour in Carmen's breast' – *just* – 'and then draw the chemo going for the tumour in the breast' – *Monty Python! I'm in a Monty Python sketch* – 'and then visualize what crosses your mind' – *that someone's taking the piss, that's what's crossing my mind.*

'Does that suit you, Carmen?'

'Yes, I – I think so.'

'You too, Dan?'

'Yes, it seems a very good idea.'

'Fine, then, till next week!'

'Yes, till next week.'

She shakes us both by the hand.

'Bye, Carmen! Bye, Dan.'

'Byeee,' we call over our shoulders.

In the lift I carefully dart a look at Carmen. She's laughing her head off.

Thank goodness. Her brain's still working.

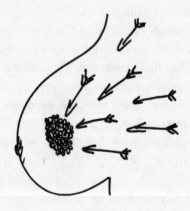

Seems kinda funny sir to me,
that at the end of every hard day,
people find some reason to believe . . .

Bruce Springsteen, from 'Reason to Believe' (*Nebraska*, 1982)

Nineteen

But I have to admit the conversation with Gerda did us good.

It gave Carmen and me the brilliant idea of keeping each other a bit more up to date with our feelings. So I can tell Carmen I hate the idea of going to Bloemendaal this summer, that what I'd like best would be for Dr Wolters to develop galloping Arab consumption on his left heart valve, and that I think it's great that every time I go to MIU I step inside a cancer-free zone. And Carmen tells me honestly she really can't bear it any more, and that even days before she's due to take the chemo she's already terrified at the thought of the needle.

The subjects that remain taboo are all things that could become reality after the chemo – metastatization, breast amputation and death, to name but a few. I get support from an unexpected quarter: negative thought has an unfavourable effect on the development of the illness, Dr O. Carl Simonton writes in his book. Simon, as Carmen has christened him, brooks no opposition; with chapter headings like *Mental forces can influence cancer*, *Take charge of your health* and *The scientific proof for our approach*, Simon is the Louis van Gaal of medical science.

But sometimes life is simple: if all the statistics are our enemies, and Simon can cheerfully ignore all the figures and survival rates with American nonchalance, then Simon is our friend. So over the past week we've told everyone willing to listen that Simon's method of combating cancer with positive thinking, meditation exercises and visualization techniques is scientifically proven (although quite honestly I haven't told anyone about our drawing assignment for Gerda). And if anyone is a champion of positive thinking, then Carmen is that person.

We were right about that, everyone said.

If anyone can do it, Carmen can.

We're telling everyone the mind can be stronger than the body. What am I saying – *is* stronger than the body! We're going to make it! Let all those who love us follow us in our battle for superior knowledge, and join us in clutching at this single straw! Hallelujah, Simon!

Blonde hair, blue eyes,
straight from a book of fairy-tales . . .

Bloem, from 'Even aan mijn moeder vragen'
(*Vooral jong blijven*, 1980)

Twenty

Carmen's hair is starting to fall out in considerable quantities
now. In the morning, when she wakes up, her whole pillow's
covered with it. Since yesterday she's been able to pull whole
bunches out of her head, quite painlessly.

'Pay attention,' she says when I come home in the evening,
holding up her index finger with a serious expression on her
face, 'I've been practising all day . . .'

She comes and stands in front of me, pulls a blank,
scared face, looks at me with her eyes wide, bites her lip
to suppress a pretend scream, and pulls a bunch of hair out
of her head with both hands. A new joke in her Mr Bean
repertoire.

'Good, isn't it?' she says, roaring with laughter.

∎

In the evening in the bathroom she stands and looks in the
mirror, her head lowered slightly.

'It's getting really thin now, isn't it?'

'Hmm. But you've still got lots left.'

'No, not for long. Take a look at this,' she says, and pulls aside a bunch of hair on the top of her head. I see a centimetre without any hair at all.

'OK, when you part your hair you can see it, fair enough—'

She's barely listening.

'I don't think I can go on like this. I'm so scared I'll be at work some time, or in the pub, and people will see it.'

She's caught between anger and tears. Mr Bean has left the building.

'What do you want?' I ask.

The moment I've feared for weeks is coming worryingly close.

'Should we just cut it off?' she asks hesitantly.

'Do you want me to do it?' I say, looking at her in the mirror.

Gulp. Do I mean that?

'Can – is that what you want to do?' she asks nervously, almost embarrassed.

I don't know how I manage, but I nod and smile.

'Of course I'll do it for you.'

She looks at herself in the mirror again, waits for a moment and says, 'Just do it.'

'Fine,' I say, and take my electric clippers out of the cupboard beside the mirror.

'How do you want to do it?' she asks uncertainly.

'Clippers first, then scissors?'

'Yes, I reckon that's the best idea, don't you? It has to be really smooth. I don't want to itch under a wig.'

I take a white handkerchief and lay it over her shoulders. She is still looking at herself in the mirror. I examine the top part of the back of her head, moving my head like a trained barber from left to right and top to bottom. Where in God's name are you supposed to start, can anybody tell me? At the back of her head anyway, so she doesn't see the first bit of scalp straight away when I pass the clippers across it? Yes, the back first.

'Here we go, then, darling.'

I sigh deeply, switch on the clippers and shear away a strip about four centimetres wide, starting at the nape of her neck. At the same time I kiss her on the cheek. In the mirror she sees the long hair falling on the handkerchief, throws her hand to her mouth and starts crying. I swallow, but continue resolutely on with my shearing, kissing her on the head every few seconds. We say nothing.

Ten minutes later Carmen is bald.

You can hide neath your covers and study your pain,
waste your summer praying in vain...

Bruce Springsteen, from 'Thunder Road' (*Born to Run*, 1975)

Twenty-one

'*Aaarrrggghhh!* This wretched thing itches like hell, it's going to drive me completely round the bend!'

I look up from my music magazine.

It's hot on the terrace behind our house. Because of the neighbours' extension on one side and the high hedge on the other there's never any wind. Only right at the back of the garden, down by the little brook that separates the city from its forest, the Amsterdamse Bos, do you sometimes get a little gust of wind, but we hardly ever go down there. When you do, it feels as though you're in the middle of the forest. Most unnatural. I go there sometimes with Luna to feed the ducks, but otherwise the garden actually stops before that as far as we're concerned, beyond the wooden planks of our terrace. We're sitting under the big rectangular parasol. Even I think it's hot, and I'm not wearing a wig.

Prickly-wig, Carmen's been calling it since yesterday. She's been wearing it for a week now, but yesterday was the first day the temperature went above twenty degrees. Before that, it was a wonderful summer from the point of view of wig technology: seventeen degrees or so at the most, a lot of rain and not a single day at the beach.

'Couldn't you take it off?'

'And what about Maud? She's about to turn up with the little one.'

Luna has spent a night at Maud's, and today she wants to go to the zoo. I was over the moon when Maud suggested it. There was another course of chemo on Tuesday, and just as Carmen starts feeling better, around about the weekend, I'm shattered. Three days of looking after Carmen and Luna full-time, and the odd few hours at MIU in between, are starting to take their toll. Thanks to Maud I was able to sleep in this morning, and as a result I've got so much energy now I might even drop down to the Beachpop dance party this afternoon. So far I haven't told Carmen anything about my wicked plan.

'So? Isn't it your house? Everybody's going to have to get used to the fact you're bald,' I say. And then I drop in, as casually as possible: 'By the way, Maud won't be staying all that long, she wanted to go to Beachpop this afternoon. In Bloemendaal, you know the one. It's starting up again this afternoon.'

'I don't even want to think about it.' Carmen isn't having the loveliest of days. 'And I don't want you to go, either. I'll be stuck on my own here with Luna.'

'No, that wasn't the plan, darling,' I lie. Fuck.

'OK, just so you know,' she says, not looking up from her fashion magazine.

'Yeah . . . Didn't I say that wasn't the plan?'

Silence.

'Oh, this FUCKING THING!' she yells, and claws at her wig with her fingers.

'Christ alive, Carm, then take the bloody thing off!'

'No! I don't want to look ridiculous. Get that into your head right now.'

Then you must be aware of it yourself, I think.

A few minutes later the doorbell rings. I get up and walk to the front door.

'She's such a little darling,' says Maud. She strokes Luna's hair. The little girl's asleep in her buggy.

Maud stays for another hour or so. She's going to go home and change into her hippest clothes. She's already jumping up and down at the idea of going to Beachpop. Carmen babbles and laughs happily along with her. I smile.

'Frank and a few others from MIU are coming too,' says Maud.

'We're going to have a nice time at home,' says Carmen.

I do nothing and I do nothing, I just hang around,
I look out the window from time to time,
and I scratch my arse, I stare into the distance,
I grab a beer, and I play on my flute for a bit . . .

De Dijk, from 'Bloedend hart' (*De Dijk*, 1982)

Twenty-two

'And now?' I ask.

On the bed there's a pair of scissors, a sort of pizza-box that held the thick gel bandages, and a few loose, snipped-off pieces. And there's a young, naked, bald woman with one beautiful, healthy breast, and one breast covered with blisters, sores and a patchwork of sections of burnt skin in a range of colours: yellow, pink, purple, red and claret. The black lines drawn on it five weeks ago for the radiotherapy are still visible through the volcanic landscape.

Carmen tilts up her head and looks at the side of the part of her breast that has still not been wrapped up. The bandage is covered with gel on the underside, to make sure the layers of burnt skin don't come away next time the bandages are changed. She holds the piece already on her breast in place with one hand, while with the other she points to the bandage.

'The nurse made some sort of notch, around about here I think it was. Otherwise it doesn't quite fit around my breast, and that stuff gets creased.'

'OK. About how far in do I cut?'

'Ooh – about five centimetres, I'd say?'

Dr Scheltema wasn't too unhappy when Carmen had had her series of four courses of chemo. The tumour markers in Carmen's blood looked hopeful, and the tumour in her breast had shrunk slightly. She even dared to drop the word 'operate' into the conversation. 'But first of all let's make sure the tumour in the breast gets even smaller, or else we risk letting it get into the skin when they operate. And then we'll be really much worse off than before,' she said. A radiologist was brought in from the Antoni van Leeuwenhoek Hospital, and he agreed with Scheltema. Radiotherapy. For seven weeks, to Antoni van Leeuwenhoek every day. Then we'd see.

The first four weeks of radiotherapy were a walk in the park compared with the problems after each course of chemo. But after twenty exposures of radiation, as the radiologist predicted, Carmen's skin started to give out.

'Should I cut in any further, do you think?'

'Umm – no, that's fine,' says Carmen anxiously. 'Stop! Stop!' She's terrified I'm going touch the painful, burnt skin of her breast by accident. I set the scissors down and, with the tip of my tongue between my lips, I lift one flap from the bandage with the notch cut into it, and let the other drop very gently on to the breast, without pressing down on it. Then the second flap in cleanly beside it, and Bob's your uncle. The breast is hermetically sealed.

Carmen inspects my handiwork. 'Yes,' she nods. 'Good. Thanks.'

I wipe the drops of sweat from my forehead, put the pieces of protective foil and a leftover bit of unused bandage back in the pizza-box and walk to the bathroom to throw the mess in the bin. When I come back Carmen's asleep. The radiotherapy's starting to kick in.

On the radio alarm clock I see it's just half past eight. It's still light outside. Last night she went to sleep at eight o'clock, a quarter of an hour after Luna. To show solidarity I went to bed too. I still hadn't got to sleep by midnight.

I gently walk over to her and kiss her on the forehead. 'Night, love,' I whisper. She goes on sleeping.

Downstairs I get a bottle of beer out of the fridge. Though, actually, I feel more like a glass of rosé. I put the beer back and open a bottle. I take a little bag of Japanese crackers out of the cupboard. I check to see if I've got any text messages. One from Ramon.

► Frank and I know **Ramon** from BBDvW&R/Bernilvy. Ramon was brought in as Frank's account assistant. Where Frank has too much style, Ramon has too little. He's built like a brick shit-house, and you only get to look like that if you're either a prole or a poof, and Ramon's certainly no poof. He's proud of his body, and I have to admit he's right to be. It gives him more self-confidence than is good for him. He can sometimes get aggressive if he's in a bad mood and someone accidentally touches him (or his car or his beer). Ramon acts like the whole world belongs to him, and the world usually falls for it, too. He's also got an enormous cock, and that helps him radiate more self-confidence than is quite sensible from the objective point of view.

Ramon isn't actually a true friend in the way Frank and Thomas are, but we belong to the same blood group. Ramon's wild about clubs like La Bastille, Het Feest van Joop and the Surprise Bar. I know only one person with the same aberration, and that's me. Another thing we have in common is the fact that, like me, Ramon has an omnivorous appetite for women. We grab whatever comes our way, and don't let relationship duties get in the way. Ramon and I reckon moderation is a virtue only practised

by those who always come away empty-handed.* The last similar-
ity is that we both come from the south: I come from Breda, and
Ramon comes from Chile. When he was nine, his father fled to
the Netherlands with his whole family. Ramon's father was a
teacher, and too bright for the Pinochet regime. The family settled
in the high-rise projects of south-eastern Amsterdam. His little
friends tended to be drawn to coke and related substances,
whether as users or as dealers. Ramon went to university. He
wanted to have a career, he said. Ten years later, not Frank but
Ramon was appointed director of the advertising agency
BBDvW&R/Bernilvy. Frank couldn't cope with suddenly having a
flash git like Ramon as his boss, and resigned. Since then he can't
stop showing off about MIU Creative & Strategic Marketing
Agency, and going on like a TV commercial whenever Ramon's
about. Ramon says he couldn't give a monkey's about what Frank
(or anyone else on the planet) thinks.

Are we still going out Leidsepleining on Friday? he wants
to know.

Wahay – Is the Pope Catholic?

I've dropped my weekly evening football match in the
Vondelpark since the chemo courses began, I've stopped going
for a drink after work, but Danny's Friday Night Out remains
thoroughly in force.

But it's only Tuesday, and I haven't the energy. I switch on
the TV. On the Yorin channel there's a repeat of tonight's *Big
Brother*. I've seen it already, we always turn it on at seven
these days. You've got to do something. There's a real Thomas
film on RTL. Jean-Claude van Damme. I text him to see if
he's watching. On SBS6, Everton–Southampton for the FA

---

* Boccaccio, previously misused by Ronald Giphart in *Ik omhels je met duizend
armen*.

Cup. I watch it for a moment. Rubbish game. On Canal Plus there's a French film. Nothing doing there, then. Which leaves MTV. R&B, sod that. The sports news on Channel 3 doesn't start till a quarter past ten.

I pick the newspaper up from the floor and take a look at the article about the Amsterdam transport system in the supplement. I get about halfway. In the drawer of the table there's a copy of that Harry Mulisch novel, *The Discovery of Heaven*, which I've been busily reading for the last two months, and have managed sixty-seven pages. I open the book with a feeling of distaste, read to page seventy-one and put it away again with a sigh. Ah, a text! Thomas, saying he is indeed watching the film and how is Carmen. I click away and tell him she's in bed because she's exhausted by all the radiotherapy, and I'm bored to sobs. Before I send it, I delete the bit about being bored. Thomas has been sitting on the sofa at his house for years. And Anne wouldn't have the first clue what I was on about.

I pour myself another glass of wine and switch on teletext. Page 601. Not much news. 703. It's going to stay nice this week. All we need. Back to SBS. Still 0–0. What about AT5? Oh God, some cow listing all the road works in Amsterdam this week. In the meantime I've switched on my computer and opened Outlook. I leave unopened the four mails from an American chat group about inflammatory breast cancer. I open a mail from Anne. How is Carmen today? She can tell her herself tomorrow.

Hakan mails Frank, Ramon and me to say he's coming with us to Miami in the last weekend of October.

A reply from Frank, saying we'd better book soon, in case, and we should take a look at www.pelicanhotel.com, because it's the hotel that belongs to Renzo Rosso of Diesel, and it's just great.

> ▶ **Hakan**. Second-generation Turk. Successful, and it shows. Motto: dress to impress. What we have in common is our BBDvW&R/Bernilvy background and an excessive interest in football and women. Just enough, between men, for us to consider ourselves the very best of friends.

The following reply is from Hakan again. He's heard the Pelican is already out of fashion. I mail the guys back to say I couldn't care less which hotel we stay in, as long as we go. I miss the sports news because Carmen's mother phones to ask how Carmen is. Exactly a quarter to eleven. I don't feel like sleeping in the slightest. I take a look at Bol.com. The new Manic Street Preachers is out. I click on order. I read an online review of The Prodigy. Order. A CD by Eagle Eye Cherry, there's that one song that Carm's so fond of. You see, going out's cheaper than staying at home. I pour myself another glass of rosé, and put away the Japanese crackers before I eat the whole bag out of boredom. Quarter past eleven. The porn on Canal Plus starts in half an hour. I flick through an old copy of *De Tijd* and read a bit from *The Healing Journey* by Simonton. I manage a quarter of it. Carmen has read both of them already. I put the bottle of rosé, three-quarters empty, back in the fridge, clear the table, turn on the dishwasher, lay Luna's little table for the morning, and walk back to the sitting-room. Ah, they're getting down to it already. Italian porn tonight. They're mostly good-looking girls with real tits. I don't like inflated American porn-tits. Carmen and I are in touching agreement on this: sooner big tits that are real and droop a little than fake tits that stand up

86

and don't move when you're screwing. It's been months since we abandoned our communal scientific analyses of TV tits. When Carmen accidentally zaps to porn on Canal Plus, she can't zap away quickly enough. For Carmen, porn is passé. Not for me. I watch two scenes, come, take a piece of kitchen paper, wipe my belly clean, walk to the bin, shove the wet paper under a stack of old newspapers and go to bed. After about ten minutes I fall asleep next to Carmen.

I do declare,
There were times when I was so lonesome,
I took some comfort there . . .

Simon and Garfunkel, from 'The Boxer' (*Sounds of Silence*, 1970)

Twenty-three

Carmen barely knows Ramon. They've seen each other a few times, at BBDvW&R/Bernilvy parties. Carmen seriously impressed Ramon. ('Hey, amigo, how about swapping partners some time?' 'Don't be daft, I really don't fancy giving you a blow-job.')

He never comes to our house. We always arrange to meet in the Leidseplein, at the Palladium.

▶ **Palladium.** The Ajax team have been taking their girlfriends there for ages. It's rumoured that even Wim Jonk* once scored there.

There we spend half an hour talking about Bernilvy and MIU, and look at the firm young girls that fill the Palladium, and then we go to the hunting-ground where, as fat guys in our thirties, we feel more at home: La Bastille.

▶ In **La Bastille** they realize nothing in life is as important as regularity, so they play something by André Hazes† at least once

---

*   The most boring Ajax player of all time. Later found PSV more to his liking.

†   Amsterdam folk-singer, hugely popular but disdained by the critics.

every quarter of an hour. The clientele consists primarily of second-time-round women (30–40, divorced, recognizable by their heavy investments in cosmetics and sunbeds with a view to getting a bit more out of things. High chance of scoring.

Once we're in there, we move on to the order of the day. We spot a little coterie of cocktail-drinking women at the bar. Ramon chats to a girl with a Moschino belt. I talk to one whose blouse Carmen would find far too revealing (I think it suits her), and whose bum is too big for the skirt she's wearing (even I can't wriggle out of that one). In the context of the Bastille it isn't even all that vulgar. After talking bollocks for half an hour we're snogging. After an hour I ask her her name for the third time and for the second time whether she lives in Amsterdam. I can't shake the impression my popularity's starting to wane. She has a boyfriend, she says at one point, and her girlfriends are there. Then she starts talking about how ridiculously full it is here, and she just had to stand in the line for the toilets for ten minutes, and when she got there she had to pay for it, too. I've got enough complaining voices in my head already. I ask Ramon whether he and his gang feel like going along to the Surprise. He shakes his head. I shrug and leave the Bastille.

▶ The **Surprise** is the antechamber of the Bastille. If second-time-round women mostly populate the Bastille, in the Surprise the average woman is ten years younger. Girls who have just split up with their boyfriends, and who are entering a brief and intense period of partying. Always with a mate, who is usually in the same post-relationship boat. Two or three times a week they'll go together to the Surprise (and after three o'clock to the Cooldown or Het Feest van Joop). There they are soon recognized by the always affable bar staff, spend a decent amount of money at the bar and – the status symbol for female visitors to the Surprise –

are allowed to leave their handbags and jackets behind the bar. The barman treats the girl and her friend to free shots and winks each time they visit. An extremely pragmatic approach, because the more of this kind of girl you have at the bar, the more men you'll get. Soon the girl falls in love with a male visitor to the Surprise, the couple continue to go to the Surprise for form's sake, although less and less frequently, and then end up on the sofa in their new house in Almere. A few years later they get divorced, and then it's the Bastille's turn. That's how the Leidseplein sensibly recycles its clientele.

I last ten minutes in the Surprise. Clearly, even by the standards of the Surprise, I look like a randy baboon. The girls don't react. So should I go to the Paradiso and dance away on my own? Or should I . . . Oh, what the hell.

'De Ruysdaelkade,' I say to the taxi-driver.

Out of shame, I ask the taxi-driver to let me out not on the side where the prostitutes are, but at the top of the canal, and pretend to go into a residential house. When the taxi's out of sight, I cross over and, after walking up and down three times, discover the women who are still working at around this time of night aren't exactly the pick of the bunch. Finally I choose an African woman. She's wearing a black negligée that's too small for her meaty breasts. When she gets undressed they sag about five centimetres, but hey, at least there are two of them and they aren't burnt.

Half an hour later I undress at home. I leave my clothes in the sitting-room and walk upstairs as quietly as possible. Silently I creep into bed.

'Good time?' Carmen asks sleepily.

'Yep. Nattering and dancing. It was nice to be out with Ramon.'

'Mmmm,' she says with a warm voice. 'Great. You've deserved it.'

In the dark I kiss her cheek.

'Goodnight, love of my life.'

'Goodnight, my best friend in the whole world.'

What is it about men and breasts? How can you be so
interested in them? Seriously, they're just breasts.
Every second person in the world has them. They're
odd looking, they're for milk. Your mother has them
too. You must have seen thousands of them. What's
all the fuss about?

Notting Hill (1999)*

Twenty-four

Who could ever have thought I would be spending a week's
holiday in Center Parcs in Port Zélande? I can explain it
perfectly to everybody and to myself, that's not a problem.
Could you follow our inescapable logic for a moment?

1. It's too risky for Carmen to go far, with all the chemo
   still in her body.
2. Because of Carmen's wig, all destinations with an
   expected temperature of more than twenty-five degrees
   are out of the question.
3. A doing, walking, going-out or visiting-things sort of
   holiday is ruled out because of Luna's age (one) and
   Carmen's condition (nil).
4. Center Parcs is a client of MIU, so I can declare part of
   my stay as field research.

---

* Julia Roberts to Hugh Grant. To which we might point out that Julia herself has
no tits, or at least none that can be seen with the naked eye.

92

Besides, in a month I'm going to Miami with the guys, so I should be able to cope with a week in Port Zélande, I reckoned.

Wrong. Port Zélande isn't nice. Everything about it's disappointing. The people here are driving me round the bend, the weather's great and consequently far too hot for pricklywig, Carmen's just as prickly as her wig, and to make the party complete, Luna has recently started refusing to take a nap during the day, which makes her tired in the afternoon and stops her enjoying anything, which has a cumulative effect on the rest of the family.

Last of all, it doesn't help that Carmen has to call Dr Scheltema in three days to find out whether her breast really will have to come off or not. That's how it is.

Dr Scheltema, along with the radiologist and Dr Wolters, thought along the following lines. Compare it with 'backburning', the technique that's used to tackle big bushfires. An area of forest is burned deliberately to halt a forest fire that has broken out some way away. And as soon as that's been done, the whole of the bush is levelled. With the irradiation of Carmen's breast, Dr Scheltema, Dr Wolters and the radiologist want to achieve exactly the same effect. The chemo had already ensured the tumour got smaller. After that, the radiation would make the tumour even smaller in such a way that the apotheosis of the whole process could be brought to fruition: the removal of the tumour by operation, and the backburning of Carmen's breast.

And Carmen had the advantage, Scheltema said, of having considerably large breasts. Then there's a greater chance that with the amputation of her breast, the surgeon will later be able completely to remove the tumour, which begins with the nipple.

In three days, on Thursday morning, the Scheltema–Wolters commission goes into conclave with the radiologist and the surgeon.

Not only medical Amsterdam, but also our complete circle of friends and family, is intensely involved in the wider social discussion of my wife's breasts. Everybody hopes the doctors will give a green light for the operation (no one calls it amputation).

'What did I hear, is there a chance they might be able to operate on Carmen?'

'Yes . . .'

'But – that's a good sign, isn't it?'

'Yes, basically, because at first they weren't going to risk it, and now they probably will, so yes, that is good.'

'Oh, how fantastic! So that's going to be great, then, isn't it?'

Now! My boy, how great it's all going to be, and how relieved Carmen will be! Relieved she soon won't be able to make those jokes any more like the time I came out of the bathroom and she lay naked on the bed with a big grin on her face and two yellow Post-it notes on her nipples with 'nice' on one, and on the other, 'aren't they?'

And then there's me. I'm going to be sooooo relieved!

Relieved that along with her breast, something else is going to be amputated – her ability to be unrestrainedly, unashamedly, vulgarly horny, a process set in motion when Carmen lost her hair. Don't ask me why, but Carmen has found herself a bit less attractive since she's been completely bald. Although I'm constantly reiterating she's beautiful even without her hair. In fact, to celebrate her baldness I shaved off the few pubic hairs she still had after the chemo, and told

94

her under the sheets how lovely her pussy looked like that. That got Carmen going, too – at least on the first evening. After that, her unhappiness over her bald head won out over her excitement over her bald fanny. End of sex. Great, huh?

After the amputation of her breast it's going to be one big party in the bedroom. However often I tell her I still find her attractive, every time she looks in the mirror she'll see she's no longer Carmen.

Carmen is afraid of losing her breast, I'm afraid of losing the Carmen I know. A lonely anxiety I don't dare share with anyone. Maybe I attach more importance to Carmen's breast than I do to Carmen's life?

And Carmen and I barely talk about the operation, which is coming closer and closer. We both know what we're thinking about when we eat mussels in the Port Zélande restaurant, when we're lying on the beach, when we watch *David Letterman* in our bungalow in the evening – every minute of the day we're thinking about the breast. And when we're sleeping, we're dreaming about the breast. Each of us knows the other's doing it, and neither of us talks about it.

The evening before The Phone Call we're lying in bed. I kiss Carmen and turn over on to my side.

'Shall I turn out the light?'

'Yeah, do that.'

'Night, my love.'

'Night, treasure.'

Click.

A few minutes pass.

'Danny?'

'Yes?'

'Are you asleep yet?'

'No.'

'Oh.'

'What's up?'

'What d'you think they're going to say tomorrow?'

'I don't know, darling.'

'And what do you hope?'

'Well, yeah, I hope they'll risk it.'

'But you're a tit-man, Dan. And soon you're going to have a wife with a bald head and one tit.'

I turn over and hold her tight.

'I hope they'll take the risk, Carmen.'

'Really?'

'Really.'

I feel a tear fall on to my shoulder.

'What do *you* hope they'll say tomorrow?'

'I hope it can come off.'

'Then that's good.'

'But it's pretty awful, isn't it?'

'. . .'

'Danny?'

'Yeah – it's terrible, darling. But I'd rather have you with one breast than not have you at all.'

■

The next day we're lying on the beach. It's already midday. Every now and again I look at Carmen, but don't dare to ask if we should make the call in a minute.

'I'm going back to the bungalow to ring them,' she says.

'Wouldn't you rather do it here?' I ask, pointing at my mobile.

She shakes her head.

96

'I'd rather not. I want to hear exactly what Scheltema has to say, and it's so windy around here.'

Of course she doesn't want to call from here, you pillock, I think to myself. Sitting on a nice beach full of people and hearing you're going to lose your breast.

'Shall we go back to the bungalow together?' I ask.

'No. I'd rather go on my own. You stay here with Luna.'

She pulls a skirt on over her bikini and walks away down the beach.

I watch after her till she reaches the edge of the forest and disappears from sight.

She doesn't come back for almost three-quarters of an hour. I've kept Luna amused with buckets and spades and water. It's as though I'm sitting in the waiting-room while my wife's having a baby.

'Hi,' I hear unexpectedly behind me.

'Hi!' I say and try to read from her facial expression what Scheltema might have said.

'They don't know yet.'

'They don't know yet?'

'No. Scheltema says the surgeon wants to take a look at my breast before he decides whether they should risk it.'

'Jesus,' I sigh, 'when's he doing that?'

'Next week. I've got an appointment with him on Monday.'

Another four days of suspense.

'Hm. Why did it take so long? You've been away for three-quarters of an hour.'

'Scheltema was on her lunch-break.'

We'll go on, in a lightless trench, to go on again...

Ramses Shaffy, from 'Wij zullen doorgaan'
(*Wij zullen doorgaan*, 1972)

Twenty-five

The surgeon's called Dr Jonkman. His office is next to Dr Wolters's, in the Oncology Department. Not bad, judging by Carmen, who licks her lips behind his back and gives me a wink.

'Bit of a looker?' I whisper quietly in her ear. She nods enthusiastically.

'If he touches your tits, I'm decking him,' I whisper. Carmen laughs.

Jonkman is a doctor out of a hospital romance. He's about forty, boyish face with collar-length hair, greying at the temples. Put him in a Paul Smith jacket and he could be an account man in an advertising agency. He can imagine our situation more easily than Dr Scheltema and Dr Wolters, who are about fifteen years older. He probably has a wife Carmen's age and – given his appearance – she's bound to be pretty gorgeous. That creates a bond.

But he's still a doctor. As soon as he opens Carmen's file – which by now I recognize from the outside – and switches from Carmen the person to C. van Diepen the patient, he starts talking like a Euro MP. Choosing his words carefully, he explains he's only going to operate if he knows for certain it will strongly improve her chances of survival.

'You're a beautiful young woman, and after the ablation' – we stare at him uncomprehendingly – 'that is, erm, the amputation, after the amputation, OK, you'll have a little scar, ten centimetres or so, running horizontally where your breast is now' – no, we don't like the sound of that, we really don't – 'and then perhaps we can insert a breast implant, but it'll never be like it is now.' He pauses for a moment and looks Carmen right in the eye. 'It's a terrible piece of mutilation.'

Terrible piece of mutilation. His words make me start, but I realize he's being so direct deliberately. He wants to know whether Carmen's ready for it. I like him. Jonkman is the first one who understands that a breast, for a young woman and her husband, is more than a protuberance with – in Carmen's case – a swelling inside it.

'Shall we take a look at your breast?'

Carmen takes off her blouse and her bra, and goes and lies on the narrow examination bed in his surgery. Jonkman starts feeling my wife's breasts with his hands. Carmen winks at me, and I smile.

'Hmm . . .' he says after a while. 'OK. Get your clothes back on.' He washes his hands. 'I'd say that right now the tumour measures six centimetres by two.'

'So . . .?'

Carmen doesn't dare finish her question.

'I think we've got to take the risk and, to optimize your chances of survival, move on to the amputation of the breast.'

Carmen shows no emotional reaction, but I can see it's a hard blow. Jonkman swiftly continues. 'The ablation can be carried out in the third week of October,' he says, glancing at a roster hanging on the wall, 'although I myself will be on holiday then. Which means Dr Wolters will be performing the operation.'

The sound of the name Wolters in combination with the word operation is enough to make Carmen burst into tears.

'I don't think so,' I say grimly.

'Why not?' asks Jonkman, startled. I can tell from his face he doesn't know anything about it. The great clodhoppers. Wolters and Scheltema have kept it under their hats.

'A year ago, Dr Wolters made a mistake when diagnosing my wife's condition. That's why we're here now. My wife and I don't want him to get his hands anywhere near her body.'

Sobbing, Carmen stares at the floor. Jonkman quickly recovers his professional demeanour.

'Fine. Then I'll operate on you, a week later,' he says without asking any further questions.

Carmen nods and whispers, barely audibly, 'That's great – thank you.'

'My assistant will arrange a precise date with you.'

The operation is set for Thursday, 31 October.

Four days after Miami, it suddenly shoots through my head. So I can forget that. Fucking cancer. One tit and the best weekend of the year, both lost in a single conversation.

When I'm out in the streets,
I talk the way I wanna talk,
when I'm out in the streets,
I don't feel sad and blue,
when I'm out in the streets,
I never feel alone,
when I'm out in the streets,
in the crowds I feel at home . . .

Bruce Springsteen, from 'Out in the Streets' (*The River*, 1980)

Twenty-six

And on the eighth day God created Miami.

Yeah, you bet, and I'm there! Ocean Drive, Miami Beach, Florida.

In the taxi on Ocean Drive, Ramon, Hakan and I can't turn our heads quickly enough to catch all the gorgeous girls all around us. It's one great big sweetie-jar, even Frank agrees.

Carmen brought the subject up herself. 'You just go off with the guys, while you can. Later there'll be the operation, and after that I'm really going to need you,' she said. I jumped in the air, and the next day bought up all the roses in the flower stall opposite the Olympic Stadium. Carmen was so impressed she asked if I didn't fancy a weekend away every month.

We were dropped off at the Pelican Hotel. The hotel is mint green. The next one along is pink, the one after that pale blue. A waitress with dark-blonde hair and enormous hooters showing through her white V-necked Diesel T-shirt comes skipping up the steps to the terrace. She sees me staring, laughs and says, 'Hi.' 'Hi,' I say back.

Sitting at reception is a Puerto Rican girl. Christ almighty, they don't look like that at the Hans Brinker Hotel in Amsterdam. 'Lord, I'm not worthy,' stammers Ramon. The girl laughs, flashing her teeth, and gives us our keys. I feel exactly as I did twenty years ago, the first time I went to Lloret de Mar.

Because Ramon and I are suspected of having the same nocturnal interests, Frank puts us in a room together. We are given 'Best Whorehouse'. Frank and Hakan take 'Me Tarzan, You Vain'. The rooms aren't big, but this place is about hip rather than comfort, Frank explains to me.

Everyone has been given instructions to shower quickly and be back down within half an hour. Frank has booked a table in the Delano, and apparently they expect you to turn up on time.

And to dress properly, I realize when I see Frank and Hakan. Frank's wearing a black pinstripe jacket, and proudly names the label – a Japanese designer I've never heard of before. He casually remarks that he bought it on Madison Avenue in Manhattan. Hakan says he thinks it's a nice jacket, but the jackets of another label – which I've never heard of either, although he himself just happens to be wearing a shirt and shoes of the same make this evening – are even nicer. Obviously I stayed with my snake leathers. And my white trousers and purple shirt may not be in quite the same price range as Frank's outfit, but I reckon I look cool enough to check out my market value among the women of Miami. Ramon is wearing a tight T-shirt. It really suits him. Fortunately, in terms of the competition, he's also wearing his black leather trousers, which were last in fashion when Ajax played in their old De Meer stadium.

∎

Over dinner, outside under the palm trees around the Delano's swimming-pool, we have our first in-depth discussions. Can the Netherlands become European Champions (me: yes, Ramon and Hakan: no, Frank: doesn't know); how is MIU doing (Frank: fantastic! me: OK); who, when we were at BBDvW&R/Bernilvy, did it with Sharon (me: me, Ramon: of course! Hakan: just a blowjob, Frank: fuck off!); is the St Martin's Lane hotel in London hipper than the Delano (me: don't know, Ramon: don't know, Frank: no, Hakan: yes) and are we going to take the ecstasy Ramon brought with him this evening (me: yes! Ramon: really? I thought you weren't going to? me: stop nagging and just let me have one, Hakan: not tonight, Frank: of course not)? Ramon gives me a pill. I'm a bit nervous. Until this point in my life I've only ever consumed alcohol. Carmen is against anything to do with drugs. I swallow the thing down with a slug of beer. Frank looks at me and shakes his head.

> ► The **Delano** – pronounced Dèlano, certainly not Delááno, which is what I say – is even more expensive than the Pelican. That's because it's one of Ian Schrager's hotels, Hakan tells me. He utters the name with such respect I don't ask who the hell Ian Schrager is. The Delano's customers consist of Ocean Drive estate agents, advertising people and business groupies. Nobody laughs. The food, the cocktails, the décor and the women in the Delano are prohibitively expensive. But money isn't important this weekend, we've decided.

We go to Washington Avenue, beyond Ocean Drive. That's where most of the clubs and discos in Miami Beach are, at least according to Frank, who usually knows things like that. How he knows them is a complete mystery to me, but he does. We seem to be headed for Chaos, where it's all happening (according to Frank). Hakan mutters reservations. He says he heard the barman at the Delano saying Washington Avenue is passé, and we should go to Club Tantra, in a completely different part of town. Ramon and I wave Hakan's objections aside; we've observed with delight that there are bunches of beautiful girls standing in the long queue waiting outside Chaos. Standing behind a velvet rope, arms folded, a brother of Mr T is standing watch. I don't know why, but I'm dying to get in. Ramon clearly is too. He creeps forward and starts straight in with his spiel about 'I spin at the RoXy in Amsterdam.'

> ▶ **The RoXy.** The late RoXy – clubbing's answer to Marco van Basten, who, because of severe injuries (third-degree burns), had to quit early. Consequently, like Marco, it won larger-than-life status. I've heard loads about it, but never managed to see it. I missed out on the RoXy. Carmen was never a big fan of house. Neither was I, though I must say my interest perked up when even Frank waxed lyrical about the gorgeous girls that used to go there. Ramon went there every week, too, after his tour of the Leidseplein with me. Then I went to Paradiso to dance to the Cure with ugly women. And now it's too late. I'll have to make do with Ramon and Frank's stories.

Without even looking at him, Mr T clearly indicates with a nod of the head that we can kiss his fat black ass and we have to go to the back and then ask him if he'll let us in when we finally get back to the front.

And half an hour later, he won't.

'There are four of you guys?'

'Yes.'

'No way.'

Ramon is about to go for the man, but works out just in time this isn't a good plan. I can't see anything funny about it. I *have* to get in there. I don't make a fuss, certainly not to Frank, but if I have to spend another five minutes waiting in a queue, I'm going to jump over it like Tigger in Luna's storybook.

Right next door to Chaos is Liquid. There were only about five people waiting outside when we arrived in the taxi, Frank remembers. Now there's a queue the length of the canal around the field in the ArenA. Fuck. And Jesus, that pill's starting to kick in. Hakan tries to talk us into a taxi to Tantra. We don't reply, and continue walking along Washington Avenue. Each time we pass a club Hakan protests. Too many people, not enough people, doesn't look like much, looks crap, and so on. Fortunately Frank threatens to go home if we don't go to the first club we get to *right now*. That's Bash. There's no queue, and Ramon's DJ spiel works on this bouncer. Though not quite as he planned.

'The RoXy?'

'Yeah man! In Amsterdam.'

'So what do you spin at the RoXy?'

'Deep house. Every Thursday.'

'Every Thursday?'

'Yeah, I did a five-hour set last week!'

'You did?'

'Yeah!'

'Didn't the RoXy burn down a while ago?'

Silence.

'Hahaha, come in, you cocksucking fucking motherfuckers.'

Even Ramon falls silent. We meekly pay the twenty dollars per person entry, not too expensive in Miami terms. A bad sign. And it's a bad sign that we can get in as a group of four men.

In the toilet, we get our shirt collars just right, check our haircuts from all sides, high-five each other to shouts of 'yo!' and 'my man!' and walk, full of good cheer and E, through the big black door to the main room. There are nine people inside. Ourselves included.

Hakan immediately starts grumbling. Ramon scans the two girls sitting at the bar, I go on to the dance floor on my own and Frank stomps back to the girl in the ticket office. There'll be more people here in half an hour, he comes back and tells us.

And he's right. Half an hour later there are thirteen people. Hakan starts piling on the pressure to get out of this miserable place. Frank says his jetlag's starting to get him down. It isn't affecting Ramon and me. We're going like lightning.

The light goes on in Bash at about seven in the morning. Ramon leaves with a girl; I walk, completely drenched in sweat and with a smile from ear to ear, from Washington Drive to Ocean Drive. I've been up for nearly thirty hours. I've had a fantastic evening, I haven't even been unfaithful, and I'm about four hundred dollars poorer. Well, what the fuck. I grab a beer from the mini-bar and slump on to the bed, where I try to have a wank. Images alternate of myself with Sharon, with Maud and with Carmen a year ago. Halfway there I fall asleep with my half-erect cock in my hand and a half-full can of beer on the designer table next to the bed.

You think that I'm strong, you're wrong . . .

Robbie Williams, from 'Strong' (*The Ego Has Landed*, 1999)

Twenty-seven

An hour and a half later I'm awake again. Wide awake. The day can't start quickly enough for me. Ramon isn't there yet. I pick up the phone and dial the number of Thomas and Anne, where Carmen's staying this weekend.

'Anne speaking.'

'Hi, Anne, it's Danny!' I shout enthusiastically.

'Oh. Hi, Dan. I'll just get Carmen for you,' says Anne, a bit less enthusiastically. Have I woken her up? No, it's afternoon in Holland.

'Hi,' says Carmen. I feel a distance between us, but act like I haven't noticed anything and say the hotel's completely crazy and there's house music playing there all the time, even in the toilets. Laughing, I tell her about the meal at the Delano, and about going out, and I say I'm very tired now. She barely reacts. I ask how she's getting on at Thomas and Anne's. With an undertone I don't recognize in her, she tells me they're sitting at home, it's nice and they've had a good conversation. For a moment I wonder if I've got through to the wrong Anne.

I can't bear it any longer, and ask her what's up, and if I've said or done something wrong. I hear her asking Thomas if she can use the phone in the bedroom for a moment. There's

107

a short silence. Then I hear a click and she's back: 'I'm feeling bloody awful, Dan,' she says, blowing her nose. 'I'm finding it harder than I thought – the idea you're running around among all those sexy women with enormous tits while I'm sitting here with a bald head and a burnt tit...'

I say I don't really know what to say. And I haven't got off with any girls at all.

'You say that like it's an achievement,' she snaps. I hear a sigh. Then, in a slightly friendlier voice, she says, 'Just leave me for a bit. It'll be OK. Have a lot of fun there and give Frank my love.' She tries to make it sound as sincere as possible. I say I love her and to say hi to Thomas and Anne. She's quiet for a moment.

'I don't know if that's such a good idea, Dan,' she says and hangs up.

■

Downstairs Hakan and Frank are already sitting in their swimming trunks having breakfast on the terrace. I join them. We eat together and then go to the beach. There we run into Ramon and his irritatingly athletic body. With a big grin he tells us he's been shagging his conquest senseless all night and all morning, and hasn't slept for a minute.

On the beach, Frank reads *Wallpaper*, a magazine I've never heard of. It's full of all the things I recognize from his penthouse. Hakan, Ramon and I talk about the important things in life. Should Ajax stick to a 4–3–3 formation or not, what percentage of women swallow, what percentage of men and what percentage of women are unfaithful. I mouth off, loudly announcing one Dannian theory after another. Then Ramon brings up the subject of how often we have sex with our wives. Hakan makes it four times a week, Ramon six (Hakan: 'No, just the times with your *own* wife!'). Just before it's my turn, I say I've got to take a piss, and take a dip in the sea with that end in view.

■

'Danny, d'you fancy going and grabbing a drink together?' Frank asks when we get back to the Pelican. Ramon and Hakan are having their beauty sleep. Frank orders two margaritas from Our Favourite Waitress. 'It's not like you to run away when it's your round.'

I look at the curves of the waitress's breasts as she bends over to set down our margaritas. 'I didn't come all the way to Miami to talk about cancer.'

'I can see that. Have you phoned Carmen since you've been here?'

'This morning,' I sigh. 'She wasn't happy. And Anne certainly wasn't.'

'I'm not surprised,' Frank replies. 'Anne thought it was ridiculous you were going to Miami as though nothing was up. So did Thomas. He can't work out how come you're not bothered, how come you're fine.'

'Christ almighty!' I shout. 'I'm not fine at all!'

Frank puts an arm around my shoulders. 'You don't have to explain it to me.'

All at once it all comes out. I tell Frank how unbearable I think it is that Carmen and I don't go out drinking together any more, don't go out eating any more, and never have sex any more. He nods.

'Can you imagine what things are going to be like when her breast comes off, Frank?' I go on. 'Even if the cancer's gone, Carmen will never be the same. And I think things between us are going to be shot to shit—'

He grips my hand. We look at each other. I see there are tears in his eyes. We don't say a word. It's the most beautiful moment in Miami.

We clink glasses and take a sip of our second margarita, which Our Favourite Waitress has just put down under our noses without our asking.

'She's pretty gorgeous, but Carmen has bigger tits,' I say as she sways up the steps from the terrace. 'At least she does at the moment . . .'

Frank's margarita sprays all over the table.

I'll be home on a Monday,
somewhere around noon,
please don't be angry . . .

The Little River Band, from 'Home on a Monday'
(*Diamantina Cocktail*, 1977)

Twenty-eight

That evening we managed to get a table in Tantra, thanks to
the guys at the Pelican. It's a Turkish restaurant, and Turkish
food is incredibly hip in Miami, we learn from the Pelican
barman. Hakan swells with pride.

After dinnertime, Tantra seems to be a really happening
place this evening. Roger Sanchez is spinning, Hakan
announces with delight. Frank is equally enthusiastic. I've
never heard of the man. I know about as much about DJs as
Clarence Seedorf* knows about penalties. The food in Tantra
is fantastic, I have to admit. So's Roger Sanchez. And so are
all the women. And the pills top it all off. I'm even more
relaxed than I was yesterday. I tell the guys how brilliant I
think it is, and we should do this every year, and next year we
could go to Barcelona or New York. No, Tel Aviv, says Hakan,
that's as hip as it gets these days. No, Rio, says Ramon. Yes,
Rio, I say. Then we say we love each other and would never

---

*   Dutch–Surinamese footballer. His ego is the only thing higher than his penalties
as they fly over the goal.

leave each other in the shit and after that Ramon says he's made a date with his girl from yesterday, and he's off now. Frank looks daggers at him. I spot a plump girl with a black see-through blouse. After swapping three cheerful glances with her, I get up on the floor. She's wearing a black bra (C-cup) under her blouse.

'Hi. What's your name?' I say, original as ever.

'I'm Linda. And you?'

'Dan,' I reply, suddenly aware I have absolutely nothing more to say to her. I can't imagine what sort of things I'm supposed to ask a kid like this.

'Where are you guys from?' she asks. Oh, yeah. That kind of question.

'Amsterdam.'

'My sister's been there! She says Denmark's such a nice country.'

'Yes, it is,' I agree, ashamed of myself and happy the guys can't hear this conversation. But it's fine by me, and I can tell intelligence isn't going to be taking pride of place this evening.

'And where are you from?' I ask. Why should I make an effort?

'North Carolina. But I moved to Florida this summer. Love the weather and the beach.'

'Ah – yeah!' I answer. What am I doing here?

Suddenly she grabs me by the neck and kisses me full on the mouth.

Oh, yeah. That's what I'm doing here. Now I remember. I clutch her tightly to me. She's pretty substantial. Her friend winks admiringly. That's the first test passed. Whether she'll pass Hakan and Frank's test I really don't know yet, so I quickly push her in front of me to a corner. On the way I see she's got an arse it would take you a weekend break to walk around. Once we're out of sight I start snogging her. My hand glides over the smooth material of her black see-through blouse. She breaks away from my embrace for a moment, and says bashfully she isn't very slim. You're not joking, I think, but I say I don't like skinny women, and pinch her arse. She titters with embarrassment. Then I take her hand, put the palm to my mouth and start licking. When she realizes what I'm up to, she starts giggling.

'You are *dir*ty,' she says with a shake of her head.

'Thanks,' I say. Time to go.

'Are you married?' she asks in the taxi on the way to the Pelican.

'No,' I say, putting my wedding ring hand behind her back. After that I stick my tongue into her mouth for fear of losing sexual momentum. At the same time I wriggle around behind her back until I've got my wedding ring off and put it in my trouser pocket.

In the lift I unbutton her blouse and push her bra up over her breasts. Linda has big areolas. I like that. And Linda is horny. I like that too. Panting, she opens my trouser buttons and drops to her knees. Just as she gets my cock, which is by now as hard as the seats in the ArenA, deep into her mouth, the lift door opens and I find myself looking straight into Frank's eyes. Frank's gaze falls to Linda's head, which is bobbing up and down. Linda notices I've frozen, looks up in shock and blushes like a beetroot. I clumsily hoist up my trousers and put my hard-on away.

'Linda, Frank. Frank, Linda.'

'Hi, Linda,' says Frank, looking straight at Linda's breasts.

'Hi, Frank,' says Linda, buttoning up her see-through blouse.

'So. That's enough chat,' I say quickly. 'See you tomorrow, Frank!'

Frank nods.

'Bye, Frank,' says Linda.

'Bye, ah . . .'

'Linda.'

'Bye, Linda.'

I walk down the corridor arm in arm with Linda. I feel Frank watching after us. I take the key of my 'Best Whorehouse' room, and spend the rest of the night giving Linda from Tampa, Florida the shag of a lifetime.

■

Ramon wakes me coming into the room. I nervously check beside me. Phew. Linda's gone. Ramon would have laughed his head off at fat Linda and me. He plops down on the bed, where Linda and I have just been swapping body fluids. Ramon is too tired to feel the wetness there, and falls asleep. I can't sleep. I get up, pick my trousers up from the floor and feel around in the left pocket.

It hits me like an electric shock. There's no ring there. Right-hand pocket. Nothing. I start sweating. Back pockets. Nothing there, either. I go and lie on my belly and look under the bed and under the radiator. Ramon wakes up and asks what I'm doing. I say I'm looking for my contact lenses. He falls asleep again. I look through my pockets again. And again. The drawers of the designer bedside table. The bathroom. Nowhere. Fuck. Think, Danny, think. Where can I have lost it . . . That woman! Linda! The cow's nicked my ring! Oh, my God! Oh, no. Carmen . . .

I lie down on my belly again and search the whole of the

floor. Then I go and lie on the bed. This is a national catastrophe. The end of Carmen and Danny. I feel like committing suicide, but I don't need to, because Carmen's going to kill me anyway. My wedding ring's lost. I won't be able to bullshit my way out of this one.

■

Downstairs Hakan and Frank are already having breakfast on the terrace.

'Stay up late?' asks Hakan. 'I lost you all of a sudden.'

That's nothing compared to what I've lost, I think to myself.

'So-so,' I say, relieved Frank has clearly said nothing about the scene in the lift. Frank looks at me quizzically. I love the bastard. Ramon comes downstairs and goes into great detail about what he did with his date last night. There's a lot of laughter. I join in, but really I feel like crying. What's worse? Ramon betraying his friends by disappearing for half a weekend because he'd rather be screwing some floozy, or me betraying my wife by taking my wedding ring off for fear of missing a fuck with another floozy? Cock-a-doodle-doo (times three).

For the last few hours before we head for the airport, Hakan, Frank and Ramon want to go to the beach. I walk apathetically along with them. We lie ourselves down. Ramon and Hakan talk about cars, Frank reads a men's magazine. I look at the sea, feeling like I could burst into tears at any moment.

'I'm going for a little walk.'

Ramon nods, Hakan goes on talking and Frank doesn't look up from his magazine. Isn't even Frank wise to me?

Maybe he is, but it doesn't matter. I don't want to talk. A hundred yards further on I glance around to check whether they can see me. I go and sit on the hot sand and feel like the loneliest, most miserable man in the world. Three days of laughter with the guys are almost over, the alcohol and the ecstasy have left my system, a woman I've just had screaming with satisfaction has robbed me, and tomorrow I'm going to be murdered at home. I see my tears falling into the sand between my legs.

■

At Schiphol we say goodbye. In the taxi I break into a cold sweat. Another ten minutes and I'll be home. What am I going to say? That I took it off when I went into the sea? Or for a metal detector in a disco? The taxi turns off by the VU Hospital. Another few minutes. Luckily the lights are red. Or I could say that—

I get a text. **FRANK MOB**.

> **Feel in the left-hand pocket of your jacket.**

I feel quickly. Nothing. Another text.

> **I mean the right-hand pocket;)**

I briefly feel in my other pocket. I feel – Yes! My ring! MY RING! My own lovely, beautiful, wonderful wedding ring.

Another text comes in.

> **Found it in the lift in the Pelican. Dan, Dan – stop doing it. Good luck for today. X.**

Girls, they finish us off, sir,
they drive us round the bend, sir, girls do . . .

Raymond van't Groenewoud, from 'Meisjes'
(*Nooit meer drinken*, 1977)

Twenty-nine

I don't know whether female intuition is as well developed as men sometimes fear. Carmen didn't even casually ask if I'd been unfaithful when I came home. On the contrary, she apologized for being so abrupt on the phone.

I did once fess up. About Sharon.

▶ **Sharon** was the receptionist at BBDvW&R/Bernilvy. Blonde, a bit provocative, and she had truly magnificent breasts. D-cup, black piste.* From day one I yearned to see those breasts in a live context. Sharon had no problem with that. Sharon never had a problem with that. Not even with Ramon. Or Hakan, as I've just discovered. And who am I to sit in judgement?

I was stupid enough to put an anonymous phone number in my diary for an evening when I was 'out with a client'. A beginner's mistake. Carmen had called the number the following day, heard the words 'Sharon here', hung up, consulted the phone-list in my Filofax to see if there was a Sharon working at Bernilvy, and compared the numbers. Bingo. That

---

* Wrampled from Youp van't Hek, New Year's Eve speech, 2002.

evening, out of the blue, she asked me which of the girls at the office Sharon was again? I did my very best not to blush, and said Sharon was the blonde girl at reception.

'No, really?' she said, holding up my diary with Sharon's number in front of my nose. 'That incredibly vulgar looking thing with the huge knockers spilling out of her dress? And you've been to bed with her?'

I turn bright red. I didn't fancy lying about this one. 'Erm ... Yeah.'

'How often?'

'Erm ... once.'

A Clintonian truth: my director's office, the toilets at the Pilsvogel and the sofa at her house still don't count as 'bed'.

> ▶ **De Pilsvogel.** A good pub (disguised as an old-fashioned Amsterdam café, the yuppie girls from De Pijp go there), a good terrace (lunch in the sun, till half-past two, another hour in the sun between five and six, on the other side of the terrace), a good crowd (but avoid Friday around drinks time, when the suits from the financial district take over De Pilsvogel.

Carmen was absolutely furious, and I was naïve enough to be surprised. Hadn't I told Carmen I was regularly unfaithful? OK, that might have been on our first date, and I never mentioned it again, but didn't she know what I was like? Frank once told me this form of reasoning wasn't entirely kosher. An opinion in which Maud supported him. But they've both kept my escapades quiet from Carmen, including the ones after Sharon.

I've become a bit more cautious with Thomas over the last few years, though. He doesn't know a bit of necking features on my weekly 'to-do' list. Let alone regular shagging. He does know about Sharon, but that goes back to the days when he used to score occasionally himself. For that matter, Anne knows about Sharon as well. When Carmen found out about Sharon, she went and stayed with Anne for a few days.

Ramon is monophobic himself. But unlike me he can't see that the frequency of our infidelity has stopped being a hobby and become a kind of addiction. Always having something on the go. Names, phone numbers, email addresses. Like an alcoholic who won't accept he's addicted, but who keeps a bottle of vodka in his office drawer to get him through the day. And keeps it hidden from the outside world. Like Carmen, Ramon's wife hasn't the faintest idea how serious things are with him.

A monophobe is addicted by the kick he gets from infidelity. Feelings like regret and guilt – in normal people, a built-in brake to keep them from regular infidelity – are things he's managed to shake off. A monophobe convinces himself he (or she, but usually he) is doing his partner no harm whatsoever with extra-curricular screwing. With excuses like 'as long as she doesn't notice', 'I really don't love her any less when I do it with someone else' and 'I can separate sex and love', he throws sand in his friends' eyes, and his own. Deep down, a monophobe is fully aware this is a kind of moral survival, a way of continuing to see himself as a good person. Because nobody could sustain a lifestyle he thought was completely despicable. A monophobe doesn't see himself as a bad person.

That's changing in my case. That business with the wedding ring is the lowest I've ever fallen. My monophobia, which I've always seen as a nice, innocent, controllable aberration, is becoming an obsession. The kick I get from scoring is becoming more addictive than the women or the sex as such.

Every week for the last few months, since Carmen and I have spent almost every evening at home, I've been counting the days until it's Friday again. Danny's Friday Night Out. And when it comes round again, and we're drinking Budweisers at MIU at the start of the evening, or sitting eating in a restaurant, I start growing restless and can't wait until it's midnight. The time of the evening when Vak Zuid, the Bastille, Paradiso and Hotel Arena are all in full swing. That's the only time I feel good. Chatting up girls becomes a compulsion, and it's getting easier and easier. Even Frank, whom I've kept informed of every adventure for years, no longer knows how bad it is. That's why just recently I've much preferred going out with Ramon. It isn't that he's my best friend now, but at least he doesn't make me feel ashamed.

Tears on her cheeks, grief on her face,
desperate eyes, gleaming in the light,
come here, stop crying, I'll kiss your tears away,
safe in my arms, believe me when I say,
we always have each other, then she said sssssssst,
and she whispered through her tears,
you've said all that before . . .

Tröckener Kecks, from 'In tranen' (*Met hart en ziel*, 1990)

Thirty

'The blisters have almost gone.'

Carmen stands looking in the bedroom mirror. She lifts her breast up, pushes it a little bit to the left and to the right, and examines it from all sides. I lie in bed and watch with her. The worst burns are healing. The skin on the breast is starting to grow back. She takes another good look, puts her bra on and, otherwise naked, joins me in bed. Tomorrow she has to go to the Sint Lucas. Then her breast will be amputated.

This is the last evening I will sleep next to my wife while she's still double-breasted. Neither of us really knows whether we want to talk about it or not. At any rate, neither of us feels compelled to celebrate this with a good bout of sex, as a farewell party to her breast. Carmen lies with her head on my shoulder. A moment later she breaks the silence by sniffing loudly. It isn't long before I feel her tears running down my shoulder for the millionth time since the cancer entered our lives. I hold her even tighter and we don't say anything.

There's nothing to say. This is love in the time of cancer.*

---

*   Freely wrampled from *Love in the Time of Cholera* by Gabriel García Márquez (1985).

I don't want to spread any blasphemous rumours,
but I think that God has a sick sense of humour...

Depeche Mode, from 'Blasphemous Rumours'
(*Some Great Reward*, 1984)

Thirty-one

Under Luna's watchful eye and with Maud's help, I'm decorating the sitting-room with paper-chains.

'And how was it yesterday, in the end?' Maud asks.

'She lay there like a little scrap of humanity under this kind of pale blue sheet. Every now and again she emerged from her sleep, usually to throw up. I held her head up with one of those little containers under it, you know, one of those foetus-shaped egg-boxes.'

Maud hugs me. 'Has she – has she seen what it looks like?'

'No. The doctor recommends we take the bandage off together. Apparently it helps with the coping process.'

'Christ – isn't that an awful lot for you to bear?'

I nod. 'I'm so worried I'm going to be horrified by what I see, and Carmen's going to notice.'

I look at Maud through my tears. She holds me tight and kisses me on my forehead. I lay my head on her shoulder for a moment. She rubs her hand over my back. 'Danny, Danny,' she whispers quietly, 'come here, darling...' After a while I pull myself together and kiss her on the mouth. She laughs, taps me on the nose in mock anger and wipes a tear from her cheek.

'I'd better be off,' I say. 'Will you give Luna another jar of baby-food?'

■

Carmen's already dressed. She's sitting in the TV room, wearing a loose black jumper with a collar. The difference between the bump on the left and the one on the right strikes me immediately. Carmen sees me looking, and says she's stuffed the breastless side with half a pair of tights with three rolled-up pairs of socks stuffed into them. Until she can wear the bra with the prosthesis, the socks are frantically attempting to make the difference between a D-cup and Ground Zero as inconspicuous as possible. As a piece of DIY, it's not at all bad.

The operation was successful, says Dr Jonkman. In a while, when the stitches are out, Carmen will have to wear her new bra with the prosthesis. Dr Jonkman says she'll have to do that as soon as possible because given the size of Carmen's breasts (I assume he means 'breast') there's a risk her spine will grow crooked because of the weight. So the cancer's going to give her a herniated disc on top of everything else.

The bra has a pouch that's closed with a Velcro strap, which the prosthesis has to go into. The prosthesis itself is a flesh-coloured silicon bag in the shape of a drop of water cut down the middle. Well, yeah, if there was such a thing as D-cup drops of water. In the middle of the drop there's a little dot that's supposed to represent a nipple. The bag feels like a balloon full of jelly. When Carmen first collected it, we threw it back and forth to each other, shrieking with laughter, the way you do with balloons full of water on hot summer days.

■

Dr Jonkman asks if Carmen and I want to take the bandage off together, in a little room in the hospital. I say we do.

Carmen asks if I'm ready, before she takes off her bra.

'Go on, then,' I say reassuringly. I hardly dare to look. But it's about to happen. Then I see my wife with one breast.

She undoes the clasp of her bra and lets the straps hang from her shoulders. As inconspicuously as possible, I take a very deep breath.

And there it is.

It's terrible. Next to her familiar, big and oh-so-beautiful breast, there is now a flat patch with a big piece of bandage on it. It's just like what I imagined a flat patch would look like, but I'm horrified to see it on my wife's chest. Big breasts are magnificent, but a woman's body with one big breast looks like a sadistic joke on the Creator's part. I look for a long time, on the one hand because I don't want to give Carmen the impression I don't dare look, on the other because it means I won't have to look in her eyes. I feel I have to say something.

'What shall I say, Carm . . .'

Not that I like it, anyway, because I don't like it.

'It's, umm – flat, isn't it?' she says, looking at the bandage in the mirror.

'Yes. It's very flat.'

I stand next to her as she pulls away the sticky tape at the edges of the bandage. The bandage comes slowly away.

What emerges from underneath it is woman-violatingly

ugly. It's the biggest disfigurement I've ever seen live. A big slit runs across her breast from left to right, about ten or twelve centimetres long. At the stitches, the skin is pulled unevenly tight, making creases in some places, like a child's first toddler-school attempt at embroidery.

'The wrinkles will go when the scar forms,' says Carmen, reading my mind.

'...'

'It's ugly, isn't it, Danny?'

There's no option but honesty. I think quickly for a way of putting it that isn't embarrassing while still being candid.

'It's – not pretty, no.'

'No. It's not pretty. It looks awful,' she says, still looking at her own ex-breast.

Then she looks at me. I can see in her eyes she's humiliated. Humiliated by the cancer. God, this is dreadful. She who wants to be beautiful must suffer pain. She who wants to stay alive must be distinctly ugly.

Those are the laws of cancer.

So here it is, merry X-mas, everybody's havin' fun . . .

Slade, from 'Merry X-mas Everybody'
(*The X-mas Party Album*, 1973)

Thirty-two

After an hour with Luna watching a *Teletubbies* video, I think that's enough. Before you know it, you end up talking like Tinky Winky.

It's half past ten on Christmas Day. I look into the bedroom. Carmen's still fast asleep.

'Luna, shall we have a bath together?'

'Yeaaaahhh!'

We play with Tigger and Winnie and use my shinbone as a water-slide until the water gets cold. I dry Luna and myself, and put her party dress back on her.

I don't generally like Christmas much, but today I feel like making it nice. If we can't get life's pleasures outside, then let's do it at home, I've decided. I've bought Carmen two nice bottles of bath-oil. One of them is scented with balm ('restful for body and spirit'), the other with orange and lime blossom ('total relaxation'). Luna's giving her the new Madonna CD. I put Luna's hair in two bunches, and tie them with elastic bands and Christmas balls we bought this week. Luna thinks it's fantastic.

When I glance into our bedroom, I'm pleased to see Carmen isn't in bed.

'Let's go downstairs, to Mummy!' I say enthusiastically to Luna.

'Hurray! To Mummy, to Mummy!'

'Are you holding Mummy's present tightly?'

'Yes!' she coos.

'And do you remember what you say when you give it to her?'

'May Kismis?'

'Something like that, yes.' I chuckle and kiss her, touched.

Downstairs, Carmen is sitting at the kitchen table in her long grey dressing-gown, reading a newspaper. She hasn't put on her wig yet, and I can see she isn't wearing her prosthetic bra.

There's a little plate of flan in front of her.

'Are you eating already?' I ask in surprise.

'Yes, I was hungry,' says Carmen unsuspectingly.

'Is something up?' she asks after a short silence, taking a bite from her flan.

'Yes. Christmas . . .' I say, embarrassed.

Luna stretches out her little arms to give Mummy the wrapped CD and a drawing. I'm holding the two bottles. They're wrapped in gold gift-paper, with a curly red bow.

Carmen gives a start. 'Oh – I haven't bought anything for you . . .'

'That doesn't matter,' I lie gently.

Luna helps her unpack the CD. I go and sit at the table and look around. The place is a tip. There are CDs, a *Bij* magazine, a *Flair*, a newspaper and the little appointment book from Sint Lucas. On the dinner table there's half a brown loaf from yesterday and two bags of cold meat from the supermarket. There's an opened carton of milk and a jar of peanut butter. Out of misery, I take a slice of brown bread, go to the fridge and get some butter, and then I butter my bread and put a slice of meat loaf on it. While Carmen is busy unwrapping my present, she watches what I'm doing.

'I could have got Christmas breakfast together, couldn't I?' she asks timidly.

I can't help it. My tears give me away.

'Yes,' I mumble disappointedly, with my mouth full of stale bread and meat loaf, 'that would have been nice, yes ...'

'Oh, my God ... Oh, how stupid of me ... Oh, how awful,' she stammers, now completely distraught. 'Oh ... sorry, Danny ...'

I feel so sorry for her, take her arm and tell her it isn't so bad. We hold each other tight and comfort one another. Luna looks at us happily.

'I've got an idea,' I say. 'I'll call Frank and ask him if he fancies coming over today. Then I'll pick him up, and go to the late-night shop and get something nice. It'll be open today. And then I'll come back and we'll start all over again.'

■

Frank kisses me three times when I get to his penthouse.

'Merry Christmas, my friend!' he says cheerfully.

'Thanks. You too,' I answer flatly.

Frank looks at me closely. 'Not good, then?'

Looking at the floor, I shake my head. I burst into tears on his shoulder.

In the car I put on 'Right Here, Right Now' by Fatboy Slim at volume 18. In the late-night shop on Rijnstraat we buy everything we see that looks nice. At the florist's on the corner I buy a bunch of roses. With four arms full of food and drink and flowers, we sing as we walk into the sitting-room.

Carmen's wearing the black trousers and the white jumper I think suits her best. She's put make-up on and she's wearing her wig. She comes over to me and hugs me. 'Happy Christmas, darling,' she says, beaming. 'And tonight I'll give you the best Christmas blow-job anyone's ever had,' she whispers.

They say two thousand zero zero, party over, oops . . .

Prince, from '1999' (*1999*, 1982)

Thirty-three

We're celebrating the millennium in Maarssen, in the middle
of the Netherlands. Thomas and Anne are organizing a party.
I really don't see the point. Thomas hasn't phoned me since
Miami, and Anne asks after Carmen as soon as she gets me
on the phone. Fortunately Maud and Frank are there as well,
along with some old friends of ours from Breda.

When the clock strikes twelve, Carmen and I become
emotional. We hug each other for several minutes. We don't
know what wishes to make for each other. Then I go to Frank
and hug him for ages. He wishes me a better year than the
last one. Maud kisses me and strokes my cheek. 'I've been
proud of you this year, Danny,' she whispers.

A bit later Thomas comes over to me. He slaps me on the
shoulders, wishes me a happy new year and asks how I am. I
give him a probing look. Does he really not know? Or does he
not want to? I hesitate for a moment. Shall I play hide-and-
seek with him, or shall I tell him things at home are seriously
crap, and tell him straight out I'm seriously pissed off with him
for not calling me since Miami? We've known each other for
thirty years. I've got to make it clear to him how I feel.

'It's not always that brilliant, Thomas,' I begin.

'No, that's life, I guess . . . Did you have a good Christmas?'

I try again. 'No, not fantastic. Christmas really wound us up. It's more symbolic than I thought and . . .'

'Yeah, there are duties involved, aren't there?' he quickly interrupts me. 'Same with us: Christmas Day at Anne's parents', Boxing Day at mine. I always call them National Boredom Days, hahaha.'

'Well, I actually meant something else,' I say. Let's change tack. 'Hey, Frank told me you didn't think I should have gone to Miami now Carmen's got cancer?'

He gives a start. He looks nervously around. 'Well, look, it's . . . Oh, shit, I've just got to get the – the doughnut balls out of the frying pan. Otherwise they'll be as black as Nwanko Kanu,* and then no one'll want them, hahaha. Look, sorry. I'll be – back in a minute . . .'

And he's gone. I watch after him and grip my champagne glass so tightly I nearly break it. My wife doesn't have a case of the flu that you know will be over in a week and then life will go on as before, she's got *cancer*, you twat! C.A.N.C.E.R. As in fatally ill, bald, had her tit cut off, terrified of kicking the bucket. How the hell do you *think* things are at home, you stupid sod?

Thomas comes in with the doughnut balls. I take one, grab a bottle of champagne from the table and escape outside. I hurl the doughnut ball as hard as I can at the fence. Through the window I see Thomas passing round the bowl with a happy expression on his face. I go and sit on a wooden bench. Staring at the last rockets in the sky, I think of the year of cancer we've just been through.

---

* Nigerian favourite with the public when Ajax were in De Meer. Made inimitable movements with legs like stilts and feet like Coco the Clown's.

'Still love me?' Carmen asked me late on Christmas Day, after she'd given me her Christmas present.

'Of course I love you, darling,' I replied with a smile.

I was fibbing.

The truth is I'm really not absolutely sure if I do love her. Yes, it hurts me when I see Carmen crying, when she's sick, in pain, frightened. But is that 'loving'? Or is it just pity? And no, I don't want to let her down. But is that love? Or a matter of duty?

But we can't split up, even if we wanted to. It's me and nobody else Carmen wants around her if things start going downhill. No one understands me like you do, she says.

Inside I hear Prince singing that the party's over. Great, rub it in, why don't you, I mumble to myself. I've always lived according to Dan's Principle: if I don't like something in my life, I change it. Work, relationships, everything. And now, at the start of a new millennium, I'm seriously unhappy for the first time in my life. And there's absolutely nothing I can do about it.

Happy New Year, Dan.

I feel fantastic, I feel fantastic,
the world is mad and I'm OK,
so stop talking about hunger, cancer and violence,
put on your hat and sing along,
I feel fantastic, I feel fantastic...

Hans Teeuwen, from *Hard en Zielig* (1995)

Thirty-four

'Goodness, Carm, I think it's really amazing the way you cope with it,' I hear Maud saying to Carmen when I go back in. 'You do everything, you're so cheerful, you're still working just like you did before—'

Thomas nods in agreement.

'Oh, of course you can let it get you down, but that doesn't do you much good,' says Carmen, giving the answer people like to hear. 'Nothing really bothers me at the moment.'

This afternoon she wasn't in the land of the living until half past twelve.

'You're so positive, it's really admirable,' says Thomas. Frank looks at me and winks. Carmen adds a bit more.

'What else are you supposed to do? The more positive your outlook, the nicer your life is.'

She's walking on hot coals.

But this evening it isn't working. I can see she's exhausted by the long evening.

'Darling, shall we make a move?' I ask.

Carmen's happy she doesn't have to make the suggestion.

Luna simply goes on sleeping when I take her out of her bed and carry her carefully to the car. Frank helps me with my stuff. 'Chin up, mate,' he whispers. 'She needs you.'

'Why the hell do you act like you're doing just fine when you talk to people about it?' I ask her angrily before we're round the corner. 'They'll all be sitting in there talking admiringly about you now. How optimistic you always are, how you never complain. You must know yourself, but in the end they are our friends. They ought to know that for three-quarters of the day you aren't well at all, damn it!'

She says nothing for a minute. I'm about to pursue my argument further when the bomb goes off. She suddenly starts crying hysterically and striking the dashboard with her hands. I'm shit-scared, quickly pull in to the filling-station we're just driving past, and pull up in the deserted car park. I try to hug her, but she wildly slaps my arms away. I look round at Luna who, miracle of miracles, goes on sleeping.

'But I don't want people to think I'm fine! I'm *absolutely not fine*. I feel absolutely crap! Seriously crap!!! Can't they see that? I'm bald, my tit's been cut off, for fuck's sake and – and – I'm so scared it's never going to be OK – and I'm going to be in pain – and I'm going to die! I so absolutely don't *want* to die! Surely they understand that?' She weeps, taking long sobs.

'Come on, darling, come on,' I say gently. Now she lets me put my arms around her.

'I really don't know what's what any more, Danny,' she sobs. 'Am I supposed to go around the place complaining all the time? That'd go down well ... And then nobody would ask me how I was – everybody would be thinking: there goes that old whinger again.'

'Carm, you don't have to be ashamed you don't always feel well, do you? You can't expect support from other people if they don't know how you really are, how you really feel.'

'Hm ... Maybe I should be more honest with everybody ...' She looks at me. 'That's better, isn't it?'

I nod. She leans in to me and lays her head on my shoulder. 'I hardly dare say it,' she says after a moment, 'but – but I'm thinking about giving up Advertising Brokers.'

'You're absolutely right,' I say without a moment's hesitation.

She sits bolt upright and looks at me in surprise.

'Yes. You should have done that ages ago. It's your business. If you feel better, you can always start over again.'

She stares at the dashboard. I see her thinking. 'Yes,' she says with sudden resolve, 'and then I can go to the gym, and – have Luna at home with me for an extra day, and – shop and read and – just think about myself.' She taps the dashboard again. 'Yes! I'm going to stop. They can manage on their own!'

I grin contentedly.

And so it happened, on the first day of the new millennium, that Carmen (thirty-five) stopped working.

Part Two

DAN & CARMEN
AND
DAN & ROSE

It was carnival and there was an uprising of love throughout the city, as if the agents of some giant conspiracy were goading and inflaming hearts across all levels of society . . .

Sándor Márai, from *Embers* (2003)

One

The streets of Breda are awash with drunken frogs, singing vicars, sexy chickens, randy elves and other types you tend not to come across in Amsterdam. Maud and I emigrated three days ago. Carmen, Frank and Ramon didn't come with us. Carmen doesn't like carnival (I'd be lying if I said I loved it), Frank has style, and Ramon comes from Chile. I don't care whether Thomas is coming this year.

Maud and I have been looking forward to it. On the way south we listened to *The Worst of Huub Hangop*.* I've had a super-slick tiger outfit made, I'm wearing a black, ruched shirt, and I've had my hair sprayed silver. Maud's wearing a nurse's costume with the kind of short skirt I've never seen nurses wearing at the Sint Lucas. We dump our stuff at the Hotel van Ham, and head straight for De Bommel.

▶ **De Bommel** is the best pub within our national boundaries. In Breda, going out is called Bommeling, a little glass is a Bommeltje, and the barman from De Bommel enjoys more respect than the

---

* See also www.kluun.nl.

centre-forward with NAC. And they know it, too. 'For God's sake leave us alone,' it said on a printed leaflet I was handed one evening when the place was full to the gills, and I'd had the nerve to trouble the barman with something so trivial as an order for drinks. At carnival, every self-respecting (ex-)Breda-ite comes here to see and be seen. Throughout those days, the public is prettier and hornier than in any club in Amsterdam, and it's in Brabant: the people there are authentic.

Rose is here again. She's wearing her hat again. A greyish-blue soldier's hat. The kind the sergeant dolls wear in Stratego. Except it looks sexier on her. Last year, while three sheets to the wind, I spun a whole yarn about that hat, that I hadn't seen such a sexy hat since *The Incredible Lightness of Being*. Fat lot of good it did me.

▶ **Rose** lives in Amsterdam too, she once told me. Sadly I've never spotted her there. I only ever see her at carnival. And every year I fall in love with her for three days. And every year she turns me down with a laugh. I haven't the faintest idea why.

This year my outfit is so cool I don't see how I can fail. You've got to sweep them off their feet, is my motto.

'Hi, Rose' – *that blonde hair* ...

'Erm' – *those blue eyes* – 'ah – it's Dan, yeah?' – *those long lashes* ...

'Yep' – *those sexy lips* ...

'Danny from Amsterdam' – *I see her looking at my outfit, it's all going according to plan* – 'who was married.' She takes my hand and points to my wedding ring. 'Correction. *Is* married.'

Oh, yes. That was it. She has principles. I hate principles.*

---

* Wrample from *The Smurfs*.

'And?' she asks me teasingly, 'Are you going to try and chat me up this evening?' *Change of plans.*

'No, because you don't like wedding rings. I've got an idea – why don't I invite you out for a drink in Amsterdam some time? I'm really good company.' I put my arms demonstratively behind my back. 'And one hundred per cent definitely, purely platonic.'

She bursts out laughing. *Bingo!*

I take a business card out of my tiger-suit, write on it *entitles the bearer to one platonic drink*, and give it to her.

Grinning at my own cool, I walk back to Maud. She's busy snogging an enormous bear in an NAC shirt. When she stops her examination of his tonsils, I see the boy's face.

So Thomas is here, too.

Ich bin so geil, ich bin so toll,
Ich bin der Anton aus Tirol ...

DJ Ötzi, from 'Anton aus Tirol' (*Das Album*, 1999)

TWO

The carnival high is so addictive that even in advance I always dread the comedown I'm having right now. I'm lying alone in my hotel room. Maud's bed hasn't been slept in. I can barely resist the urge to text Anne and tell her that if she wants to speak to her husband, Maud's mobile's her best bet. With greetings from Danny.

I get up and look out of the window. The street is full of detritus from yesterday's procession. A drunken clown lies in a doorway, and I see a giraffe walking past arm in arm with his freshly shagged witch.

I'd more or less promised Carmen I would be home today. Carnival Tuesday in Breda is a twilight zone. Officially it's still carnival, but the town is already displaying signs of closure. The only people who go today are the ones who really can't get enough of it, and the ones who really don't want to go home. Normally I fall under the first of these categories, and this year I fall under both. I don't want to go back to my everyday life. I want to stay here. I phone Carmen.

'Hi, darling!'

'Hi!'

'How are you?'

'Pretty good.' She doesn't sound unfriendly.

'And how's the little one?'

'She's fine. She's been sleeping well for the last few days. And how was Breda?'

'Absolutely fantastic. It's really very nice again this year.'

'Great. Glad you enjoyed yourself! What time will you be home?'

'Erm – I was thinking about staying on for another day or so. I don't have to be back at MIU until Wednesday. Is that OK?'

Silence.

'Carmen?'

Beeeeeeeep.

I heave a deep sigh. Putting it off. But tomorrow's going to be worse than the day after the 1974 World Cup Final.

I'm so excited, I'm about to lose control,
and I think I like it . . .

The Pointer Sisters, from 'So Excited' (*So Excited*, 1982)

Three

I saw Maud this morning when she came to pick up her stuff. 'So,' I teased her, 'was Thomas up to much?'

She shrugged. 'He begged me not to tell you I'd been with him,' she said. The contempt in her voice did me good. I told her I'd made Carmen really chuffed by deciding to stay on another day.

'What are we all doing here?' Maud laughed with a shake of her head, and then took the train back to Amsterdam.

An hour later I was standing on my own in De Bommel. Apart from me there were three blokes and a giraffe's head. Towards evening people started slowly trickling in until the place was half-full. Out of boredom I tongue-wrestled a girl with a huge witch's nose. And she wasn't even dressed up as a witch.

Now it's Wednesday. I'm in a deserted breakfast room, where cleaners and carpenters are clearing away the remains of carnival. So, back to Amsterdam on my own, and this evening I'll be back under Carmen's watchful eye. I texted her to say I was going to go to work for another few hours, and I'd be home at about six. She didn't text me back.

In Amsterdam I head straight for the stadium. At MIU

they're just having lunch. I pull up a chair and tell some carnival tales, in so far as they're suitable for a wider public. After that I go to my PC and open my mail. Holland Casino, KPN, Center Parcs, a lot of nonsense and a mail from someone I don't know, roseanneverschueren@hotmail.com. I open it and grin. Roseanneverschueren is Rose!

From:	roseanneverschueren@hotmail.com
Sent:	Wednesday 8 March 2000 11:47
To:	Dan@creativeandstrategicmarketingagencymiu.nl
Subject:	Slept well?

Hi there, Tiger, I found your card –

I'm sitting shivering over my fourth cup of coffee and eightieth cigarette with a lot of complaining, far-too-serious people around me. I want to go back south! So, did you enjoy the rest of it? Plenty of girls to kiss?

Best, Rose

ps: you wanted to go for a platonic drink? Go on, then. Can you make Friday evening?

YESSSSS! Successful strike, right on target! My day is saved. I read the mail through three times and carefully formulate my reply. Don't be too eager, now. Make a date without too much pressure or expectation. I spend about three-quarters of an hour over the mail, before I think I've found the right mix between enthusiasm and platonic sociability and innocent excitement. I read it through once more, put in another spelling mistake to make it look spontaneous, and then press *send*.

Frday is OK!
See you, Dan.

Then I walk home with a heavy heart.

Luna's nice to me. Carmen isn't. Best not to mention my plans for going out again on Friday.

I'm driving in my car, I'm pullin you close, you just say no,
you say you don't like it, but girl I know you're a liar,
'cause when we kiss . . . fire . . .

Bruce Springsteen, from 'Fire' (1978, on *Live 1975–1985*, 1986)

Four

'I'll see you tomorrow evening after dinner. There's a nephew
of mine from Breda's in Amsterdam this afternoon, so I'm
going to have a beer with him first,' I say to Frank over lunch,
as casually as possible. 'I'll text you to find out where you're
going afterwards. What time did you arrange with Hakan and
Ramon?'

'Seven o'clock at Club Inez,' says Frank.

▶ **Club Inez**. The food there is so trendy each dish on the menu
contains at least one ingredient I've never heard of. Fortunately
Frank's usually there too.

I send Rose an email and ask if she fancies popping in
to MIU to take a look at our office, before going on to Vak
Zuid – and to call if she wants to come any earlier, in case
she's standing at the door at half-past six and I have to give
a red-faced explanation to this mob here about who this
lady is.

It goes like clockwork. It's a quarter to seven and everyone's gone home. Frank's leaving too, he says. Then Rose
calls to say she's going to be half an hour late. That's all very

neat, though it's a shame I'm in the toilet when the phone rings, and Frank takes the call.

Frank shakes his head and laughs as he puts his jacket on. 'Have fun with your nephew,' he says as he walks out the door.

My blush slowly fades. I put Daft Punk on, loud, and grab a Budweiser from the fridge. Once again, I'm curious to see what she looks like without her carnival costume. I can't imagine she's going to be a disappointment.

And she isn't. The bell rings, and there, when I walk over to the glass office door, there stands the Blonde Goddess from Breda. She's wearing a long, black jacket and a black cap over her long blonde hair. She laughs. I grin and open the door.

'Hello, madam.'

'Hello, sir.'

I kiss her as platonically as I can three times on the cheeks. I give her a beer and a guided tour of our office, and talk cod-nonchalantly about MIU. She likes that. It's going well.

■

There's a big crowd in Vak Zuid. I plan to join Frank and his cohorts at about nine, particularly since I have the feeling Rose is beddable. I get that feeling very quickly. That is, Rose is eminently beddable, but not by my wedding ring and me. I tell her I'm beginning to fear I'm going to have to move her name definitively from my *to do* file to my *platonic* file.

> ▶ **Vak Zuid**. Yeah. Because it's opposite MIU in the Olympic Stadium, geographical necessity has made it our local. It's a thank-God-it's-Friday sort of place. Every Friday at five it fills up with men in striped shirts with white collars and cuffs, and women in

twinsets. I thought it was appalling the first time I went there. Until I worked out after five Bacardi breezers women in twinsets are just as randy as the average nail-studio-blonde-with-Moschino-belt you find in the Bastille. I've really liked it since then.

'You're such a big puppy,' she laughs.

'A puppy?'

'Being playful all the time, jumping up at everybody, licking them all over . . .'

'I get the feeling you're rather fond of puppies,' I say, looking her straight in the eyes. She starts to blush. She's mine for the taking!

'Erm – yes. But *married* puppies are too phoney for me.'

I think I might as well join the guys. What's the good of staying here? I'll just tell her I've got to be home in half an hour. Yes, that's what I'll do.

'Ah, Rose . . .'

'Yes?' – *That hair. Those eyes. Those divine teeth.*

'Shall we grab a bite to eat?'

■

We go to De Knijp on Van Baerlestraat. The only people who usually go there are on their way to the Concertgebouw or just coming back from it, and I can't imagine there'll be anybody I know. We both order steak and chips. She tells me about her last relationship, with a boy from Friesland. She says she hopes it sorts itself out.

'And you, tell me about your wife.'

You asked for it. 'Are you ready to hear a nasty story?'

'None of that "my wife doesn't understand me" stuff, though, eh?'

'No!' I say, slightly irritated. I start talking. About the cancer. About the chemo. About the fear. The breast amputation. And about our relationship.

As she listens she lays her hand on mine.

Outside I see Ramon's sent a text.

So, are you shagging, you randy git?
We're off to the NL. You?

I text back I'm not coming. I already know Zinedine Zidane's* chances of getting a contract with Ajax are considerably better than my chance of shagging Rose this evening.

'Fancy going dancing?'

She says she's wild about dancing. So am I, since Miami, although I've no idea what house sounds like on E. I've never been to the More, but I don't dare go there, it's where Frank goes after two o'clock. I say I'd like to go to the Paradiso.

> ▶ Some people still don't believe man has walked on the moon. I'm a bit like that with **Paradiso**. I consistently refuse to believe the Stones and Prince and my own Springsteen sometimes appear there just for a laugh after a gig at the Kuip stadium in Rotterdam, and conclude that everyone who says they've been at one of those concerts must have been paid by Paradiso to get that rumour floating around the world. Or to piss me off. God help us, I'm happy as a pig if I manage to get tickets for De Dijk.

We go on talking on one of the little seats in the upstairs room. She puts her hand on my knee, quite naturally, like we'd known each other for years. I put my hand on hers, and

---

* Ex-European footballer of the year, nearly as good as Rafael van der Vaart's going to be.

do my best not to make it look like I'm making an unambiguous move.

'Fancy dancing?' I ask.

We go down to the dance-floor. We talk more than we move. Very soon we're standing talking at the side. We go on talking. About this and that. But our eyes haven't been involved with the conversation for ages. They're full of yearning. There's nothing to be done about it. It's overwhelming. Mid-sentence I press her against the wall and kiss her. She goes limp and surrenders. We kiss. And kiss. And kiss. For several minutes. Then I look at her and shrug my shoulders like I don't know either. She shakes her head. Neither does she. We start kissing again. A little later we go.

She lives on Eerste Helmersstraat in Oud-West. I park the car in a free place, open her zip and slide my hand into her trousers. She's dripping wet. All at once she pushes my hand away. She's cross-eyed with lust.

'We're not going to do it,' she says.

I lay her hand on my trousers. My cock nearly jumps out. She laughs and pulls her hand away. I sigh deeply. We haven't even got time. It's ten past four. I never get home later than a quarter past. Carmen knows all the clubs I go to shut at four.

I kiss Rose once more, she gets out, I watch after her, blow her a kiss through my window and then drive home.

I'm completely lost.

Red alert red alert, it's a catastrophe,
but don't worry, don't panic...

Basement Jaxx, from 'Red Alert' (*Remedy*, 1999)

Five

I'm sitting in the car. She's at home, she says. We've mailed each other a lot this week. She wrote on Monday to say she'd enjoyed herself, but she should have gone home earlier. She didn't regret what had happened, but repeated she didn't want an affair with a married man. She didn't know whether it would be such a great idea to see me one more time, she wrote. I didn't believe a word of it, but I didn't care to go into it in an email. Now that I phone her, I realize I've done the right thing. She's glad I've called. It's Thursday evening. We chatter on about nothing in particular. I tell her a bit about my work and about Luna, she talks about her colleagues. Meanwhile I get out of my car with the flowers I've just bought at the late-night shop on Stadionplein.

'Hey, which number Eerste Helmers did you live at again?"

'Umm – seventy-nine. Why?'

I ring the doorbell.

'Hang on a second. There's someone at the door.'

'I'll wait.'

From the first floor she calls on the intercom: 'Hello?'

I say 'Hello' through my mobile and through the intercom. It's quiet for a moment.

'Hey?!?'

'Just open the door.'

'Is – is that you?'

'No, it's Harry Belafonte.'

'Christ . . .'

She presses the button and I open the front door.

'You're mad,' she says, watching me come up the stairs with a big grin on my face. Her eyes reveal this was a very good move on my part.

I put the flowers on the table and kiss her. She's wearing a dressing-gown and her hair's wet. Still kissing, I push her backwards until we fall on to her sofa. Her dressing-gown falls open a little. She sees me looking, pulls it closed with a laugh and huddles herself tightly against me. I stroke her hair and kiss her on the top of her head. I haven't sat with Carmen like this for ages. I like it.

We kiss again, more wildly now. My hand slips inside her dressing-gown. She doesn't object. I knead her breasts. They're soft. I fall in love with them right away. I kiss her neck and gently bite her throat.

Suddenly she stands up. 'Erm – do you want some coffee?' she asks.

'If there's nothing better on offer, then yeah,' I laugh.

I look in her CD box and see *Ray of Light* by Madonna. She pours two cups of mocha and comes to sit next to me, the buttons of her dressing-gown done up this time. I press her to me again. The process repeats itself. Madonna sings. *Wanted it so badly, running, rushing back for more . . . the face of you . . . my substitute for love.** I stroke her tenderly. She's lying

---

*   From 'Substitute for Love'.

stretched out on the sofa now, her head on my chest. I open the button of her dressing-gown and, eyes closed, she whispers, 'Don't . . .'

Two Madonna songs later she kisses me again. My hand inches towards her breasts again. *And I feel like I just got home...** And lower. She sighs and throws back her head. This time she doesn't stop me when my hand slides down her belly. *Put your hand on my skin – I close my eyes – I need to make a connection – touch me I'm trying – to see inside of your soul – I close your eyes – Do I know you from somewhere...*† I go and kneel between her legs. I press my middle finger against her crotch. She shakes her head.

'I can't stay away from you. Tell me to go, or I'm not going to stop,' I sigh. I'm as randy as Patrick Kluivert‡ after a night's clubbing.

She looks at me for a moment. Then she grabs me by the shirt-collar and presses me to her. Her dressing-gown has slipped from her shoulders, and she's now completely naked. She unbuttons my shirt, I nervously undo my trousers and push her legs apart. I'm nervous. For a brief moment I wait to give her one last chance to shake her head. *Watching the signs as they go* . . . She doesn't shake her head. She gives me a troubled look and nods once, almost imperceptibly. *I think I'll follow my heart* – I slowly slip inside her. *It's a very good place to start...*§ It feels heavenly inside Rose.

---

*   From 'Ray of Light'.

†   From 'Skin'.

‡   Footballer (Ajax, Barcelona) whose libido in his teens was just as impressive as his goal-scoring capacity. Over the past few years both have subsided to moderate proportions.

§   From 'Sky Fits Heaven'.

I discover this once again on her bed, and three more times the next Saturday afternoon when I'm supposedly in town. The fat is in the fire.

What in God's name have I started?

She says her love for me could never die,
that would change if she ever found out about you and I,
oh, but it's so damn easy making love to you,
so when it gets too much,
I need to feel your touch,
I'm gonna run to you . . .

Brian Adams, from 'Run to You' (*Reckless*, 1984)

Six

Infidelity doesn't mean a thing. It's like having a wank, except a woman's body happens to be involved.

An affair is a whole different ball game. Then screwing turns into *making love*. It's no longer just about a female body you like poking your dick into, it isn't even about a *woman*. It's something I always wanted to avoid. My compulsive need for physical infidelity was already bad enough. Other women could reach me anywhere except my heart. My body and mind might be monophobic, but my heart was monogamous. That was for Carmen. Rose knows we would never have had an affair if Carmen hadn't been ill. But Carmen *is* ill. In the spring of 2000, Roseanneverschueren@hotmail.com, real name Rose, nickname Goddess, name on my mobile Boris, is the first affair I've ever had in my life.

We complement each other perfectly. With Rose I get what I'm lacking at home, and thus – even if it is part-time – regain my pleasure in life. She spoils me with all her feminine qualities, she's exactly the woman I need in this time of cancer. Rose is my surrogate queen.

From my side, I shower her with all the attention I can muster. She gets the highlights of Dan, with me she feels more of a woman than ever before. 'You call me Goddess, and that's how I feel when I'm with you,' she says delightedly when I show up with a rose and a gift token from a lingerie shop. She's enjoying her role, she plays it to the full. She lets me decide what we're going to do and where, when and how. She asks me what she should wear when we go out. She asks me what colour lingerie she should buy. She shaves her pubic hair into the shape that turns me on the most.

The relationship is like heroin. Within a few weeks I'm addicted to Rose, I'm addicted to the feeling she gives me. I try to be with her as much as I can. All the clichés about infidelity come out of the box. Now and again I go 'to the office early'. I go 'into town to listen to CDs'. I use Danny's Friday Nights Out as a cover. Or an Ajax home game. Then I read up on the match on teletext and learn it off by heart before I go home. We arrange to meet late in the evening after dinner with a client. Every now and again, sometimes twice a week, we spend a whole evening together. When we do that, we go to a pub or a restaurant where there's the least chance of bumping into anybody and talk all evening. Mostly about sex. About the sex we've had, the sex we're going to have, the sex we fantasize about having. And if we're not talking about sex, we're having sex. We shag till we drop. At her house, in my car, in my office, in the Vondelpark, in the Amsterdamse Bos, everywhere.

In the daytime we do nothing all day long but mail each

other. Dozens of emails per day. We mail about how things are going for me at home, about our next meeting, about her work, about my work, about her train that was late. The things you talk to each other about over dinner in a normal relationship. Half the time I'm busy checking whether there's any new mail from her in my inbox. My efficiency quotient at MIU plummets to Bryan Roy levels.*

At the weekend, when I can't check my mail, I text her. Ten, twenty times a day. When I go to the toilet, when Carmen goes to the toilet, when I pop out to the car for a moment because 'I've forgotten something', when I'm putting Luna in the bath, when I'm brushing my teeth. Every minute I'm alone.

> Mornin Goddess, dream of me again? I'll
> call you when I'm back from the crèche.

> Foof – Can I nominate you for the Nobel
> Prize for blowjobs? You were divine. Have
> a good weekend, Goddess.

> Can't phone now, I'm afraid. Carmen at
> home. Tommmmorrow I'll be all yours
> again. We'll text again. X.

For her part, Rose can do nothing but wait. Wait till I call, wait to find out whether we're actually going to meet up, or whether I'm going to have to cancel at the last minute, wait till I text.

We've agreed a strict code: Rose can never phone me, and

---

*   Played for Ajax in the early nineties. Fair-weather outside left with individual feats to celebrate, and an overall performance to make you weep.

she can only text me back if I explicitly put a question mark at the end of a text, and never leave it longer than five minutes after I sent mine.

x. are you at home?

I'm terrified it's all going to come out. On my mobile phone, one month Rose is listed as 'Boris', after a boy who's training with us, and the following month 'Arjan KPN', after a client of mine. I delete my Last Numbers Dialled after each phone call. I immediately delete every text I get from her. A few times a day I delete the emails I've received from her. I never mail her from our home PC.

When I ask, she shows up. At any time of day, wherever I happen to be. If I'm on my way back from a client in Eindhoven, she takes the train to Utrecht to spend three-quarters of an hour sitting with me at a pavement café and then drive back with me to Amsterdam.

She cancels dates with girlfriends because she doesn't know how late my dinner with a client has run and whether we're going to be able to see each other. It could be half past ten at night, or half past twelve.

My meetings with Rose always end the same way. I go and shower, give my cock and my face a good scrub, and then leave the warmth of Rose's bed for the cold of the night. Alone. In the car, still glowing with the excitement, the willingness and the sex with Rose, I dread going home. Those are the most terrible moments of the whole week. With a knot in my stomach, I look for a parking space on the Amstelveenseweg. Before I get out of my car, I sometimes wait for a few minutes to double-check my story, inspect it for bugs and to repeat it to myself, terrified that holes are about to appear in my alibi for the evening.

Then I undress downstairs to make as little noise as possible, creep upstairs, brush my teeth specially well, slip silently into bed and lie awake for at least half an hour with my back to Carmen, my eyes wide open. Anxious I might have missed something, that I still smell of Rose. Particularly as I've been getting home later than a quarter past one during the week, when Carmen knows the pubs close at one.

I finally relax in the morning, when I feel the atmosphere in the house is OK and my alibi has apparently worked once again. Then I'm at my best. I'm nice to Carmen, I play with Luna, I'm cheerful and energetic, however much I've drunk and however late it might be.

Then my shot of pleasure, the enjoyment of life, has done its work once again.

It's you and the things you do to me,
now I'm living in ecstasy . . .

Sister Sledge, from 'Thinking of You' (*We Are Family*, 1979)

Seven

I've been planning for weeks, and I've prepared everything down to the smallest detail. Luna's away at my mother-in-law's for the weekend, I've got hold of some vitamin E from Ramon's dealer, and found out where Frank and Ramon are going out to on Saturday, and therefore where Rose and I have to stay away from.

Carmen is at her annual staff weekend with Advertising Brokers in Monaco. The girls went wild when they heard Carmen was actually going along. Wherever Carmen is, that's where the fun is. Everybody knows that. After I've taken her to Schiphol, I go straight to Rose's.

When I walk in, she calls from the kitchen to tell me I'm to go and lie in bed. That doesn't sound like much of a punishment, and I'm quite pleased to be ordered about for a change. A few minutes later she comes into the bedroom. She's wearing a shirt with nothing underneath, and carrying a tray that's almost too big to get through the door. I see bagels, salmon, avocado, cream cheese, freshly squeezed juice and a bottle of champagne with a bow around it.

'That's because it's your birthday next week,' she says. 'I couldn't give you a present you could take home. So I'll just do it like this . . .' She gives me a mischievous look and slowly unbuttons her blouse. 'What do you want to do first?'

I feel both touched and incredibly horny.

'Eat,' I say, plunging my head between her legs and staying there for a good few minutes. After a whole morning and afternoon of pleasure, screwing, eating, sleeping, talking, laughing, shagging, sleeping and fucking again, I feel like the happiest man in the world.

Just before Rose and I head into town for an evening out, I get a text. Carmen. She writes they're having a great time, and she's bought a little skirt for Luna in Monte Carlo, and a very expensive pair of boots and a Diesel denim jacket for herself. I grin, tell Rose why – she laughs, touched – and send a text back to Carmen:

> **I'm proud of you and happy you're having fun, love of my life. X!**

Enthusiastically, I let Rose see what I've texted to Carmen. Mistake.

'Hm. Nice name you have for Carmen,' she says bitterly. 'At least I know my place now.'

I'm about to deliver a whole lecture about the concept of time, that Carmen's the love of my life *so far* and you never know how the rest of a life will be played out, but that kind of exposition doesn't strike me as such a great idea right now. In the one weekend she has me all to herself, how on earth could I bring her down from cloud nine?

'Ah,' she says with fake nonchalance when we're sitting at Café Weber on Marnixstraat, 'a text like that doesn't actually change anything. I know very well I'll never have what Carmen has with you.'

'But you do know you're very important for me . . .'

'I do. But no one else does. Your friends don't even know I exist. Not as a woman, not as a person. How do you think that feels?' She gives me a probing look. 'And I can't even tell my own mum and dad. An affair with a married man whose wife has cancer. They'd really love that. My sister didn't even want to hear about it when I cautiously started to mention it. She cut me off short. And a girlfriend I told thinks it's scandalous. She doesn't understand how I can do it, or why anybody would do anything like that while his wife is ill.'

'Pff . . .' I say, taking the last sip of my port.

'Yeah. Pff. Easily said. And then you'll make me read those sweet little texts you send to Carmen. That really gets me going,' she says with a wink. 'So don't you dare try and go home early this evening. At last you're mine, for once.'

> ▶ **Weber and/or Lux**. The lounge cafés on Marnixstraat. I can never tell if I'm in one or the other, they're so much alike. For the umpteenth time I'm coming to the conclusion I don't understand the whole lounge thing. If you want to lie on the sofa, you're better off staying at home!

Because I don't have to be home before four o'clock, we have all the time in the world. We go to Lux, where I used to go with Carmen from time to time. Luckily, as I expected, we don't run into anyone we know. That's the reason I avoid the Bastille in the evening. I don't want to find myself bumping into Ramon. As my regular alibi, he knows how often I'm unfaithful, but he doesn't know it's been with the same girl for the past few months. And I want to keep it that way. Fortunately Rose is keener on dancing than on listening to André Hazes. Paradiso is out of the question for this evening.

Maud might go there. And More is out too, because it's Frank's regular haunt. I suggest Hotel Arena. As far as I know, it isn't a place anyone from MIU goes to.

> ▶ Until a few years ago **Hotel Arena** was a no-go area for trendy Amsterdam. Eighties music, backpackers and little teams of girls from Purmerend with handbags. I used to go there a lot. Now it's got considerably hipper, they play house and the beer's doubled in price. Given that the gorgeous woman quota has risen in line with the place's metamorphosis, I've decided to ignore that factor.

'What do you reckon to one of these, now we've got the whole night together?' I ask Rose, and offer her a party smartie.

'Oh? Mmmmm. Good idea . . .'

An hour later DJ Roog is God and I'm finding my own Goddess more beautiful than all the Ajax footballers' wives put together. I make that clear to her by having a permanent erection and – in the few moments I don't have my tongue in her mouth – whispering to her how gorgeous she is, how tender, how feminine, how lovely, how clever and how often I'm going to take her later. When I look at my watch, my blissful smile gets even bigger. At this rate my face is going to split across the middle. Just three o'clock! When you're having an affair, you learn to value time. Especially at night. Normally at about this time you have to choose between going on drinking/dancing/chattering on and screwing, because you have to be back at four fifteen at the latest, but tonight time is on our side. As the place starts closing we head off at a gallop towards the waiting taxis. Even though there's plenty of time, there's still no time to lose.

■

A bit later we're at her place putting my erection to all kinds of imaginative uses, and we keep it up throughout the small hours.

It's light by the time I head home, not tired but certainly satisfied. Carmen's mother is coming with Luna in an hour. Well, after twenty-four hours of Rose, Papa is Papa once again. I can sleep tonight.

When I get home I ring Carmen. She's happy to get the call. 'It's *fan-tas-tic* here,' she coos down the phone. She tells me they're having lunch in the gardens of a castle overlooking the Bay of Monte Carlo, and they're going to go to Cannes that afternoon. I tell her I danced till four in Hotel Arena. I don't mention the pill or Rose. Carmen hates drugs and Carmen hates infidelity.

That evening, when I'm waiting to pick her up from Schiphol with Luna, it hits me immediately. She's exhausted. When she's saying goodbye to her colleagues, she puts a brave face on it. She kisses everyone and makes jokes about the weekend. Her broad smile doesn't vanish for a moment. Until we're out of sight. 'Oh Danny, I'm shattered . . . Is the car far away?'

I say I've parked it in a disabled space, just by the P1 entrance. She kisses me.

That evening she goes to bed at half-past eight. Fine by me. I go to sleep too. I wake at nine in the morning. Carmen sleeps till late in the afternoon.

Her colleagues have been able to enjoy a weekend of Carmen in top form. Rose enjoyed me. I enjoyed Rose.

Yes, Carmen and I still enjoy life.

But, sadly, no longer together.

Now everyone dreams of a love lasting and true,
but you and I know what this world can do...

Bruce Springsteen, from 'If I Should Fall Behind'
(*Lucky Town*, 1992)

Eight

Carmen seems to have reached the conclusion I'm taking refuge in work and clubbing. She isn't exactly happy about it, but she accepts it, and she's found a solution. She does exactly the same. A few weeks before Monaco she and Anne went for a relaxing weekend on the island of Schiermonnikoog. The week before, she went shopping with her mother in London. And at Ascension she was with Maud in New York.

She never gets bored. When Luna's at home, they do the same nice things. On days when Luna goes to the crèche, Carmen goes for coffee at Advertising Brokers or has lunch with Maud. Or else she goes and spends a day with her mother in Purmerend. And she escapes into shopping. 'Shopping is healthy' is her new motto. Carmen's portrait probably hangs in the boardrooms of DKNY, Diesel, Replay and Gucci.

For my second birthday since the cancer, I got a bicycle from Carmen, but no sex. We haven't done it since her Christmas present. I've forgotten how it feels to be in Carmen's hand, Carmen's mouth, or in Carmen herself. And oh, let's be honest, I'm not making much of an effort in that direction. Neither of us has a great need for it any more. Carmen has cancer and only one breast and I've got Rose.

We're still living together, but more like brother and sister.* We know we can't manage without each other, given the situation, and try to row as little as possible. Carmen does everything she can to keep the cancer from taking over our lives, and to be cheerful at home. So now and then the cancer, her prosthetic breast or my going out gets too much for her, and then I'm an arsehole. I completely understand that. I'm happy she lets me out of the house every now and again, however much she might gripe about it. I know she has to make a big effort to do it.

For my part, I try to do everything within my power to ensure Carmen doesn't notice any of the things I get up to when I'm not at home. I don't know whether Carmen believes me when I say I was out with Ramon until four, had to have dinner with clients again, that I'm going to work at eight more often and making more trips to the late-night shop, but she rarely asks.

What I do know is it can't go on like this. It's getting too much. MIU, Rose, Carmen, Luna, my sense of guilt: everything and everyone is clamouring for my attention. Carmen and I have to talk, although I can't see what could change in our situation. I can't leave her in the lurch, but neither can I tell her I'm having an affair, because that would mean ending everything. And then I'd go completely to pieces.

But we do have to talk. Perhaps next week, when we're taking Luna for a week at Club Med in the South of France. A while away from Rose, a while away from Amsterdam, and

---

*   Wrample from 'Redding' by Tröckener Kecks (*Met hart en ziel*, 1990).

no three-way meetings. Just Carmen, Luna and me. Yes. Next week, we'll have to have the conversation.

I'm scared of a week without Rose, but it's what I want.

I'm scared of talking to Carmen, but I know it has to be.

Something's got to change. Cancer or no cancer.

Bloody cancer.

So need your love, so fuck you all . . .

Robbie Williams, from 'Come Undone'
(*Escapology*, 2002)

Nine

Before I go to Club Med with Carmen and Luna for a spot of marriage therapy, another night out's being planned. The notorious occasional MIU drink, where we're all supposed to think of something to celebrate. This time it's my birthday we're celebrating – from a month ago. We're going out in Rotterdam and all staying in a hotel.

But there's a problem. This bash means I won't be seeing Rose for nearly ten days. I have to come up with something. The previous evening, there's no way I can get out of the house. I certainly wouldn't score any points with Carmen.

I rack my brains, and all of a sudden I've got it. I'll *cancel* sleeping on Friday night.

I mail Rose to say that a whole evening this week is out of the question, but on Friday night I'll drive back to Amsterdam and then reserve the period from about half past five in the morning until a quarter to nine for her. She sulkily agrees.

I promise Carmen I'll definitely be at home half an hour before we go to Schiphol. She isn't wild about my tight schedule either. I note in my head:

Day / time	Activity	Location
Thursday		
19.00–22.00	husband / father	A'veenseweg (sitting-room)
22.00–08.00	sleep	A'veenseweg (bed)
Friday		
08.30–18.00	work	MIU (Ol. Stadium)
18.00–04.30	eat / go out with MIU	R'dam (De Engel, Baja)
Saturday		
04.45–05.30	drive / drink RedBull	A4 R'dam–A'dam (car)
05.30–08.45	sex with Rose / breakfast / shower	A'dam Oud-West (bed)
08.45–09.00	drive / eat mints	Overtoom / A'veenseweg (car)
09.00–09.45	pack suitcase / sort things out with Carmen	A'veenseweg (sitting-room)
10.00–10.50	check in / drink black coffee	Schiphol
11.10	fly / rest	A'dam–Nice (plane)

After work I go with Frank to pick Luna up from the crèche and pack my stuff at home. Frank talks to Carmen as I pack my case upstairs. I catch scraps of the conversation. I hear Carmen say she isn't happy about me staying in a hotel in Rotterdam tonight. Frank puts her mind at rest and tells her he'll be sharing a room with me.

I kiss Luna and say Papa will be back tomorrow, and the three of us will be going on holiday after that. When I kiss Carmen, she barely looks at me.

'Will you be home on time tomorrow? It'd be nice if we could catch the plane,' she snaps at me.

Once in the car I sigh the way I did in the last minute of the UEFA Cup Final against Torino in '92* when the ball bounced over Stanley Menzo,† hit the bottom of the net and bounced back into the field. Frank grips my hand for a moment, I put on the Fun Lovin' Criminals, loud, and we join the Friday evening jam on the A4. I couldn't care less. I'm away from home.

The drink ends disastrously. I've taken an E, and I'm horny. All my colleagues watch with delight as I engage in a thorough snogging session with Natasha in the Baya.

> ► **Natasha** (23) is our new trainee. She has a navel piercing, and it suits her unusually well.

Maud whispers in my ear that it would be good for my image if I stopped right now. I agree. It's almost half past four, and Rose is waiting for me. Before she knows what I'm doing, I quickly slip Maud my tongue as well. Frank pulls me away. I laugh at him.

> ► The **Baya Beach Club**. Bar staff (m/f) with Miami-style chests spend their day at sports college and serve cocktails in beachwear in the evening, under strict look-but-don't-touch rules. Even by Rotterdam standards it's pretty much on the vulgar side.

---

* Ajax-Torino 0–0, Olympic Stadium, 13 May 1992. Score 2–2 (Jonk, Pettersson). Menzo, Silooy, Blind, F. De Boer, Alflen, Winter, Jonk, Kreek (Vink), Van't Schip, Pettersson, Roy (Van Loen).

† Stanley was better at dishing out advice than he was at saving goals, and that's not great in a goalkeeper. He was such a nice guy that nobody dared tell him. Apart from Louis van Gaal. The whole of the De Meer stadium was secretly grateful to Louis.

'Come on, let's go back to the hotel,' he says.

'I'm not going to the hotel. I'm going back to Amsterdam.'

'You've been drinking, and you've taken a pill, for God's sake!'

'I've got another date.' I give Frank a challenging look. 'With a girl.'

'Let me guess. You're having an affair.'

'Yes. Four months now. And her name is Rose. Anything else you want to know?'

'No. I know already. The girl I spoke to on the phone at MIU, when you were on the toilet, the one you've spent whole days emailing since then.'

'Yeah. So what?' *OK, give me a full-scale bollocking if you dare, you twat.*

Frank doesn't bollock me.

'I hope Rose is giving you what you need to survive, Danny.'

A bit later I'm driving at 180 km per hour down the A4 towards Amsterdam Oud-West. Halfway there I get a text. **MAUD MOB.**

> **Dan old mate, I knew already. The girl from carnival. Take care Carmen doesn't find out. Or Thomas and Anne. Good luck your holiday with Carmen. X.**

God have mercy on the man
who doubts what he's sure of . . .

Bruce Springsteen, from 'Brilliant Disguise'
(*Tunnel of Love*, 1987)

Ten

With a buzz and a happy cry of 'Hello!' the front door opens. I run upstairs and see she's already opened the door for me. When I come in she's lying in bed, her arms spread in welcome. Her soft breasts peep out over the top of the blankets. I quickly undress, not taking my eyes off hers for a second. When I climb on top of her, I feel how soft and warm she is. We do it straight away, without wasting any time on foreplay. Afterwards she rests her head on my chest, and a moment later we both fall asleep.

When I wake up, I feel something being put on the bed. I open my eyes, still half asleep, and see she's taking off her dressing-gown. She slides back in beside me and kisses me on my forehead. There's a tray with croissants on the bed. I start getting emotional.

'What is it, darling?' asks Rose.

'When I see everything you do for me – it's so nice with you, so warm.'

'You deserve it,' she says gently.

Bang, that's it. The floodgates open. My self-pity has everything it could wish for. I start crying, the first time I've done that in Rose's presence. She comes and sits next to me, hugs me and gives me my tea. I don't dare tell her why I suddenly feel so crap. That I can't even bring myself to be faithful to her. Or at least honest. I don't say a word about my trainee or about Maud. Instead I start talking about Carmen.

'I think this week I'm going to tell Carmen how unhappy I am, and maybe that I've been unfaithful throughout the whole of our relationship. I can't keep it in any more, it just can't go on like this. I'm beginning to hate myself.'

Rose looks thoughtfully at her cup of tea.

'I'd think very hard about whether you really want to be so honest,' she says after a while. 'Is Carmen supposed to be happy you're being hard on yourself just because you've suddenly started feeling guilty after all these years? What's she supposed to do with that? You can't do that to her. Not now.'

I shrug. 'Maybe I'll even tell her I'm having an affair. At least that would give her a reason to hate me.'

She gives a start. 'But – you really can't do that! That would . . .'

'Yes, that could mean the end of my marriage. So? Perhaps that's what I want. I don't think I love Carmen any more.'

There, it's out. It's the first time I've said it out loud.

Rose looks me straight in the eye.

'You do love Carmen,' she says calmly. 'I can tell, from the way you talk about her, the way you let me see her texts. You bring each other love and happiness. You're not happy now, but you do love her. Otherwise you could never do all the things you do for her.'

'Like having an affair with you?' I say cynically.

'Nonsense,' she replies fiercely, 'that's got nothing to do

with the way you feel about Carmen. With me you get the warmth Carmen can no longer give you. That's why you escape to me. You can't do without that warmth.' I see her lower lip starting to tremble. 'And increasingly neither can I – at first I could cope with it, that dull rumble in the background. But I've started feeling more and more for you . . .' She sniffs. 'I think we should think hard about whether we should stop, while we still can . . .' She leans her head against me. I feel a tear fall on my cheek.

'I don't want to stop seeing you, Rose,' I say softly. 'I can't live with –'

All of a sudden my phone rings. I take a look and my heart leaps.

CARMEN MOB. 'Oh, fuck! It's Carmen!' I push Rose roughly away.

'Fuck, fuck, fuck!' I shout. My phone rings again.

'Pick it up!'

'No! I don't know what to say! Hang on – let me just – let me just think . . .'

Trrringg. 'Why don't you say . . .'

'Shut up for a second!' I snap, 'let me think . . .'

The mobile rings for the fourth time.

'Let it ring! I'll call her back. I just need to get a story together.'

Fifth time. Sixth time. The mobile stops ringing.

Naked, I pace back and forth in the bedroom. I think feverishly. What now – At any moment I expect to hear my phone beeping to say I've got a voicemail.

Instead the mobile rings again. I barely dare to look.

FRANK MOB. Phew . . .

'Frank?'

'Yes.' He sounds downhearted. 'Carmen just rang. I think you should give her a quick call, or you're going to be in big trouble.'

'What did you say?'

'That I was still asleep and didn't know what time you went out.'

'OK – thanks – what time is it now, by the way?'

'Just turned eight. Listen, Dan . . .'

'Yes?'

'This isn't cool.'

'No – Sorry.'

Rose has put on her dressing-gown. I sit on the edge of the bed staring apathetically in front of me, clutching my phone.

'Call her now!' says Rose nervously.

I stand up and shake my head. 'No. I'm going to head off now. I'll come up with something.' By now I'm half dressed.

'Shouldn't you shower?' Rose asks cautiously.

■

Before I get into my car, I look up one last time. Rose is standing on the balcony in her dressing-gown. She blows me a kiss. There's an anxious look in her eyes.

In the car, my brains are firing on all cylinders. Before I get to de Overtoom, the main road in the middle of Amsterdam, I've got my story ready. I call Carmen.

'Hi, darling! I saw you called?' I say as casually as possible.

'Yes. Where were you? I've rung Frank, too.'

'I just popped out for a cup of coffee in that restaurant over the A4, near Schiphol. You know the one? I nearly fell asleep driving. But I left my phone in the car.'

'Hm.'

'It was brilliant yesterday! It's nice, Rotterdam is.'

'Oh. Are you running late?'

'No, I'm nearly there, in fact. I'm just driving past Schiphol,' I say as I tear down de Overtoom. 'See you in a bit, love!'

'Yeah. See you in a bit.' She snarls and hangs up.

Leave me alone, even if it doesn't always turn out fine,
loneliness is sometimes worse with two . . .

Klein Orkest, from 'Laat mij maar alleen' (*Het leed versierd*, 1982)

Eleven

We've been everywhere together. South Africa, Kenya,
Mexico, Cuba, California, Nepal, India, Vietnam, Malaysia,
you name it. Even when Luna had just been born, we went
diving with Thomas and Anne in the Dominican Republic.
Since we've had cancer, Carmen's been in New York and
London without me. And I've been in Miami without her.
When we're together, we don't do anything that calls for any
kind of effort.

Even with the holiday destinations. One week in Center
Parcs last year and this spring a weekend in Texel or Ter-
schelling, can't remember which. At any rate there were more
cows than people, and there was a very long, deserted beach.

And now we're in Club Med. Right near Cannes, so there's
that at least. But I can tell we're not going to get out of this
sodding club all week.

When we take our cases to our room, there are two GOs*
doing aerobics with a group of people by the pool. Everyone
looks happy.

Carmen doesn't. She still spends her whole time in her

---

*   GO: Club Med host. Stands for Glib and Oily.

why-should-I-be-nice-to-you mood. I remain indefatigably nice. Just go on smiling like a Buddhist, I've been telling myself every day, even if they're crapping on you from a huge height.

Luna's moody too. She's completely exhausted from the journey, and as difficult as Mido.* Luckily she quickly goes to sleep in our room. Carmen and I take the baby-monitor with us and go to dinner. We take a look at the kind of people walking around here. They all look like they're at a funfair. Carmen slowly thaws. Laughing at people together creates a bond. I even get a goodnight kiss in bed. The first day could have been worse.

On the second day the atmosphere in the team is, admittedly, a little better. We lie on the loungers by the pool, we eat, we play with Luna. There are a few topless women by the pool who aren't unappealing, so visually I can't complain. When I pop up to the room to get Luna's doll, I quickly send Rose a text.

> **A lot of women here, but it's beyond dispute: you've got the loveliest tits and you're the most gorgeous woman.**

There's one in my inbox as well. Let's see, from Thomas, wishing us a nice holiday. Pfff – OK, nice of him. I'll give him a call after the holiday.

In the evening we go to the auditorium for a toe-curling performance of *Titanic* (pronounced Tee-tan-*eek* according

---

* Egyptian footballer formerly with Ajax. Self-styled super-talent. Unmanageable, and they must have lost the user's manual. By the time you're reading this he's probably playing for some second-rate European club for an enormous fee.

to the French GOs). Luna thinks it's brilliant. Carmen and I drink our vicarious shame away. We're nice to each other. I keep reaching my hand behind Luna's back for contact with Carmen. After the show we put Luna to bed, drink a bit more and watch a movie in our room together. I grip Carmen's hand. When we're going to sleep, I stroke her face.

'That was a nice evening, wasn't it?'

'Yes.' She runs her hand over my chest.

'Night, lovey.'

'Night, my friend.'

On the third day I start getting a bit bored. Carmen and Luna are sleeping in the room. I lie by the pool texting Hakan, who brings me up to date on how the Dutch team opened yesterday – the European Cup starts in two weeks! – against Turkey. Out of boredom, I text Ramon a dirty joke I heard from one of the guys at the office. And first to Thomas. He likes that kind of humour. After that I send Rose a text.

> **I feel like giving you a good hard shag and then being really nice to you. X.**

I click my thumb on Options, Send, Search, OK, and off goes the text.

To Thomas.

I see it in a tenth of a second. Holy Christ, please not that! I turn red. My heart thumps in my throat. I try to stop the message going through. Too late. The 'Send Message' envelope has been replaced by the 'Message Sent' envelope. I start sweating. I want the ground to swallow me up.

I consider calling Thomas and telling him not to read the text, but I get a text myself. **THOMAS MOB**.

180

Glad things are better again between you and Carmen. ;)

I laugh. Good old gullible Thomas. At the same time I see Luna and Carmen walking towards the pool. Laughing cheerfully after their afternoon nap. I smile, touched. They wave. Just like a normal, happy, cancer-free little family. Carmen kisses me and winks at me. For a moment I'm happy. It almost scares me. God almighty, in the name of love* might we give each other a chance? After all, we're Dan & Carmen! We're not going to let my unbridled sexual desire or a little bit of cancer get us down? Are we?

■

When we've got Luna in bed and plugged in the baby monitor, we go to the outside bar by the pool. I order an amaretto and an armagnac. Carmen takes a sip of amaretto and looks at me. I feel it coming. This is it. The Conversation. I barely dare to make eye contact.

'Danny, what's been up with you lately? I feel you slipping away.'

'I don't think I am, am I?'

'Yeah,' she says quietly, 'you do everything you can to be away from home. And when you do go out, you abuse it.'

'Where's all this come from?'

'Who's Tasha?'

Shock.

'Tasha? Oh, yeah – Natasha. She's our new trainee. Why?'

'When you didn't pick up the phone on Saturday morning

---

*   Wrample from 'Stop in the Name of Love' by The Supremes (1965).

181

I got worried. And when you were packing your case I heard you'd got a text. I opened it for you. Look.'

With trembling fingers I open my message folder. In it I find a number I don't recognize. I open the message and blush.

> **Dan, I think you're pretty damned hot –**
> **yesterday tasted of more to come. X.**
> **Tasha**

Carmen sees my blush as a confirmation, just in case the text hadn't been quite unambiguous enough. Her eyes fill with tears. 'Is she good in bed? Does she have nice tits?'

'Carm, I haven't slept with Natasha. I really haven't.'

'Just stop,' she says, weeping. 'I understand. Of course you'd rather shag a hot little Monica Lewinsky than a woman with one tit and a bald head.'

I'm about to answer, but she waves a hand to say she isn't finished yet.

'That's not even the worst thing,' she goes on, her voice trembling. 'It hurts me to realize you can only be happy, apparently, if I'm not there. I know I'm not nice to live with these days. I wish I could make you happy again, but I can't and it's driving me mad. And making me sulky. I don't want that. I don't want to be a horrible old bitch.'

'You're not a horrible old bitch,' I say.

She brushes it aside. 'Wherever the problem lies, whether it's you, the sodding cancer or me: you think being with me is terrible. You run away. Can you look me in the eyes and say you still love me?'

'I – I don't know, Carm – '

She pauses for a moment. 'I thought that would be your

answer. Dan, listen. I've thought long and hard about what I'm going to say now – '

I feel myself growing smaller in response to her courage. I hadn't expected this. It's like I've been caught off-guard because my opponent has suddenly appeared on the field with three strikers rather than the expected two. She's caught up and equalized.

'I don't even want to know what you get up to when you're hanging out in the pub till half past four. I don't want to know who's sending you texts. I don't want to know where you are when you don't pick up the phone. I've always suspected you were unfaithful as a matter of course. If you were ill I might well do the same myself. I might have started seeing someone else ages ago.'

I look at her, startled. Does she know? I look for clues in her face to show me what she knows and what she doesn't. But I don't have time. She goes on.

'But I'm *not* you. I'm a woman with cancer with one breast, and perhaps only a few years to live. For those few years I'd rather be alone than with a man who isn't sure whether or not he still loves me. It would be difficult, it would be terrible, but I can do it, of that I'm sure—'

She pauses, looks at me and then comes out with it.

'Perhaps we should get divorced, Dan.'

She's said it. The D-word. *Divorce.*

The opposing team has now suggested what I've always dismissed as an impossible option. She's put the ball in front of an open goal. All I have to do is run up to it.

Everything runs through my head. How relieved I am every time I walk out the door to go to work at MIU. How happy I am when I can go out for the evening again. How good I feel when I'm with Rose. How tense I am when I come home, never knowing what the mood's going to be like this time. How often I've really felt like running away for good.

And now I can. If I say yes now, I'll be released from the chill. From the lack of intimacy. From the cancer.

'No.'

I say no. – *I say NO!?*

'No. I don't want to get divorced.' – *But you do!*

'Christ alive, then what *do* you want, Danny? Do you want more freedom? Then in God's name *say* what you want!' – *Yes! Say what you want!*

'How should I know what I want? No cancer, that's what I want!' I answer angrily.

'If you get rid of me, you'll be rid of the cancer,' she says dryly.

'No, I don't *want* rid of you!' I'm dumbfounded, because I realize I mean it, from the bottom of my heart.

Carmen says nothing for a moment and takes my hand. 'This week, have a good think about what you want, Danny. I don't feel like sitting and waiting until you know whether you still love me. Of course I want to stay with you, but something has to change. Otherwise we'll both go our own way. You and I are too good for this misery.'

'Jesus, Carm,' I say gently, 'to think it could have come to this.' I draw circles in her palm with my thumb.

'Let's not talk about it any more tonight. Let's just have a good time,' she smiles. 'See if we can still do that.'

'Yes,' I grin, 'let's go out clubbing and get rat-arsed.'

'Good plan, Batman.'

It's a long time since the two of us went to the pub. Carmen has gin and tonic and I hit the Kronenbourg. We have a lot of fun, we drink and we dance. We have a laugh. Together!

Swaying slightly, we walk back to our apartment. On a carpeted landing near our apartment, Carmen takes off her skirt and panties and goes and sits, legs parted, on the stairs. She gives me a look I haven't seen on her face for ages. We have the hottest sex we've had in years.

Have I got a little story for you,
and I'm glad we talked . . .

Pearl Jam, from 'Alive' (*Ten*, 1992)

Twelve

Carmen is cheerful. She keeps referring to the sex we had last night, and she's been winking at me all day long. We haven't mentioned last night's conversation. Not even now Luna's in bed. We're sitting reading on the little terrace in front of our apartment. Carmen has taken my hand, and is stroking it. I can't imagine us splitting up. *No fucking way!*

But I'm still tense. I've got one last card under the table, and I'm going to have to play it before we can start on the next game. Every time she looks at me I want to start talking. Again and again my nerve fails me. All at once I summon all my courage.

'Listen, Carm, I want to talk to you about something I've never dared to bring up . . .' I can't restrain myself now. 'My, erm – infidelity.'

'I saw it coming,' she smiles. 'I think it's good for us to talk about it. Come on, then.'

Christ, she's strong. I'm not. My nerves are about to explode.

Carmen sits straight up. 'So? Give it to me, baby!'

I laugh and decide to start the easy way. 'I'm sure you've never been unfaithful, have you?'

'You really want to know?' she asks.

'Yes,' I say innocently, already formulating my own confession.

'Then yes.'

She sees her words haven't got through to me.

'Yes, I was once unfaithful, Dan.'

I look at her with my mouth wide open. Carmen who has always, since Sharon, always said she'd leave me if I did it again, that same Carmen coolly replies to a question that was just a warm-up, a courtesy question, the 'are-you-sitting-comfortably' ice-breaker you use with a nervous interviewee, by saying she's played away from home too.

'Um – I – erm – I don't know – ah – when?' I stammer.

'A few years ago on Koninginnedag. A boy I saw at Café Thijssen. No one saw. We went outside and just kissed for a bit.'

'Phew.'

'But I did it with Pim.'

'Ah . . . What?'

'It.'

'Oh. When?'

'A few years ago. He kept asking me out for dinner, but I always kept him at bay. And when you were in Thailand I gave him a call. And then something happened.'

'At our place?'

'Yes. And in his car and – and once in the toilet.'

'God almighty.' – *Look who's talking.* 'All on one evening?'

'No. We met up another two times.'

'During those four weeks when I was in Thailand?'

'Yes.' She says it as though she's telling me she forgot to empty the dishwasher.

I should have known? In Miami, let's not forget, I'd said as much myself: women do it out of revenge. I had so urgently wanted a month's partying in Ko Pangang, with Frank, just before we started at MIU. Carmen wasn't happy about it because she'd worked out I wasn't going there to polish statues of the Buddha. Weeks later, when I saw her at the airport, she burst into tears and flew into my arms. An hour later we were screwing, and I acted like I hadn't had sex for weeks. In retrospect, so did Carmen. The slut.

'And you?' she asks.

'What?'

'How often?'

'Oh.' I'm still getting my head round that sleazebag Pim, who does it in toilets and cars. How cheap. And my wife joining in. Yuck.

'Hello? Earth to Danny?' says Carmen impatiently.

Hm? Oh, yeah. My turn. Where to start. First of all the exes I kept sleeping with after I started going out with Carmen. So – once or twice with Merel. Every Friday for six months with Emma, after I bumped into her on the Leidseplein. And now and again with Maud after parties Carmen didn't go to. And – there was – umm – Christ, where do you begin? Replays don't count, I reckon. That makes things a lot easier. *Three, then.*

I'm not counting that time with the prostitutes, either. That was circumstances beyond my control. But those two with Ramon in the sauna in Noord weren't actually professional prostitutes, so I do have to count them. *Five.*

Then my work. Lisa and Cindy at BBDvW&R/Bernilvy, and the couple of times with Sharon. Oh yes, and Dianne. Give me a minute ... *Five and four makes nine.* So, at MIU, so far just Maud after the Christmas party. But I'd already

188

counted her among the exes. And I haven't done it with Natasha yet. So that's still nine. Shit, Maud's assistant with the tattoo on her belly, the one we had to fire after three months. I can't even remember her name. *Ten.*

The holidays. That crazy kid from the Hague. Then there was that weekend with Ramon in Gran Canaria a few years ago. *Eleven.* Then Thailand. Hmmm. Let me think. Let's do it island by island. Ko Samui. The Irish girl with the spotty arse and the ugly old German woman. Oh, how Frank laughed. I'm still ashamed. *Erm – thirteen.* Ko Samet. The Swedish woman. Oh no, she just wanted to give me a blowjob. Then Ko Pangang. The Finnish girl. *That makes fourteen.* Mmmmm, what a gorgeous . . .

'*How often*, Danny?'

'I'm counting.'

So, fourteen. Miami, Linda. *Fifteen.* Anything else? Skiing with Ramon, nothing happened. With Frank in New York? No, nothing that time either. Oh yeah, Turkey with Hakan. The waitress. *Sixteen.* Hm. So far that's the holidays.

Now going out. Christ, and I've got to sixteen already. Ahem. The girl at the Christmas party in Vak Zuid. *Seventeen.* Ellie, Thomas's sister, last year at carnival. *Eighteen.* That Surinamese girl from Paradiso and the one with the eyebrow piercing from De Pilsvogel. *Twenty.* A good thing I'm not counting the snogs in De Bastille, Surprise, De Bommel and Paradiso, or we'd be here for hours. Oh, wait a moment, the one after the Basement Jaxx concert. I actually went back to her house, fuck, how far have I got? Oh, yes, twenty. Plus one is *twenty-one.* And maybe three or four I've forgotten. And Rose, of course. *Let's round it off at twenty-five.* I look at Carmen. Fasten your seatbelts. Welcome to Monophobia.

'And?'

'Umm – a good bit more than the fingers of one hand.'

'More than the fingers of one hand?'

'Two hands' – *Five hands, you dick!*

'Christ almighty.'

'Are you disappointed?'

'I hoped it would be less. Danny . . .' she says with a shake of the head. She's not as angry as I'd expected. 'Do I know them?'

Gulp. 'Do you really want to know?'

'Yes.'

'So, erm – some exes. Merel, Emma . . .'

'You see!' She brings the palm of her hand down on the table, almost triumphantly. 'I knew it, I knew it – Emma, that butter-wouldn't-melt-in-her-mouth face of hers! I knew you were still doing it! And I knew about Merel, too. I'm glad we never see her any more.' – *Let's keep Maud out of this for now.* 'When was all this?'

'Both in the early days, before we moved in together.'

'Oh – Danny! Christ, we used to shag like crazy in those days – we were like rabbits! Why did you need all those other women?!'

'I don't know. I couldn't stay away from women' – *Couldn't? Can't, you twat!*

'God almighty, that's a proper addiction, Danny.'

I sit and nod, head bowed.

'Any other girls I know?'

'Well – Ellie.'

'Ellie?'

'Thomas's sister.'

'WHAT?! Ellie? When!?'

'Last year at carnival.'

'I bet Thomas didn't notice, did he?'

'No, of course not! I was careful,' I say quickly. I can still see him cursing at his sister there in De Bommel when all we were doing was having a snog.

'That was lucky. Otherwise you might as well have put it on the front page of *De Telegraaf.* I assume Frank knows everything?'

'Most of it, yes . . .'

'Fuck. Christ alive, I'm seriously pissed off about this, Danny.'

'But Frank won't tell anyone . . .'

'That's not the point! How would you like it if your friends knew I'd done it with Pim? Well at least, thank God, Thomas doesn't know anything. And what about Maud? Does she know? Or hang on a minute' – *Oh, no, please don't ask* – 'You're not going to tell me you've done it with her too, are you?' – *Ouch.*

'With Maud? God, no!'

'Thank Christ for that. But she knows you've been unfaithful.'

'Yes. She knows.'

'Shit – OK, when you were going out with Maud you slept with tons of girls, isn't that right?'

I nod.

'Always without a condom, of course?'

'Almost always with one,' I lie. 'And what about you, with Pim?'

'Without.'

'Fuck.'

'Hang on, you're not intending to lay into me, are you?'

she says crossly. I quickly shake my head. She bursts out laughing. 'OK. That really would be the cherry on the cake,' she says with a laugh. 'You randy little sod – I'm glad you've told me. Though I'm willing to bet you've left out a few.'

'Well – I think that's probably enough, don't you?'

'OK, let's drop it. But you've got to promise me one thing, Danny.'

'And that is?' – *Oh Jesus, I can feel the storm coming. Oh, no, please –*

'That from now on you're not going to be unfaithful, for the few years I still have left.'

Shit. Shitshitshitshit. Hi, Rose.

'I promise,' I say, apparently without hesitation, and with the most reassuring smile I can muster.

It's raining but there ain't a cloud in the sky
must have been a tear from your eye . . .

Bruce Springsteen, from 'Waiting on a Sunny Day'
(*The Rising*, 2002)

Thirteen

I told Carmen I was going out with Ramon tonight. She kissed me and said she hoped I'd have fun. On the day after our infidelity conversation she cried a bit, but she said she wanted to put it behind us. She was proud of me for admitting everything. Carmen trusts me again.

I don't trust myself. That's why I arranged to meet Rose at Vertigo, rather than at her place. I haven't the faintest idea how this evening's going to go. Do I dare say goodbye to my sex-machine, my periodical shot of the pleasures of life, my croissant-baker, my surrogate queen, my shrink?

> ▶ **Vertigo** is the catering industry's equivalent of what Frank calls a 'butterface' (i.e. everything about her is lovely but her face): it's an absolutely rubbish pub in a fantastic location (the Vondelpark pavilion). It isn't even a lounge café, and it still manages to be boring. Stick it anywhere else and not a soul would go there.

I have butterflies in my stomach as I cast my eyes over Vertigo to see if she's already there. This isn't a first date. There she is, at the bar. She waves and smiles nervously at me. I ask her what she wants to drink.

'I'll have a white wine. This *is* our last evening. Am I right?' she asks anxiously.

'Sweet or dry?' I ask.

I can't bring myself to look at Rose. But she looks at me. I feel her eyes on me as I watch the barman pouring the wine. He finishes far too quickly as far as I'm concerned. I pick up my glass and clink it against Rose's. 'Cheers.'

'Just tell me the verdict,' says Rose.

'Carmen and I are going to have another try.'

'That's good. I'm happy for you both. Really.'

'And I've admitted I've been unfaithful for much of my life.'

'So. And how did she react?'

'Not bad. I had to promise I'd never be unfaithful again.'

'So – to our last evening, then, eh?' she says mockingly, raising her glass.

'But we can go on seeing each other, can't we?' I say, and try my best, good as I am at bringing bad news, to introduce some lightness to the proceedings. 'Now we've really got everything. You've got a secret affair with a married man you can't go to bed with, and I've got a platonic girlfriend I can't tell anybody about, otherwise I'm going to have to go home and explain how we met,' I laugh.

Rose doesn't. Rose isn't amused. Her face clouds over. 'I don't think there's anything funny about it, Dan,' she says fiercely. 'Don't be so naïve! Don't you understand we can't see each other any more? Surely you can work that one out all by yourself? You can't stay away from me, and I can't resist you. Later you'll spend your whole life feeling guilty, and I'll spend my whole life feeling like a slut.'

It's a tough one to deny. Not seeing each other is the only

way for me to keep my promise. I know myself. I should really be glad. I rest my hand on her leg. She takes it and puts it back on my leg.

'We should go home, before we start making mistakes.'

'Can I call you or email you from time to time?' I ask her, embarrassed, like a schoolboy, standing outside with my bicycle.

'Better not to,' she whispers, eyes fixed on the ground.

I bend towards her and give her one final French kiss. Then I get on my bike. I look round once and see Rose still standing there with her bike.

She's crying.

It's the final countdown . . .

Europe, from 'The Final Countdown'
(*The Final Countdown*, 1986)

Fourteen

A week later we learn Carmen's dying.

'Tell me exactly where it hurts,' says Dr Scheltema.

Carmen points to just under her ribs, the place she'd pointed out to me the day before. A bit to the right of the middle, to the viewer's left. 'Isn't that where your liver is?' she asked me. No idea. I know more or less where my heart and my lungs are, I can point to where my stomach is because I can feel it when I've eaten too much, but I've no idea where the rest of it hangs out. I did arts subjects at school.

'Hm,' says Scheltema. 'Get undressed in the room next door.'

I stay where I am. Scheltema flicks through Carmen's file. There's an uneasy silence. Then she stands up and says, without looking at me, 'Let's go and take a look.' She closes the door behind her, so I assume by 'us' she means herself.

A short while later she comes back, washes her hands in the wash-basin, goes and sits down, says nothing and starts flicking once more. Carmen comes in, too. Scheltema closes the file, puts on her glasses and looks at us.

'What you're feeling is in fact your liver,' she begins. 'I'm afraid you've got a metastasis.'

Sometimes you hear a word you've never heard before, but you immediately know what it means.

'So it's spreading?'

'That's right. It's spreading.'

Carmen and I look at one another. For a moment Carmen doesn't move a muscle. Then her lower lip begins to tremble, she brings her hand to it and the first tears come. I take her other hand and keep looking at her. It's a déjà-vu from a year ago. Same room, same chairs, the same silent Dr Scheltema in front of us. Then we learned the forty per cent chance of survival Carmen had read about on the internet was a bit on the high side. Now it's no more than zero.

'Is it definitely spreading?' I ask.

'The best thing would be for us to have an immediate ultrasound of your liver. And then you come back to me.'

Meek as sheep, we allow ourselves to be guided through the hospital. We sit down in the ultrasound waiting-room. Carmen says nothing. She sits with her head bowed, looking at the handkerchief she's rolling up and opening again like a cigarette paper. Rolling it up, opening it out. A nurse comes out of a door. She's holding a file, looks at the name on it, looks at Carmen's and asks, 'Mrs van Diepen?'

Carmen nods.

'Shall I come with you?' I ask.

'Please,' says Carmen.

We walk into the room. Carmen has to get undressed and go and lie on a gurney. The nurse rubs her belly with pale blue gel. I stand next to Carmen and hold her hand tightly. With my other hand I stroke her shoulder. She looks at me and starts crying again. I feel my own eyes welling up, too. The nurse picks up an apparatus I recognize from the echograms we had done when Carmen was three months pregnant. That time we turned happily to the screen and the obstetrician explained which parts of the body were already recognizable in the little worm tumbling about on the screen. Over and over again. Carmen and I both thought it was hilarious. We'd gave the little worm the working title 'Woopsy-daisy!' Carmen thought that captured the motion best.

Today there's not much woopsy-daisy going on, and we don't feel the slightest need to look at the screen. The faces of the two nurses (or doctors, I've no idea what their rank or status is) tell us everything we need to know. They point to something on the screen, mumble something incomprehensible to each other, which one of them writes down in Carmen's file, glancing now and again from the screen to the file.

'You can get dressed again.'

'And?' I ask.

'You'll get the results from Dr Scheltema,' she says.

■

'It doesn't look great,' she says as soon as we sit down. 'A metastasis measuring three by four centimetres, on the upper side of your liver.'

I look over at Carmen, who has by now put her hand back to her mouth, signifying the approach of a crying fit, but I decide to ask Scheltema anyway.

'How – erm – how long does my wife have left?'

'If we don't act quickly, two months at the most . . .'

'And if we do act?' I ask combatively.

'If I'm totally honest, it's really just a matter of putting things off. A few extra months on a course of Taxotere. It's a different kind of chemo from the CAF you got last year. You can have no more than twelve of these. Your body won't stand more than that. And the metastasis will start growing again as soon as the treatment stops. We can stretch it out to a year at the most.'

'Will I be in a lot of pain?' asks Carmen through her tears.

'No. Almost certainly not. You must imagine your liver as a factory that cleanses the body of poisonous materials. The tumour eventually stops the liver from working. And then you get less and less energy, you sleep more, and finally you slip into a coma. And then you die. It's all very humane.'

'Well, that's something positive at least,' Carmen murmurs through her tears. Be grateful for small mercies.

'What are the side-effects of the treatment?' I ask Scheltema.

'The same as the CAF. Nausea, exhaustion, hair loss, loss of taste and smell. And with this treatment your muscles may protest, and the skin of the palms of your hands and your fingers will become very sensitive,' says Scheltema.

'Let's do it,' says Carmen.

'Oh, and your nails will fall out,' says Scheltema.

'OK,' I say. In for a penny, I guess.

So much to do,
I've still got so much to do . . .

Toontje Lager, from 'Zoveel te doen'
(*Stiekem dansen*, 1983)

Fifteen

'Mad as it may sound, I'm a bit relieved,' Carmen begins, even before we've left the hospital car park. 'At least we know where we are now. I'm dying.'

'Carm, please—' Those are the first words to have come out of my mouth since we left Scheltema's office.

'It's true, though. Last year we left here and we came out into an uncertain, impotent situation. Now we have certainty.'

I'm perplexed by what she's saying, by the fact she's actually saying it. But she has a point. I think back to last year. Then the blow was much, much bigger.

'I want to go on holiday,' she says with a blazing look in her eyes. 'As much as possible. I want to go to Ireland. And erm – Barcelona! Yes, I want to go to Barcelona, with you.'

I'm even starting to enjoy this. 'I'll ask Frank if he knows of a nice decadent hotel,' I grin. 'Will that be all, madam?'

'I want to go with all my friends to a castle somewhere in the Ardennes,' she says dreamily. All of a sudden she's joie de vivre personified. 'Oh, by the way, can you stop for a moment at this snack bar?'

'Why?'

'Get some cigarettes. I'm going to start smoking again.'

I smile and stop the car by the Moroccan snack bar in Zeilstraat.

'Ordinary Marlboro or Lights?' I ask her before I get out of the car.

'Ordinary. A bit of lung cancer isn't going to make much difference now, is it?'

I do what I do and I don't ask why,
I do what I do and maybe that's dumb,
we do what we do . . .

Astrid Nijgh, from 'Ik doe wat ik doe'
(*Mensen zijn je beste vrienden*, 1973)

Sixteen

Laughing, I walk into the snack bar. There are two people in front of me. I look outside and see Carmen sitting in the car. She's staring blankly into the distance. Stunned. As I look at her the smile disappears from my face.

What can we expect now?

All kinds of things fly through my head. Ambulances in the night. A flagging Carmen. Fear of pain. A deathbed. And death. Death. My stomach tightens. Suddenly I'm filled with a sense of panic. My wife's dying! *Carmen really is dying now!* I feel a surge of nausea, so bad I almost throw up. I become restless and start sweating.

'Hey, Ahmed, how bloody long before someone serves me? I just need some cigarettes,' I snarl all of a sudden.

'Calm down, sir, I've only got two hands!' the usually friendly man replies crossly. The two people ahead of me turn round and look at me witheringly. I quickly disappear into the toilet, and take out my phone.

It's spread, Rose. Can I call you later? Please?

I collect beautiful moments . . .

Herman Brood, in an interview with Henk Binnendijk
(*Fifty-Fifty*, EO) in 1994

Seventeen

Dear Luna

*In this book I want to write down all the things we do
together, so you'll always know how much I love you. I'm ill.
I have cancer, and when you read this I won't be there any
more. I hope this book will be a lovely memory.*

*You're just two years old, but now and again you're so
wise, partly because you're so good at talking. Over the past
year it's sometimes been difficult for us, and if Daddy or
I couldn't help crying, and you saw that, you came and
cuddled us and wiped a tear from our cheeks. Then we felt a
bit better. Or you said something that made us laugh in spite
of our tears, and then we were a bit less miserable. A lot of
people have come to comfort and cheer us, but you do it best
of all.*

*When I came to cuddle you tonight before you went to
sleep, I said I loved you very much. And then you said you
loved me too. That's so lovely! It makes me all warm inside.*

*Daddy and I talk to each other lots and lots because we
already know that in a while I won't be there any more.
That's very miserable, but in spite of everything we're doing a*

whole lot of lovely things, all three of us, in the short time we still have. I enjoy it so intensely, and then I'm so happy with my little family, I could cry with happiness.

I love you! Mama xxx

If you ask me, they're not that happy themselves...

Tol Hansse, from 'Big City' (*Tol Hansse moet niet zeuren*, 1978)

Eighteen

Carmen's joined a discussion group. She calls it the Mouflon.

▶ **Mouflon** – Tupperware, Center Parcs, *She* magazine, the Argos catalogue and so on. If she hadn't had breast cancer, Carmen would never have fetched up in a group like Mouflon in her life. Every now and again she roars with laughter when she tells me what the meeting was like. 'Spent the whole morning talking cosily with five women about breast cancer.'

The only one who's OK is **Toni**, short for Antonia. Like Carmen, she's in her thirties, lives in Amsterdam (the other three come from Zaandam, Mijdrecht and a village I've never heard of) and isn't bad-looking. I'd even say she was a bit of all right, if I didn't know she only had one breast.

All the Mouflon ladies have had one breast off. In one of them it hasn't spread (yet), with another the doctors have already given up, and the other three are in the same state as Carmen: sooner or later it's all going to go wrong. 'So the Mouflon will gradually close down all by itself,' Carmen jokes.

The women have a lot to talk about where relationships are concerned, too. Carmen tells me one Mouflon woman has already got divorced since the cancer gloom began. Her husband couldn't take it any more. And Toni's husband barely seems able to talk about it and spends whole evenings sitting at the computer in the attic. A third Mouflon member's marriage was already crap before the cancer started, so nothing's changed there. They all fell about laughing at that.

They meet at each other's houses in turn, once a fortnight. The husbands talk to each other sometimes, too, Carmen tells me. When I hear that, I pull a face that stops Carmen asking whether it might be something I'd be interested in.

Carmen gets something out of it. At the Mouflon, at least they talk openly about what it's like, as a woman, to lose a breast. Something Anne, Maud, her mother and the girls at Advertising Brokers never dare to bring up.

Last week the Mouflon met at our house. When I came in with Luna, they were all still there. I was embarrassed when I introduced myself, because I know they sometimes talk about me too.

'We gave our husbands marks out of ten this afternoon,' Carmen told me this evening. 'How they deal with the fact their wives have cancer, whether they always go along with them to the hospital, whether they're good at talking about it, whether they stay nice in spite of all the misery.'

'And what sort of mark did you give me?'

'An eight.'

'An eight?' I ask, surprised.

'Yes. Now I've heard all the group's stories, I've worked out you're not doing all that badly.'

'Perhaps we should give Thomas and Anne an account of these meetings,' I reply.

'No need,' says Carmen. 'I've already told them.'

For the ones who have a notion, a notion deep inside,
that it ain't no sin to be glad you're alive . . .

Bruce Springsteen, from 'Badlands'
(*Darkness on the Edge of Town*, 1978)

Nineteen

Summer is one big party.

Frank agreed I should only go to work for urgent matters and major presentations. Otherwise I spend as much time as I can with Carmen.

Carmen and I do whatever we feel like.

We buy black-market tickets for all the Holland games in the European Championship. When Kluivert scores his four goals in the quarter-final against Yugoslavia,* Carmen goes just as crazy as the other fifty thousand people.

> **Game was an orgasm lasting an hour and a half. Carmen thought it was great!**

'It would be nice if I died just as Holland became European champions, wouldn't it? Then I'd go out with a bang . . .' she giggles. It doesn't come to that. Carmen survives a lot longer than the Dutch team. But the great thing about cancer is it

---

* 6–1. Four by Kluivert, two by Overmars. 25 June 2000. Van der Sar, Stam, Reiziger, F. De Boer, Zenden, Van Bronckhorst, Davids, Cocu, Bergkamp, Kluivert, Overmars.

makes everything so relative. The world record for missed penalties against Italy takes its toll on our smiling muscles. If they lose, you don't actually die. Football's just a game again.

We go away for the weekend and stay in the best hotels. In Barcelona we stay at the Arts Hotel. On the top storey, looking out over Barceloneta and the Mediterranean. We take the biggest suite and play hide-and-seek. Carmen wins nearly every time. I only find her when she starts laughing because I've just walked past the wardrobe she's hiding in for the third time.

In the evening we eat divinely. I nearly cream myself when I try the tapas in the Cervezeria Catalunya on the Avenue de Mallorca.

> **Just ate fantastic tapas. Carmen ate practically nothing, but she's still enjoying it. So am I.**
>
> **Fucking cancer. Tried to walk back after tapas. Carmen exhausted after 5 min. Had to wait hours till a taxi came past. Carmen was weeping with misery. I want to call you later, Goddess –**

In Ireland we choose the most luxurious castles to eat and sleep in. Carmen has so little energy we only get out of the car to have lunch in a pub or to spend the night at the next castle, but we have a great week. We make videos for Luna, all based around the childish humour of Carmen & Dan. Carmen does *How not to be seen* behind a fat woman in the lounge of the Morrison Hotel in Dublin. Danny does the Red Hot Chili Peppers with a Castle Ballymore shower-cap on his head. Carmen does a seal impression with her prosthetic breast on her nose. Danny does Ray Charles on the Cliffs of Moher. Carmen does the What's Worse Quiz (Burn to death or drown? Never sitting again, or never standing again? Never eating or never coming? Never peeing or never crapping? Cancer or Aids?). Carmen & Danny do Dannian & Carmian conjugations (We dive into Drublin. Can & Darmen. Stuinness ginks! You're a dig barling. What wucking awful feather!)

> We're having fun, mad country. People
> here start drinking at 10 in the morning.
> Women here are ugly, according to Carmen
> the biggest point in Ireland's favour. X!

Back in Amsterdam we take our boat down the canals every day while the weather's nice. With parents, friends and a lot of bottles of rosé. We often stop at the Amstel Hotel and drink champagne on the terrace. Or else we drive to Ouderkerk and then have a decadent lunch at Klein Paardeburg. Once when we're driving past the Zorgvlied cemetery, Carmen tells me she wants to be buried there.

> Gulp. Just passed Zorgvlied. Carmen asked
> if I'd help her find a nice plot for her for
> afterwards. I can't.

Carmen invites a crowd of friends to spend a weekend with us in a castle in Spa in the Belgian Ardennes. There are twenty-three guests, almost an anthology from her whole life. Sometimes it's raining harder inside than out.

And we go house hunting. We were going to stay on Amstelveenseweg for about three years, and then, with a pile of money earned at MIU and Advertising Brokers, search for a bigger house, but the metastasized liver has thwarted our plans. It was my plan. Carmen had to get used to it, but now she thinks it would be nice to know where Luna and I will live later on.

'And perhaps I can live there for a while myself, if the Taxotere does its job,' she says hopefully.

I hope not, because if Carmen's still alive when we move into a new house, it means she'll die there. And frankly I'm worried the new house, like Amstelveenseweg now, will be infected, for me, with the association of illness and death. I'd desperately like to see a new house as a symbolic new start for Luna and me. But I don't dare share that with Carmen.

But we talk a lot about the future after Carmen's death. For hours. At home, in the pub, in our boat, on the terrace. We talk about everything.

Daddy and I have also talked about the fact there will be a new mummy for you later on. I think it's a great idea. For Daddy, of course, but it's also good for you if there's someone nice you can talk to, laugh with, make a lot of noise and do things with. And even if I'm not there any more, in thoughts and in my heart you'll always be with me. Whatever happens, you'll always be my darling, even if I'm not there myself to talk to you and cuddle you – I'll always love you, just as I'll always love Daddy.

All our conversations have made us fall in love with each other again. We enjoy each other, and we enjoy every day we still have together. Dan & Carmen as the uncrowned king and queen of enjoyment. And they lived happily briefly after.

Give me, give me, give me the power . . .

Suede, from 'The Power' (*DogManStar*, 1994)

Twenty

In between all the fun, Carmen's in a really bad way. The side-effects of the Taxotere are appalling. Carmen's gone through the menopause about fifteen years too early. All of a sudden she's got hot flushes, her periods stopped and she started turning grey. Not for long, because after three treatments she was bald again. Prickly-wig came back out of the box. This time her eyebrows and eyelashes have gone. She wore false eyelashes for a few days, but it wasn't a success because the Taxotere makes her eyes water constantly. She walks around all day dabbing them dry with a handkerchief.

Another side-effect is that all her fingers are taped up at the ends, because her nails are either loose or have already come off. Her fingertips feel 'like I caught my fingers in the door'. Carmen cried this morning because she couldn't change Luna's nappy any more. She had no strength in her fingers to open the sticky edges. After that she got angry with herself, with Procter & Gamble, with the cancer and with me because I told her irritably she could always ask me to do it. 'Can't you bloody well understand I want to do it myself?' she shrieked at me.

Another problem is coughing. Especially at night. Sometimes I'm worried she won't stop. But I'm even more worried it means it's spreading. The lungs are another favourite nesting place for a metastasizing breast cancer, I read in a pamphlet. The doctor puts our minds at rest: it's probably pleurisy. 'Pleurisy, doctor?' It seems, you've guessed already, it's a side-effect of the Taxotere.

And Carmen can't do anything that involves any effort. She barely has any energy left. The stacking-effect, Dr Scheltema called it. The body protests more and more against the chemo. And can you blame it?

But by far the biggest problem is the insertion of the needle and the little tube through which the chemicals go into her body via the veins in her hand. That needle and tube have become our symbol of the misery of the cancer. Carmen's veins seem to be deeper under her skin than most people. It gets harder and more painful every time and they spend minutes rooting around before the tube is finally in. Carmen sees it as a mountain she has to climb, higher and higher each week. I go along with her and can hardly hold back the tears when the doctor's pricking away at my weeping Carmen's hand.

Another two goes and that'll be the first six treatments over with. Then come three chemo-free weeks, to give Carmen's body the chance to recover, and then the whole circus starts up again. Another six times. The very idea of it drives her crazy.

'If only there was something I could take orally rather than having that thing stuck into me,' she says when we're sitting with Scheltema, as we do every week before the chemo begins. 'I wouldn't mind so much.' As she says it, it nearly overwhelms her again. She battles against her tears.

'Yes,' says Scheltema curtly, 'but there's no such thing.'

So I support my blubbering Carmie to the chemo room for her fifth Taxotere session.

Only seven to go.

I've just been crying in the toilet after
Carmen got punctured. It's horrible, Rose.
I'll call later.

What's amazed me for years,
that I'll never forget if I live to be a hundred,
you've fooled me, you've diddled me . . .

Wim Sonneveld, from 'Tearoom Tango'
(*An Evening with Wim Sonneveld*, 1966)

Twenty-one

Apparently there is a drink you can take.

Carmen found out via Toni. At the Antoni van Leeuwenhoek Hospital, where Carmen got her radiation treatment,
according to Toni a test's being done with the oral administration of chemotherapy. They've been doing it for months. I
can't believe it.

Carmen asks me to ring them. 'You're much better with
words than I am.'

The doctor at the Antoni van Leeuwenhoek Hospital I get
on the line confirms Toni's story.

They can't do anything for Mrs van Diepen as long as the
patient is with a doctor at the Sint Lucas. I say I understand,
and that I'll make contact with Dr Scheltema.

I put the phone down. Carmen looks at me.

'It works. There's a drink you can take.'

Carmen bursts into tears.

I feel like driving to the fucking hospital, grabbing Dr
Scheltema's hands and pinning them to her desk with that
needle Carmen's been getting in her hand every week. One.

Two. Three. Four. Five. Six. Seven. Eight. Nine. Ten. Deep breath. Then I phone the Sint Lucas and ask for Scheltema. She's on holiday.

The locum is Dr Tasmiel. I explain to him as calmly as possible that the weekly intubation of my wife is so difficult it's causing major psychological problems, that Dr Scheltema knows about this, and I end with the simple request to give formal agreement to transfer Mrs van Diepen as a patient to the doctor in charge of the oral administration of the chemo-substances in the Antoni van Leeuwenhoek.

Dr Tasmiel tells me he can't help me. He explains he can't just pass on a colleague's patients as easily as that, and says Dr Scheltema will be back in a week and a half.

I'm seething with fury, and tell him that, until today, I've been living with the naïve notion doctors put the quality of life of their terminal patients above everything else, and my wife's quality of life is almost at zero because every week, days before the treatment, she walks around crying for the simple reason she can't face having that tube in her body. And then I take an old – but in this instance not irrelevant – grudge out of the cupboard and say I had hoped for a little humility on the part of the doctors there since my wife had ended up in this state because of a mistake made by one of his colleagues, Dr Wolters, almost two years ago.

Dr Tasmiel gets irritated, says he knows nothing about it, and that in his view it falls completely outside the context of this discussion, and he also considers it far from normal for me to adopt such a tone with him.

'Have you said your piece?' I ask him.

'Yes.'

'Fine. Then let me say mine: I will have NOTHING more

to do with you.' I add that he can expect an intemperate fax, copied to Dr Scheltema and the doctor at the Antoni van Leeuwenhoek, because I consider the wellbeing of my wife to be more important than Scheltema's goddamned fucking holiday.

Carmen asks if we shouldn't just leave it. Don't even think about it! I'm in a rage. We've been royally screwed, completely fucked over.

Meanwhile I go and sit down at the PC. I say in my fax that if necessary I'll take the case to the press to ensure my wife gets the test, and I expressly reserve the right to use any means at my disposal. I haven't the faintest inkling what that might be, but I think it sounds menacing.

The morning after the fax I get a call at nine o'clock.

'Mr van Diepen, this is Dr Rodenbach, medical director of the Antoni van Leeuwenhoek. I was given your number by Dr Tasmiel at the Sint Lucas Hospital.'

Two hours later we're sitting in his office. Rodenbach is an oasis. A doctor who lets his patients talk, and listens to them, too. He tells us the results of the oral test are still uncertain, and notes that until now the Taxotere treatment has been working well for Carmen. He advises her against joining the test, and suggests an alternative to get us off the tube injection. A port-a-cath. It sounds like a chemical toilet to me, but apparently it's a handy little gadget that's applied once under anaesthetic, under the skin near the breast, a tiny operation. The Taxotere is then injected through a permanent hole straight to the vein rather than with a needle and a tube; it's painless and it always works first time. No puncturing of the veins. Carmen says she's known about this gadget for six months via the internet chat-group. She talked about it once with Scheltema, but Scheltema strongly advised her against it. The operation was pretty major, and it often got blocked. Not worth the trouble, in Scheltema's view.

'Well – erm – that sounds great to us.'

Rodenbach does his best not to let his fellow-doctor Scheltema of Sint Lucas down. The same Scheltema I once asked if it wouldn't be better to have my wife treated in the Antoni van Leeuwenhoek Hospital, the one specializing in cancer. The same Scheltema who then took serious umbrage because since the arrival of the internet all the information about cancer, all the new developments, all the new methods of all the hospitals in the world were common knowledge amongst the world's doctors within a few hours. And she'd told us she discussed her patients with doctors from the neighbouring Antoni van Leeuwenhoek every fortnight.

At best, Scheltema hasn't done her homework for months, and at worst she's callously lied to us as Carmen, weeping, begged for anything in the world to avoid the damn needle.

■

Rodenbach says he thinks the port-a-cath is better than oral administration, but the choice is up to Carmen. And he offers to take her on as a patient.

Carmen opts for the port-a-cath, for Rodenbach and for the Antoni van Leeuwenhoek. I see she's pleased, and so am I.

► The **Antoni van Leeuwenhoek** Hospital (AvL) specializes in the treatment of cancer. The doctors and nurses at the AvL understand what's going on in the heads of people with a life-threatening or – as in Carmen's case – terminal illness.

The other side of the coin is that everyone walking around

there knows you don't go there because your wife has just had a baby or because she's recovering from an appendectomy, but that it's about cancer. I even catch myself giving pitying looks to people walking arm-in-arm down the corridor, or sitting in silence beside the coffee machine in the hall. They'll have just heard it's spread in their mother, or their grandpa could pass away at any moment, or the doctors have given up on their husband or wife. In fact the AvL is just like Amsterdam's red-light district. If you see someone walking around there, you know exactly what he or she's come for.

The operation to install the port-a-cath really is a doddle, and Carmen whistles happily as she goes to the remaining chemos.

We never see the Sint Lucas again. Scheltema's voice pops up once more on our voicemail, saying she really does think it's a shame things went the way they did during her holiday, and she wishes us all the very best. I take her at her word and leave it there. So does Carmen.

Her life won't be any longer as a result, but it'll be a bit nicer.

And when I get that feeling, I want sexual healing . . .

Marvin Gaye, from 'Sexual Healing' (*Midnight Love*, 1982)

Twenty-two

To make my life a bit nicer too, I've returned to my old habits.
I'm addicted to Rose once more.

The day after the metastasis we had sat together in the
Coffee Company in De Pijp, in the morning after I'd taken
Luna to the crèche. From the monophobic point of view it's a
safe spot and a safe time, because it's a long way from Rose's
house in Oud-West.

> ▶ The **Coffee Company.** You can chat people up here, but it's
> one for the experts. The more unusual the coffee you order, the
> higher your status. Set yourself up as a connoisseur. Forget
> cappuccino and espresso. Even if you know as much about coffee
> as a cow knows about rock-climbing, order an Americano or a
> ristretto. Then you belong, and that's what it's all about.

Rose listened as I poured out all my frustration and
distress.

After that, all summer, in amongst all the holidays and
boat trips with Carmen, I had furtively arranged to meet Rose
in pubs and sandwich bars. We scrupulously avoided the cafés
in her neck of the woods, so we didn't run the risk of ending
up at her place and breaking My Promise To Carmen.

I thought it best to stay away from Rose completely for

four months. Ever since I've known Carmen, I'd never been monogamous for so long. Or rather, *zerogamous*, since there had just been that one time at Club Med with Carmen. Meanwhile, the Taxotere had driven her sex drive through the floor. So my sex life vanished, but not my sense of guilt. For the first time in my life my monophobia was laughing at me: I was still leading a double life, I still had two women, secretly, but I couldn't go to bed with either of them. Sometimes my cock nearly exploded with lust when Rose cuddled me a bit too intimately in the pub. Then, when I got home, I took myself in hand in the toilet or under the shower, and fantasized about her.

One evening after one of the chemo-dramas in the Sint Lucas, things went wrong. I'd phoned Rose, she was at home, and within a quarter of an hour I was at her place. She comforted me. The comforting turned into cuddling, and the cuddling into sex. She'd protested, but there was no stopping us. We did it on the carpet. Within a minute of slipping inside her, I came. Then we cried together.

In the weeks after that I became more addicted to her than ever. Every half-hour I yearned to be with her. My diary began to suffer from an inhuman form of time management. Carmen. Luna. The hospital visits. Viewing houses the estate agent had chosen for us. My work. Although the latter also served as an alibi to pay Rose a quick visit.

But there's one difference from the affair we had last year. Last week we were enjoying a romp in her bed, when Rose suddenly said it.

'I love you, Danny.'

Crazily enough, I was flattered, rather than seeing it as a problem. At first I couldn't work out exactly why. I'd already broken My Promise To Carmen, and this certainly wasn't going to make things any easier.

When I worked out why 'I love you, Danny' sounded so good, I was quite alarmed myself. Rose's declaration of love strokes my ego. I feel like a man again, rather than a friend. It's a compensation for my institutional love at home.

I realize this isn't going to win me any plaudits. But love in the time of cancer has its own rules, I tell myself. Rose is the only one I enjoy myself with, the only one I feel good with. And now she loves me, too.

Even Frank, De Bastille, alcohol and E are no match for that.

It's my baby callin', says I need you here . . .

Golden Earring, from 'Radar Love' (*Moontan*, 1973)

Twenty-three

At first we thought it was our imagination, but after a few weeks there was no getting away from it. Carmen's belly is getting fatter, even though she isn't pregnant and eats even less than Luna.

Dr Rodenbach confirms our suspicion. The Taxotere has stopped working. He takes his time to explain that he can see from the values in the blood that the tumour is active again. The liver isn't working properly any more, and is doing something like sweating. The sweat is called ascites fluid, and Carmen's whole abdomen is now joining the party, because the sweat contains malignant cancer cells.

Rodenbach says there's one more option now the Taxotere isn't working. Another kind of chemo treatment, called LV. The L stands for Leucovorin, the V for 5-FU. Almost without side-effects, and to be administered weekly via the port-o-cath. We look at each other and shrug. Let's do it. Let's trust to luck. It's only a postponement, Rodenbach warns. And hopefully the 5-FU won't be too late, because they won't be able to start the treatment for a few weeks. The body can't cope with two different sorts of chemo at the same time.

Soon Carmen's belly is as fat as a pregnant woman's. She has hardly any clothes she can wear. Carmen has overcome her horror, and this week she went to buy a dress from Ruim-schoots on A.J. Ernststraat. A maternity dress. When Carmen and I bump into a former colleague from BBDvW&R/Bernilvy, she says: 'Oh, how lovely! Your second one's on the way!' Carmen nods enthusiastically. 'Yes! We're hoping for a boy!'

But apart from that there's not much to laugh at. Carmen's about to explode. Dr Rodenbach says they could drain off the ascites, but he tends to do so as little as possible. The more you drain off, the quicker it returns. He wonders if she could keep going for a few days, until the first LV treatment. 'I can manage that,' says Carmen.

■

The evening before the first LV treatment I have to go away. I've been at MIU so little recently I've suggested to Frank I go through urgent matters one evening a week. That way I can drop by to Rose's afterwards.

'Will you manage this morning, with that belly?' I ask Carmen before I go to MIU.

'Well – yes, I'll be OK.'

Knowing my wife is suffering not just from cancer, but also from an overdose of positive thinking, I don't believe her.

'Do you know for sure?'

'Of course. No problem.'

I've been at the stadium for just an hour when my phone rings.

'I can't do it, Dan,' sobs Carmen.

'I'll be right there.'

Frank comes with me. We run together to my car. We get home within five minutes and I run upstairs. I see from her face the pain is killing her.

'Have you called the hospital?' I ask.

'No – I don't dare.'

Within the space of 2.34 seconds I've keyed in names – search – A – AvL ... Phone.

'Good evening, Antoni van Leeuw—'

'Van Diepen here. Can I speak to someone on evening duty in Dr Rodenbach's department?'

After I've parried the question from the duty doctor about whether my wife really couldn't wait until tomorrow morning, with a short and clear, 'No, now,' we're allowed to come in and have Carmen's belly drained.

Frank stays at home with Luna.

We have to get to the fourth floor. At the best of times, the Antoni van Leeuwenhoek can't compete with De Bastille in terms of cosiness, and its light show isn't a match for the Hotel Arena, but late in the evening it's even more depressing here than it usually is.

The doctor who's going to draw off the fluid from Carmen's belly is already waiting for us upstairs. He must be twenty-eight, twenty-nine at the most.

'Have you come for the ascites puncture?' he asks. Great, another new phrase I've learned. Carmen nods. The doctor and I help Carmen on to the gurney. She gets an anaesthetic, and a little tube half a centimetre thick is inserted into the side of her belly. At the other end of the tube there's a bucket, which fills slowly with yellow fluid from Carmen's belly. One litre, two litres, three litres, four and a half litres. Carmen is tilted on to her side like a bowl of pancake batter and shaken every now and again. 4.7 litres.

Carmen's relieved.

'Like you haven't been able to piss for a week!'

224

Now Carmen's belly is empty, she can walk a bit again. We shuffle silently down the dark, deserted hospital corridors to the exit. We're home at a quarter past twelve. Frank's on the sofa watching TV. Carmen and I have said hardly anything to each other on the way.

'Who'd like a drink?' I ask.

'A glass of water,' says Carmen softly.

'I'll take a shot of vodka,' I say to Frank. 'And you?'

'A beer would be nice.'

I go and sit down and let the evening drift past me. This was the evening I've been afraid of since the day Carmen first had cancer. Having to go to the hospital in a panic at night. This evening has gone straight in at number 2 in the Traumatic Cancer Top 5, just below the still-unbeaten number 1, by now a golden oldie: the shaving of my wife's head. I burst into tears. Carmen joins in, sociably. Frank comes and puts his arms round us.

'I should have said this morning I couldn't manage, shouldn't I?' she says guiltily.

'Yes,' I snap.

'But I hate complaining about my belly all the time . . .'

'Driving to the hospital in a blind panic in the middle of the night is much worse.'

'You've got to be honest, Carmen,' Frank adds, before he leaves. 'Then at least Dan will know you really are OK if you say you are . . .'

Carmen nods awkwardly, hugs Frank and lets him out.

A moment later I hear a sudden shriek from the toilet. 'Look what I've got!' she cries, terrified.

On the left-hand side above her groin there's a lump about the size of a snooker-ball. I'm terrified too. An infection.

A what - do - I - know - that - can - grow - in - three - hours - from - nothing-to-a-snooker-ball? I pretend to be calm. We call the duty doctor at the hospital. He has no idea what it is. We call Rodenbach.

He puts us out of our misery over the phone. It's nothing serious. The snooker-ball is the result of the puncture, which leaves holes in the various layers of the abdominal wall, and the fluid left in the belly has now dripped to the lowest part of the abdomen because of the force of gravity.

'Imagine us not thinking of that,' says Carmen drily.

The fluid will spread throughout her abdomen again if Carmen lies down, and by tomorrow morning the holes will basically have healed.

Before morning, I have Rodenbach on the line again, because Carmen has woken me moaning with pain.

'Doctor, it's Dan van Diepen again!' I shout, panicking again. 'My wife's lying here beside me, bent double with pain! She says it feels like contractions, but that's impossible, isn't it?'

Once again, Rodenbach doesn't panic. He says it'll be over in a few minutes. It's a well-known phenomenon after ascites punctures. The organs in the belly are busy nestling back into their original places.

'My stomach's heaving,' I tell Rodenbach.

'Actually that's how you should think of it,' he says.

I hold her hand tightly, pinching it hard, like I didn't at Luna's birth. Soon the cramps are over. It's light again. An hour later Luna wakes up. As though nothing had happened.

Just before I fall into exhausted sleep I realize with a shock I forgot something last night. My heart turns cartwheels.

Oh, God. Fuck. Oh, how stupid. Fuckittyfuckittyfuck.

Rose is still waiting for me.

A great big mouth behind the fence,
a great big mouth behind the fence . . .

Ajax F-Side*

Twenty-four

After a detailed account of our hectic night-time hospital visit
and sixteen apologies, Rose calms down. I'm sitting at her
breakfast table. She's still wearing her dressing-gown. I've
taken Luna to the crèche and driven to Rose's apartment. My
little plant in Oud-West urgently needed watering.

'It's getting more and more difficult, Dan – I'm never sure
if you're going to cancel an arrangement at the last minute.
I'm always worried something's wrong at home if you're ten
minutes late, always terrified Carmen might have found
out . . .'

'Do you want to split up?' I ask stubbornly.

'No.' She sighs. 'Of course I don't want to split up.'

'I don't want you ever to feel you're being used. Not now,
and not later, when Carmen isn't – isn't there any more.
Because I already know that later on I'm going to need to
spend some time thinking only about Luna and me.'

'Stop. I know that. But I don't want to hear it.'

'You have to hear it.'

---

* Wrample from the repertoire of the F-Side. Tune: *When the Saints*. When the
supporters of the opposing team say something unfair about Ajax or their supporters.

I know it's nasty, but I say it deliberately. Even if it's selfish honesty, honesty designed primarily to soften my anxiety that I may only be using her to get through this time.

And it's a wide open goal. I know Rose would never leave me in the lurch.

I wouldn't wanna take everything out on you,
though I know I do every time I fall . . .

All Saints, from 'Black Coffee' (*Saints and Sinners*, 2000)

Twenty-five

If the LV treatment doesn't start working soon, Carmen won't make it through to Christmas. The fucking Taxotere, with all its misery, will have given us less than six months' injury time, Christ almighty.

Carmen's liver is so swollen you can see it like a big bobble on the side of her belly. It's barely working now, but it's sweating all the more. Since the first ascites puncture, Carmen has had to have her belly emptied every week. Last time was a new personal record: 7.1 litres. I wouldn't be surprised if it was also a track, Dutch and European record, although Carmen would have been ruled out of participation because of her high doping levels.

The settling of the organs after each puncture makes the whole process a torture. Sometimes she walks around for days until she can't hide the pain from me any more. And then we go again.

Along with the fluid, a load of protein leaves her body every time. She's visibly in decline, and has less energy every week. On days when her belly is full, she can't walk a hundred metres. Nonetheless, last weekend she wanted to go out for a little while. We took the wheelchair we got from the home-care unit and went for a walk. I lied to Carmen that I didn't mind pushing her. The truth is I was fighting back my tears.

I've told you I can't walk so well any more, and that's why we have a wheelchair. Then you said you'd carry me. I found that so sweet and so miserable at the same time it made me cry, and now I'm describing it I have tears in my eyes again. Sometimes it's so, so hard. A little while ago you came over to me all by yourself and asked if I was still sick. And when you were there in the hospital this week and saw the doctor, you asked: 'Is he going to make you better, Mama?'

Carmen wants to do everything, but she can't do anything. Last Sunday she took over the morning shift with Luna, so I could sleep in. At half past eight she came to get me because she'd thrown up twice.

By around midday she slowly starts to get going. So I dress Luna in the morning, give her porridge and take her to the crèche. At the weekend I take Luna to the goat farm in the Amsterdamse Bos in the morning, or to the playground in the Vondelpark. Sometimes I think it's so sad for Carmen that I don't tell her where Luna and I have been.

Most days I can't get out of bed until about midday. I feel too sick in the mornings. Papa gets up with you every day and does all the work. Sometimes I snap at Papa, because I can't do any of it myself. It's the ones who are closest to you who take the worst blows, however unfair it might be. But I do have the feeling Papa and I are stronger together than we've ever been. In spite of everything he still tries to enjoy things,

and that restores my strength, so we still do as many nice
things as possible if I feel good for a day or so.

But the days when she feels good are rare. A low point comes when Carmen has to miss the Father Christmas party at the crèche. She managed to get out of bed, she got dressed, but it really wasn't working. She's sick as a dog. I'm the only man at the crèche – not counting Father Christmas (and he's wearing a dress) and his two elves – among twelve mothers.

'If I can't even do that kind of thing, then I've had it,' sobs Carmen when Luna and I come back.

A flood pours down my cheeks.*

I realize it's dawning on Carmen that the end is near. She's already working on her plans, her intentions and ideas at an accelerated pace.

She's told Maud, Anne, Thomas and Frank, for example, they should make a ring. 'See it as a memorial ring.' I've already had one made, which will later replace my wedding ring. She's having it engraved *For my great love. xxx Carmen.* When we collect the ring, the woman who made it asks if we're going to get married.

'No, it's for another special occasion,' Carmen says airily.

'Oh, then I know what it is,' says the woman with a significant glance at Carmen's belly. 'What a lovely idea, celebrating that with a ring!'

In an email to friends and acquaintances, Carmen asks them to write down something about her to Luna. The letters come flooding in. We buy a big box in which we store the letters, along with Carmen's diaries and photographs, and –

---

* Wrample from *De kleine blonde dood* by Boudewijn Büch (1985).

an idea of Frank's – two videos of friends talking about Carmen. Luna won't have a mother, but if she wants to she can find out more about her than a child whose mother is still alive.

■

In a folder from the Beyond the Rainbow Foundation that she sees lying in the Antoni van Leeuwenhoek waiting-room, Carmen reads about child psychologists who specialize in coping with grief in children. We end up with a psychologist on Rapenburgerstraat. Without Luna, because we want to talk freely.

The psychologist's consulting room is full of toys. There are children's drawings on the wall. One of them shows a big cross and a doll with wings. 'My Mama,' it says in childish handwriting. I hope Carmen doesn't see the drawing. The psychologist explains what children remember about what happens before their third birthday, what they understand of the concept of death, and what effects it has on a child to grow up without one parent. When we tell him Carmen is busy with letters to Luna, the psychologist thinks it's an excellent idea. Otherwise Luna won't be able to remember anything at all about her mama. Carmen hears that and can't hold in the tears. The psychologist waits for a moment and tells her that children of about three can be properly prepared for the death of a parent. 'Don't do it too quickly,' she says, 'but don't hide the fact that Mama is sick, and that in a while she may not be there any more.'

She gives us tips about the way to tell Luna, and warns us about something she calls 'alienation behaviour'. 'When children hear or notice they're going to lose someone they love, they sometimes become less nice, or even irritating to that person. It's an instinctive reaction to protect themselves against the pain when that person isn't there later on.'

What she says startles me, but not in relation to Luna. I recognize my own behaviour. My doubts whether I still loved Carmen, my monophobia, which was assuming increasingly manic forms. The child Danny was displaying alienation behaviour.

In the evening I read to Luna from *Frog and the Little Bird*, a book the child psychologist gave to us. The bird is lying on its back, and some think it's asleep, others that it's tired.

> Rabbit knelt by the bird and looked carefully.
> 'He's dead,' he said.
> 'Dead,' said Frog, 'what's that?'
> Rabbit pointed to the blue sky.
> 'Everyone dies,' he said.
> 'Us too?' asked Frog, surprised.
> Rabbit didn't know for sure.
> 'Maybe when we're old,' he said.*

They bury the little bird, and are very sad. Then they all go and play happily. While I'm reading it out, Luna strokes my arm with her little hand. She sees I'm having difficulties, and feels sorry for me. And I'm sorry for her, because Luna doesn't know the little bird is Mama.

∎

Carmen has her own way of telling it.

---

* Wrample from *Kikker en het vogeltje* by Max Velthuijs (1991).

We bought two fish, which I called Elvis and Beavis. You thought they were really nice. Last week Elvis suddenly lay drifting in the fish bowl, stone dead. I didn't think it was really so bad, because now, for the first time, you'd seen for yourself that animals and people die. You asked how come he wasn't still alive, and I told you that he might have been very sick, and couldn't be made better, as happens sometimes with people. Then they die too. I told you Elvis probably went to fish heaven. You thought that was perfectly normal. Then I flushed Elvis down the toilet. Papa came home in the evening and you told him the fish had died and gone to fish heaven. 'And that's in the toilet,' you said. Meanwhile Beavis has kicked the bucket as well, and we've flushed him away too, but you didn't think that was too bad, because then at least he was with his little friend Elvis again. Later, when I'm dead, I'll go to people heaven and you said yourself it's among the clouds. So you're starting to understand, a little bit.

Our own house, a place in the sun,
but I wish I was simply happy more often...

Rene Froger, from 'Een eigen huis' (1989)

Twenty-six

**Goddess, we've bought a house! In Oud-
Zuid, Joh. Verhulststraat. Carmen's happy
as a sandboy. Great, isn't it?**

Oud-Zuid is the really smart bit of Amsterdam. A bunch
of grapes at the posh greengrocer's costs more than a
month's rent in a normal bit of town like Bos en Lommer.
It's so snooty that even the snack bar has a French name, Le
Sud.

Carmen's incredibly excited. She's phoning and emailing
everyone about the house. Anne and Thomas come and have
a look, and I'm slightly ashamed. The house is magnificent,
but it's ludicrously huge. Four storeys, and twice as big as the
place we're living in now. And later there won't be three
people living there, just two.

The Saturday after we've signed the contract, we go to a
few home furnishing places on the KNSM Island. According
to Frank, there's a Poggenpohl showroom there, and he says
we should also look in at World of Wonders and Pilat & Pilat.
But after two shops, Carmen's had it. Her belly's starting to
bulge again. And so we have a great box of a house, enough

money and time to do it up, but no energy to go buy anything to put in it.

Meanwhile we drive to Frank's and ask him to help. He's happy to. He sinks his teeth into the project. Every evening we finger samples of floor covering, wood and cork, study furniture catalogues and lighting brochures. We look like the winning couple in *Honeymoon Quiz*.

The Sunday after we get the key, Carmen's mother comes to look. I knew it would happen, but I'm still startled when it does. After we've shown her the whole house, and are standing on the third floor in the room that's to be Luna's bedroom, Carmen's mother covers her mouth. Her shoulders start to tremble. I go over to her and take her in my arms in her granddaughter's future bedroom. We both know Carmen will never cuddle Luna there as she once cuddled her daughter.

Shiny happy people . . .

REM, from 'Shiny Happy People' (*Out Of Time*, 1991)

Twenty-seven

All of a sudden the LV treatment kicks in and Carmen starts feeling better.

In the morning she's still a bit sick, but in the afternoon she has a bit of energy and often goes outside. She shops till she practically gets a hernia. It'll be good when we live in our new house. At least it's got wardrobe space for all those new clothes.

The new house is a great success. I sort everything – the bank, the removal men, the notary and the sale of our old house. Carmen never has to think about anything and that's good too, because since she's stopped working her memory is a goat's cheese.* It takes up a lot of my time, but I love it. I think it's because it has to do with the future. The future. Mmmm. I look forward to it every day

Although the work on the house is actually being done by the Handymen.

▶ **The Handymen** are an illustrious duo of decorators consisting of Rick and Ron. I myself don't do anything in the house. I have odd-job dyslexia, and stick to the Johan Cruyff principle that you should improve your strong points and camouflage your weak

---

* A phrase of Johan Cruyff's: 'Their defence is a goat's cheese.'

points. I cultivate my lack of DIY skills without embarrassment. Handyman Rick regularly leaves notes like 'Look, Dan, this is a hammer.' I tell them not to get too smart and just get on with the job, and that I've already been keeping my eye on them for weeks with a webcam I've installed in the eyes of Baby Bunny, Luna's doll which, along with Maf the cuddly dog, is already testing out the new house on a sleepover basis. The next day Baby Bunny's eyes have been taped over.

The pace of things gives us little cause for complaint. The Handymen race around finishing off one room after another. Luna's bedroom is, as planned, the first one to be ready. If the Handymen and the LV-treatment go on working as they're doing at the moment, it looks as though Carmen could still end up living in the new house.

The people around us can't keep up. No one says anything, but we notice friends are starting to doubt if it's all as dramatic as we've always said. I hear via Maud and Frank that someone around the lunch table at MIU dared to bet Carmen would live to be seventy. At one point I hear Thomas telling Frank Carmen is looking 'gorgeously slim'. At a staff party at Advertising Brokers, Carmen is asked when she's coming back. Not *whether*, but *when*.

I can understand that. A year and a half ago we said Carmen had a form of cancer that had a very low chance of survival. We said it for a year. And then we said Carmen was definitely going to die, because it had spread. At the start of December it looked as though that was it: Carmen was getting more and more ill by the day. And now we're a few months on, and Carmen's flitting around the place! You can see everything's coming right. Carmen's doing terribly well. Her hair's growing back, she looks good, you can't tell she's wearing a prosthetic breast, she's incredibly cheerful and, OK, she's a bit thin and there's the belly that keeps getting so fat, and that can't be nice, can it, but things are still OK?

Friends, family, colleagues and acquaintances can only imagine somebody living with a life-threatening disease for a certain length of time. Someone like that either gets better, or dies in the course of time, it's as simple as that, isn't it?

It isn't as simple as that.

'There are patients on LV treatment who can fight cancer for years,' Rodenbach told us, 'but it's also entirely possible the treatment doesn't work the following week. We just don't know.'

The finishing-line of the marathon has been moved again. And we don't know by how many kilometres. We're thrown back into the uncertainty we lived with for the whole of the first year, from the moment the cancer was discovered.

Thanks, doc.

Twenty-eight

Now she was feeling a bit better, Carmen naturally couldn't fill the whole day with shopping, although she really did try her best. She started thinking about other things again. Like my confessions in June at Club Med. At first she'd repressed it. We were happy together, and wanted to enjoy life to the max for the time we still had together. Then her body let her down so badly that all her attention and energy were focused on physical survival.

But now the assimilation of my monophobic past is back on Carmen's agenda. Lately she's been phoning me up more and more frequently during the day to check where I am, and asking far more questions about what I've been doing if I've been out for an hour.

And she hasn't said it yet, but I can feel in my water Carmen wants to discuss Danny's Friday Nights Out. At this point! I started sulking before she even dared to mention it. The very idea. Bloody hell, is nothing sacred in this world any more?

It's Friday now. The plan is to go and get a bite to eat with Ramon and then go on to Rose's. I've put on my pink shirt and my snake leathers, and I go into the sitting-room. Carmen is lying on the sofa watching television. From the look in her eye I can see my suspicion was correct. I put on my dumbest face, and give her a kiss.

'Till tonight, lovey,' I say as sweetly as I can.

'Actually, I don't want you to go out tonight.'

'Darling, if anything happens I can be back home within a quarter of an hour. I'll bring my phone.'

'That's not what I mean. I just want you to stay at home.'

'Excuse me? I've arranged to meet Ramon in ten minutes. I told you before! I've been looking forward to my little evening out all day – it's my only relaxation in the week.'

'You should have thought about that before going and screwing all those other women,' she says coolly.

'Carm, this is ridiculous. We talked about it loads in Club Med.'

'Yes, and now I see it differently. If you do go out, how can I be sure you aren't being unfaithful again?'

I don't know how, but one way or another I succeed in being indignant too. 'Carm! Give me a break! I go along to chemo treatments, radiation, I cause a stink with doctors for you, I get them out of bed for you, I – I – do everything for you!'

'The things you do for me have nothing to do with it. That's just normal. For better and for worse. Remember, Daniel van Diepen?' she snaps.

Now I get really angry. She doesn't mean it. She can't mean it. I wait a moment to give her time to say so. Instead she looks at me defiantly.

'Fine,' I say, my voice breaking. I grab the phone, throw it on the sofa and say, 'Then you just phone Anne or Maud or your mother. Let them look after you, if you think all the things I'm doing for you are so normal. I'm going to spend the night in a hotel.'

I get up and stamp off. She throws the phone after me. 'Go on, run away again! Go and shag some other woman again,' she shrieks. 'Go fuck yourself! I don't need you!'

I don't need you. *I don't need you.* After a year and a half of hospitals, visits to doctors, crying fits, anxiety and misery, she *doesn't need me.*

Beside myself with fury, I push open the door to the hall. *I don't need you.* Then cope with the whole cancer caboodle yourself, Carmen van Diepen. I'm out of here. I furiously throw on my jacket and, cursing, open the front door.

And I stop.

My wife has cancer and she's dying. I can't go. *I really can't go.* I shut the front door and take my jacket off again. I look at myself in the mirror. *I really can't go.* From the sitting-room I hear Carmen's quiet voice.

'Danny?'

I step back into the sitting-room. Carmen is already standing by the door. 'Sorry . . .' she says softly. 'Sorry, Danny . . .'

I look at her hopelessly, walk over to her and take her in my arms. She rests against me like a limp doll and starts crying violently.

> **Ramon can't make it this evening. I'll tell you later.**
>
> **Goddess, problems at home. I won't be coming round later. Call you tomorrow. Sorry.**

After an hour's crying, comforting and making up, we decide to call Frank and ask him if he feels like coming over. A bit of a diversion. He can't. 'I'm at Café Bep.'

▶ **Café Bep.** Designer café where they've even thought hard about the waste-paper baskets. Bep's on the Nieuwezijds Voorburgwal, for about ten years the place to be for the hippy few. It started with Seymore Likely and Schuim (around the corner in Spuistraat), then came Diep and Bep. Everyone who mattered in advertising and PR (all the gorgeous accounts assistants, girls from RTF and traffic information ladies) went there at a particular time, so for a while even Ramon and I couldn't stay away. Until we had to admit we actually thought De Bastille was much nicer, and from that point onwards life – *Ordnung muss sein!* – went back to normal again.

'Oh.'

'Is something up?'

'Erm, no. Forget it. Have fun!'

'I'll do my best!'

I call Maud. I can hear it already. Pub sounds.

'Danny?' she shouts through her mobile. 'I can't hear you very well. I'm in De Pilsvogel with Tasha.'

I hang up and text her to say that it was nothing urgent.

'Everyone's out drinking in town,' I say irritably.

Carmen hardly dares to look at me.

'It doesn't matter, my love. Shall I give Anne a call?'

'Yeah, sure.' She laughs. 'If we tell her what we were rowing about, she'll personally ensure we row about it all over again . . .'

I phone Carmen's mother. She senses something's wrong, and before I can ask the question, she suggests she comes round herself. She's there within half an hour. We talk about this, that and the other, but not about our trouble earlier in the evening. At eleven o'clock, Carmen goes to bed, completely exhausted. I open another bottle of red wine and stay downstairs with Carmen's mother.

When it's quiet upstairs, she asks what Carmen and I were arguing about.

'How did you know we were?' I ask, surprised.

'Mothers sense these things,' she says with a laugh. She looks at me. 'Carmen told me all about your infidelities a while ago.'

'Oh?' I say, startled.

'If you were my son, I'd have given you a good thrashing.'

I grin, to save face.

'You know, my lad,' says my mother-in-law, 'I lie awake at night thinking about that bloody cancer and what it's doing to you. I just wish it had been me that had the chemo and the breast amputation and all the misery instead of Carmen. I completely understand if you blow a fuse from time to time.'

'Me too,' I say quietly.

'But this house arrest isn't going to work. I'll say that to Carmen tomorrow, too. And I can see how hard it is for you sometimes. And I think you're doing really well.' She holds me tight and cuddles me. 'I'm proud to have you as a son-in-law.'

I sink into my mother-in-law's arms.

'Don't you sometimes wish it was all over?' she asks.

'Yes. If I'm being honest, yes.'

'I understand too, my son,' she says gently. 'I understand that really well. You've nothing to be ashamed of.'

She kisses me on my forehead and wipes away her tears.

'And now I want some coffee, you little menace!'

Fuck you,
I won't do what you tell me . . .

Rage Against the Machine, from 'Killing in the Name of'
(*Rage Against the Machine*, 1992)

Twenty-nine

'What's Ramon's surname?' calls Carmen.

'Del Estrecho,' I call back.

'Del Estrecho – table for two, if there is one.'

Silence.

'OK. No, that's OK, I just wanted to check. Thanks.'

She hangs up.

'Now do you believe me?' I sigh, not looking up from my paper.

She sighs and nods. 'Off you go, then.'

> **I'll be at yours at about half past ten,**
> **Goddess. X!**

'What?!? How long?' exclaims Ramon, his mouth full of steak tartare.

'A year and a half,' I reply calmly.

'*A year and a half!*' he yells through Le Garage.

▶ **Le Garage.** Middle-aged suits come here with women who look just as delicious as the food served at Le Garage, but are not as fresh and contain more colour, flavourings and preservatives.

'Yes.'

'So when we were in Miami she had it already?'

'Yes.'

'Why didn't you tell me that before?'

'Because everywhere I go it's all about Carmen. I'm always having to tell people how she is. And I didn't have to do that with you. You were a cancer-free zone for me.'

'Shit, really . . .' He stares into the distance. 'Bloody hell – I thought there was something,' he says all of a sudden. He looks at me with what is, for him, an unusually serious expression. 'I just didn't know what. You've changed so much over the last year, amigo. You've started taking pills every now and again, suddenly you're wearing these lovely shirts, that expensive leather jacket you've got, your hair's a bit wild. Now the penny's dropped. You're just cutting yourself off from the shit that's going on at home.'

My mouth falls open. Ramon, who I thought I could only talk to about football and cuntfucksuckslutwhoring, understands within two minutes what friends like Thomas don't even want to understand.

'Last week, when you couldn't come out, was something up with Carmen?' he asks, concerned. It almost sounds funny coming from him.

'No, that was me playing around.' I laugh bravely. 'At the moment Carmen's practising zero tolerance. She checks everything I do.'

'She's right, with such a randy baboon for a husband,' he says, wiping his mouth as shamelessly as he can with his sleeve. 'If she ever finds out you're still being unfaithful now she's ill, I'll personally hack your head off, you lousy shit. Keep that to yourself, and to your friends,* amigo. OK, and now let's go to the Bastille and see if there are any hot chicks.'

He waves the waiter over for the bill.

'I'm not coming,' I reply. 'I've made a date with a girl, and I should have been at her place an hour ago.'

■

Obviously there's nowhere to park in the Eerste Helmersstraat. Fuck, it's already half past eleven. Why did I take the car? It's three tram stops from Le Garage to Rose's.

I'm on my way, Goddess! Chin up!

After cursing my way around two blocks, I park in a disabled space where I reckon the chance of having the car towed away at this time of night is less than fifty per cent. I call her at a quarter to twelve.

'Hi,' I call through the speaker by the bell.

The speaker doesn't reply. When I've run up the three flights of stairs to her apartment, I see Rose is as sulky as Louis van Gaal at a press conference.

'Sorry. Things overran with Ramon.'

'Sorry?!' she snorts. 'This is the second bloody time in one week I've had to sit and wait like an idiot. The whole evening last Friday, and now another hour and a half. And am I supposed to sit and stand and play dead as soon as my master appears. I'm fed up with it, Dan!'

No, I'm not up for this. I stare at her hard. 'I can get

---

*   Wrample from Hans Teeuwen (from *Dat dan weer wel*, 2001).

bollocked at home already. I don't have to come here for that,'
I say frostily.

'Oh, is that what you think?'

'Yes.'

'Well, then, just fuck off!' she shrieks.

And I do. When Carmen shrieked at me, I realized at the
front door I couldn't leave, but at Rose's there's nothing to
stop me. It's not my fault she loves me?

I drank last night and saw
that women never get what they deserve...

The Scene, from 'Blauw' (*Blauw*, 1990)

Thirty

I slam my car door and tear like a lunatic up the Eerste
Helmersstraat towards Constantijn Huygen, and then left on
to the Overtoom. For a moment I wonder whether I should
apologize to Rose. But I can't bring myself to. Instead, I text
Ramon.

Are you in the B?

I send it to Maud as well. I'd like to see her. At least she
isn't as difficult as Rose. At full speed I roar along the
Stadhouderskade with De Dijk on. '*All of a sudden you have
the feeling it might just work – no, it isn't too late, we're with the
majority, who want nothing but their head in the sun.*' Ramon
texts: YES! I grin from ear to ear – '*Everything works out, we're
just beginning – we're really just beginning!*'

De Dijk have got it right: Maud texts too. She's with Tasha
– mmmmm – in De Pilsvogel, they were supposed to be going
to More, but they fancy going to the Bastille first.

After driving round the Lijnbaansgracht I rather fancy the
Bastille. I have to keep from racing.

There's a man standing at the bar with his shirt open two
buttons too many, so he can display his ludicrously muscled

chest to its best effect. On his arm is a blonde girl blessed with enormous hooters. She introduces herself as Debbie. Where Carmen calls herself an ex-blonde-with-big-tits, Debbie's the other way round: she used not to have blonde hair or big tits. Ramon isn't going to let that spoil his fun.

'Change of plan, amigo?'

I shrug. 'A vodka for you, too?'

Ramon bursts out laughing, hugs me and finishes with a hard slap on the top of my head. He offers me a little round pill. Oh, why not. I nod and wash it down with a slug of vodka. At the same time Maud and Tasha come roaring in. They exuberantly throw their arms around my neck. They're screaming with pleasure. My Christ, I thought *I'd* had quite enough to drink this evening.

'Danny, you look really stressed,' says Maud. 'Has something happened?'

'No, nothing. Vodka and lime for both of you?'

'I'll have a Breezer,' coos Tasha, putting an arm around me. 'One of the red ones. They make your tongue sweet. You can check it out later, if you like.'

I give an embarrassed laugh.

'So Rose isn't here, by any chance?' asks Tasha casually when I give her her Breezer.

'How do you know about Rose?' I ask, perplexed, and look angrily at Maud. She hastily shakes her head to show Tasha didn't find out from her.

'Well,' says Tasha with a shrug, 'perhaps you should shut down your mailbox more often when you walk away from your computer.'

My face looks like a beef tomato. Maud explodes with laughter. Oh, what difference can it make? I'm in the Bastille,

Ramon's just given me my third vodka and lime in half an hour, the pill's starting to take effect, Maud has taken Tasha's lead and put her arm around my waist, and I'm going to More with two hot chicks, in Bastille they're playing a song called 'Just Blame the Night',* and that's exactly right.

■

It's three o'clock when we walk into Club More. Well, walk in: it's like I wanted to get into the Kuip wearing an Ajax scarf – I get the full body search, down to my crotch.

> ▶ If the RoXy was the Marco van Basten of clubbing, then **More** is its Tom Blanker.† The place never lived up to its early promise. It was supposed to be the new RoXy. But if I interpret Frank's opinion correctly, More isn't fit to polish the RoXy's shoes.

I reckon it's unlikely I'll be going home in an hour. I'm past the point of no return. Ramon's smartie and Tasha's tongue are irresistible. After another kiss I look guiltily at Maud. She doesn't react as I would have expected. I can see from her pupils she's taken one of Ramon's E-tabs, too. She grabs hold of me and starts kissing me as well. All three of us are standing tonguing on the dance floor of the More. Tasha whispers something into Maud's ear. She looks at her for a moment and nods.

'Fancy something exciting, Dan?'

■

---

*   Robert Leroy (1996).

†   In the seventies he was named the greatest Ajax talent since Johan Cruyff. And that's as far as it went.

I could have known. If you're always home before half past four and then this one time there's been no sign of you by half past six in the morning, you tend to provoke a reaction.

Tring – tring – ring.

I gesture to Maud and Natasha to be quiet.

'Where are you now, you bastard?' says Carmen, crying.

'I'm – I'm just on my way . . .'

'It's a quarter to six, for Christ's sake, Dan,' she yells furiously.

My heart's thumping in my throat. Maud is sitting shivering on the bed. Tasha, unmoved, lights a cigarette.

'Chin up,' whispers Maud as I walk out the door. Tasha just winks.

I run to my car, which is parked three streets away on the Ceintuurbaan. I check quickly to see there are no cops around, and then drive across the tram tracks towards Hobbemakade. I take out the De Dijk CD that was still in the CD player, and put on Bruce *Live*. I click through the numbers until I hear the piercing harmonica of 'The Promised Land'. The traffic lights at Roelof Hartstraat change to amber when I'm about fifty metres away. I put my foot down and tear over the crossing on red. Adrenaline is shrieking through my body. I roar along with Springsteen's despairing lyrics. *'Sometimes I feel so weak'* – I brake a little for the slight curve by the Shell station – *'I just wanna explode'* – and put my foot down again as I drive into the bend – *'explode and tear this whole town apart'* – making the car pull to the left. With a jerk on the wheel I avoid the traffic island – *'take a knife'* – but then the Chevy starts to lurch – *'and cut this pain from my heart'** – and flip,

---

* From 'The Promised Land' (*Darkness on the Edge of Town*).

and I hear a dull crash and a crunch and a tinkle of glass and the Chevy slides for several metres on its side along the tarmac.

Then everything is still. Deafeningly silent.

No more Hazes. No more Dijk. No more house. No more Springsteen. I'm hanging on my side in the seat-belt. I'm numb for a few seconds. Then everything suddenly flashes through me. I'm alive. Pain? No pain. Movement. Yes. Glass. Glass everywhere. Oh, fuck, Carmen! Fire? Get out! Middle of the road. Get out of here! Could it go up? Get out! Climb. Quick. Police. Drunk. Fuck. Oh, fuck. Fuck fuck fuck fuck.

I push up the door on the passenger side and climb out of the car. I'm almost surprised at the sight of the underside of the car. Like it's the most normal thing in the world, my Chevy is showing its underside at nine minutes to six. As if it's surrendering.

I walk to the pavement, and hang over the railing of the bridge. Slowly I begin to grasp what this means. A nuclear disaster has just happened. My car. My licence. It'll be a miracle if they can find any blood in my alcohol.* I could end up in jail. I could have been killed. Luna ... Oh, and Rose thinks I'm just at home. And my God, what will Carmen ...

I ring her. She doesn't answer. I leave a message to say I've had a car accident, that luckily I'm unhurt, but that I won't be home for a while.

A police car with a siren drives up. I stick a mint in my mouth.

■

---

*   Wrampled with some poetic licence, from 'Leo' by Ria Valk (1977).

At the police station I have to hand over my phone, wallet and keys, take off my belt and undo my shoelaces. And would I wait in this room. A door shuts behind me.

The room is a cell. The door, a black steel door with a little hole with a grid over it. I go and sit on a bench screwed tightly to the wall.

At home my wife, who will shortly die, has been waiting all night for me to come home. In Oud-West a woman who has carried me through everything for months has probably been lying in tears all night. And here I am.

It's an eternity before I'm let out of the cell. It seems to have been twenty minutes. After that I make a statement and am allowed to call a taxi home. It's a quarter to seven.

Carmen's in the sitting-room, on the Amsterdam home-care bed. With her bald head and her grey dressing-gown on, she gives me a deadly look.

'Where were you when I rang you?'

'With a girl.'

Whack.

For the first time in my life a woman has hit me in the face.

I can't blame her.

'And as if that isn't bad enough, you drive the car when you're shitfaced!' And then she says it. 'At this rate, Christ knows, Luna isn't just going to lose her mother, she's going to lose her father too!'

> I'm like fucking King Midas,
> everything I touch turns to shit . . .
>
> From *The Sopranos* (1999)*

Thirty-one

Carmen isn't lying next to me when I wake up. I look at my phone and see a text from Ramon. Fortunately not opened by Carmen. He asks if I enjoyed myself with the girls. Did I ever? You bet I did. I'm *still* enjoying it. I get up, take a shower and go downstairs. She's sitting there with red-rimmed eyes, feeding Luna.

'It's about time you went to a psychologist. This really can't go on.'

I say nothing. Carmen goes upstairs, and like a zombie I feed Luna the last mouthfuls of her porridge.

A short time later Carmen comes back down. With a big bag in her hand.

'I'm going.'

'Where to?' I ask gently.

'To Thomas and Anne's.'

'When will you be back?'

'I don't know yet,' she says tearfully, 'I don't know yet, Danny.'

I walk to the front door carrying Luna in my arms. She

---

*   Tony Soprano to his psychiatrist in episode 12 ('Isabella') of *The Sopranos*.

gives Luna a kiss, says, 'I'll call you,' gets into her Beetle and drives away without looking round.

Luna gives me a kiss on the mouth and a cuddle. I tell her I've been very naughty.

'Papa drank lots of beers and then he went driving in his car and then he and the car fell over.'

'In the Chevy?'

'Yes . . .'

'Mama's very cross with you, isn't she?'

'Yes . . .'

We hold each other tight. Softly I sing our own little song:

'Papa and Luna go together so well
They're very good friends, anyone can tell
Papa and Luna go together so well
They're very good friends, anyone can tell.'*

I phone Frank and say I'll be a bit late. I grab the bike and take Luna to the crèche. From here I cycle to the body shop, where the Chevy will probably spend the next few months. It's easier to get Ajax's customer services on the line than it is to get a spare part for a Chevrolet within a month of placing the order. And by the way, I won't be getting my driving licence back until after I've been to court, at the earliest, so it doesn't really make that much difference.

I'm scared stiff when I see the car. The whole driver's side looks like the car's done a sliding tackle on the turf at the ArenA. 'Amazed you got out of there,' says the mechanic,

---

* Lyrics: Danny. Tune: PSV club song. Composer unknown, and long may he remain so.

shaking his head. My insurance man is standing beside him, and says the insurance company has naturally refused to compensate the estimated damage of twenty-five thousand guilders, given drink was involved. He'll do his best to persuade the leasing company to keep me on as a customer. And he also says he thinks it's incredibly stupid of me. I say I agree with him. The mechanic sniggers.

Tasha's called in sick. Maud's there, though. I ask if she fancies going out. I tell her about the accident and about Carmen. She turns completely white. Then she goes to the toilet and stays away for a long time.

I tell Frank about the accident.

'Carmen must have been furious.'

'She walked out this morning.'

'Christ, Danny . . .'

Ramon calls. Maud's brought him up to date. He rings up to call me a great twat. 'If I'd known you were in your car, I'd have personally flung your keys in the canal, you stupid motherfucker. Amigo, what on earth's happening to you?'

A little later I get an email from Maud.

From: maud@creativeandstrategicmarketingagencymiu.nl
To: Dan@creativeandstrategicmarketingagencymiu.nl
Sent: Thursday, March 22, 2001 14:31
Subject: Yesterday

We should never have done what we did yesterday. I realized this morning just how far gone we were with the pills and the drink.
I don't dare to show myself to Carmen ever again. I'm furious with Tasha, with you and with myself. And I'm worried about you. You

desperately need help, Dan. I'm not condemning you, but you've got to see a shrink. You're not going to get through this all by yourself.

Maud

PS: Maybe you could take me along. We might get a group reduction ;)

A little threesome is good for what ails you.* I delete the mail with a sigh. Another one harping on about shrinks. Just shut up. What on earth would I say to them? That I had a car crash when driving five times over the limit because I was driving like a complete retard, after my wife rang me when I was in bed with a trainee and one of my exes – who is also, incidentally, a good friend of my wife, Doctor – and it all happened because earlier that evening I'd had a row with my extra-marital girlfriend – whom I'm still shagging despite the promise I made to my wife never to be unfaithful again until she dies (she's got cancer, in fact, and she's going to die in a little while, Doctor) – so what should I do, Doctor? Should I confess all this to Carmen, while we're about it, Doctor?

---

*   Wrample from *Turks Fruit* by Jan Wolkers (1973).

258

You're no good, you're no good, you're no good,
baby you're no good, I'm gonna say it again,
you're no good, you're no good, you're no good,
baby you're no good . . .

Linda Ronstadt, from 'You're No Good' (*You're No Good*, 1974)

Thirty-two

After just two days, four hours and eighteen minutes, Carmen
rings.

She says she's coming home this afternoon. She's abrupt,
but at least she's rung. I let her snap at me without saying
anything back. If someone's shaving you with a cut-throat
razor, you tend not to move about too much. And I'm still so
ashamed I almost welcome Carmen's hostile attitude. I've
deliberately forfeited my self-esteem. And after half a bottle
of vodka last night, I can cope with a telephonic poisoned
chalice.

The vodka came from Frank. All of a sudden he appeared
at my door. At MIU nothing more was said about the accident.
Last night I told Frank everything (although I censored the
names and activities of Tasha and Maud). He had put his arm
around me and I let it all out. After two humiliating days at
home, at the police station, at the mechanic's and at work, I
sobbed in Frank's arms. By the end of the evening I felt a bit
better.

Not this morning. I was woken by Luna's wailing little

voice, I had a hangover and I was seriously depressed. It was all I could do to stagger out of bed, feed Luna, get her dressed and take her to the crèche. Then I phoned Maud and told her I wasn't coming in to work today, and dived back into bed. It's hide-and-seek the way Luna plays it – with her hands over her eyes, hoping no one can see her.

I couldn't get back to sleep and now, an hour after Carmen's phone call, I feel even shittier. I'm worried about this afternoon. I feel like the little boy who's being bullied by the whole class and who wakes up knowing it's all about to start all over again, as soon as he walks into the playground. Perhaps I'd have been better off spending two days writing out lines as a form of self-punishment.

I must not screw other women or drive five times over the limit.
I must not screw other women or drive five times over the limit.
I must not screw other women or drive five times over the limit.
I must not screw other women or drive five times over the limit.
I must not screw other women or drive five times over the limit.
I must not screw other women or drive five times over the limit.
I must not screw other women or drive five times over the limit.
I must not screw other women or drive five times over the limit.
I must not screw other women or drive five times over the limit.
I must not screw other women or drive five times over the limit.
I must not screw other women or drive five times over the limit.
I must not screw other women or drive five times over the limit.
I must not screw other women or drive five times over the limit.
I must not screw other women or drive five times over the limit.
I must not screw other women or drive five times over the limit.
I must not screw other women or drive five times over the limit.
I must not screw other women or drive five times over the limit.

I must not screw other women or drive five times over the limit.
I must not screw other women or drive five times over the limit.
I must not screw other women or drive five times over the limit.
I must not screw other women or drive five times over the limit.
I must not screw other women or drive five times over the limit.
I must not screw other women or drive five times over the limit.
I must not screw other women or drive five times over the limit.
I must not screw other women or drive five times over the limit.
I must not screw other women or drive five times over the limit.
I must not screw other women or drive five times over the limit.
I must not screw other women or drive five times over the limit.
I must not screw other women or drive five times over the limit.
I must not screw other women or drive five times over the limit.
I must not screw other women or drive five times over the limit.
I must not screw other women or drive five times over the limit.
I must not screw other women or drive five times over the limit.
I must not screw other women or drive five times over the limit.
I must not screw other women or drive five times over the limit.
I must not screw other women or drive five times over the limit.
I must not screw other women or drive five times over the limit.
I must not screw other women or drive five times over the limit.
I must not screw other women or drive five times over the limit.
I must not screw other women or drive five times over the limit.
I must not screw other women or drive five times over the limit.
I must not screw other women or drive five times over the limit.
I must not screw other women or drive five times over the limit.
I must not screw other women or drive five times over the limit.
I must not screw other women or drive five times over the limit.
I must not screw other women or drive five times over the limit.
I must not screw other women or drive five times over the limit.

I must not screw other women or drive five times over the limit.
I must not screw other women or drive five times over the limit.
I must not screw other women or drive five times over the limit.
I must not screw other women or drive five times over the limit.
I must not screw other women or drive five times over the limit.
I must not screw other women or drive five times over the limit.
I must not screw other women or drive five times over the limit.
I must not screw other women or drive five times over the limit.
I must not screw other women or drive five times over the limit.
I must not screw other women or drive five times over the limit.
I must not screw other women or drive five times over the limit.
I must not screw other women or drive five times over the limit.
I must not screw other women or drive five times over the limit.
I must not screw other women or drive five times over the limit.
I must not screw other women or drive five times over the limit.
I must not screw other women or drive five times over the limit.
I must not screw other women or drive five times over the limit.
I must not screw other women or drive five times over the limit.
I must not screw other women or drive five times over the limit.
I must not screw other women or drive five times over the limit.
I must not screw other women or drive five times over the limit.
I must not screw other women or drive five times over the limit.
I must not screw other women or drive five times over the limit.
I must not screw other women or drive five times over the limit.
I must not screw other women or drive five times over the limit.
I must not screw other women or drive five times over the limit.
I must not screw other women or drive five times over the limit.
I must not screw other women or drive five times over the limit.
I must not screw other women or drive five times over the limit.
I must not screw other women or drive five times over the limit.

I must not screw other women or drive five times over the limit.
I must not screw other women or drive five times over the limit.
I must not screw other women or drive five times over the limit.
I must not screw other women or drive five times over the limit.
I must not screw other women or drive five times over the limit.
I must not screw other women or drive five times over the limit.
I must not screw other women or drive five times over the limit.
I must not screw other women or drive five times over the limit.
I must not screw other women or drive five times over the limit.
I must not screw other women or drive five times over the limit.
I must not screw other women or drive five times over the limit.
I must not screw other women or drive five times over the limit.
I must not screw other women or drive five times over the limit.
I must not screw other women or drive five times over the limit.
I must not screw other women or drive five times over the limit.
I must not screw other women or drive five times over the limit.
I must not screw other women or drive five times over the limit.
I must not screw other women or drive five times over the limit.
I must not screw other women or drive five times over the limit.
I must not screw other women or drive five times over the limit.

I look at the clock radio and see it's half past twelve. Carmen will be home in a few hours. The closer that moment comes, the less I feel able to cope with it. I want to do the right thing, I want to be there for my Carmie, but I've completely fucked up as far as she's concerned. Carmen doesn't understand the first damned thing about me any more. Nobody understands. Maud's angry with me. Frank certainly will be too, now I've phoned in sick today. Ramon called me a motherfucker. And after two days of comforting Carmen,

Thomas and Anne won't be thinking about me in particularly favourable ways, I should guess. Even Rose is cross, and she doesn't even know what everyone else does. Oh, yeah, and I think I'm a prick too. I feel guilty, hungover, miserable, furious, worried, depressed, selfish, weak, wicked, wronged, loutish, hypocritical, undervalued, overstretched, broken, immoral, asocial, misunderstood, cowardly, false and unhappy.

In short, things aren't going very well.

I sigh deeply and turn over in bed. I go to the toilet. I get back into bed. I get out of bed. I look out of the window. I go back to bed. I lie on my back. I lie on my belly. I get out of bed. I grab a glass of milk in the kitchen. And go back to bed. Twelve minutes to one. I lie on my left side. I cry. I lie on my right side. My left side. My right side. My back. I phone Rose.

Rose is furious.

'Why the hell didn't you call me before? I've spent two nights howling and waiting for a phone call or a text from you!'

I tell her I went into town and had an accident with my car when I'd drunk far too much. Rose is horrified.

'What!? You great idiot! And – were you hurt yourself?'

'No . . .'

'Thank God,' she sighs. She's the first person who's said anything nice today.

The real drama of the incident is reduced somewhat if you leave out the part about Maud/Natasha and the bit about Carmen leaving home, it occurs to me.

'Carmen walked out on me two days ago, Rose.'

'What!?'

'She was furious because of the accident and the drink, and because I was supposed to be home hours before . . .'

'You are the most unbelievable dickhead, Danny – You can be so nice, but the way you've been treating people lately really isn't normal – Why don't you go and see a shrink?'

'Not you, too!? No! I'm not going to see a shrink!'

Rose is silent for a moment.

Then she asks, 'Have I mentioned Nora?'

'No. Who's that?'

'Nora is a woman who gives spiritual advice.'

'Good for Nora.'

'She might be able to help you.'

'I don't believe in God.'

'Did I say anything about belief?'

'No, but what use is advice about spirits going to be to me? Am I supposed to ask her which type of vodka to choose?'

'Laugh all you like, but I'm still going to tell you.'

'Well, OK.'

Rose ignores my cynicism.

'You'd probably find it too woolly-headed, and it's probably not your kind of thing, but Nora's a woman with a gift. She's not a healer or whatever, not a guru, not a Jehovah's Witness type of person, but more of a sort of, how should I put it, someone who's spiritually gifted and uses it to help people. Gives them answers to the important questions of life.'

'How does she know the answers, then?'

'They come through.'

'Who from?'

'From the spirit world.'

'You don't say.' I feign indifference, but something she says interests me. I have no idea why.

'If you want, I can text you the number later on.'

'Fine by me,' I say as nonchalantly as I can.

'Good luck this afternoon—'

nora. 06-42518346. Call her now – x.

I stare at the number on my screen for a moment, shrug my shoulders and store it in my mobile. For safety's sake I save it under the code name 'SOS'. I don't fancy explaining to Carmen who Nora is, how I got hold of her number, and the fact Nora isn't somebody I've been screwing.

If you had my shoes on,
what would you have done,
go stand in my shoes...

De Dijk, from 'Ga in mijn schoenen staan'
(*Muzikanten dansen niet*, 2002)

Thirty-three

I hear the front door opening. She comes in, puts her bag down, takes her jacket off and goes and sits at the kitchen table.

'Do you want some coffee?'

She shakes her head.

'I do, if you don't mind.'

I feel her eyes following me as I make coffee for myself.

'Frank rang me this morning,' she says. 'He told me you were in a complete state, and that you called in sick today.'

'Umm – yeah...'

'Listen, Dan. I feel betrayed by you. And Anne and Thomas fully agree.'

'Hey, I wouldn't have expected *that*,' I mumble.

'It'd be nice if you'd give your friends some credit now and again. Anne spoke up for you. She told me that if I'd been in your shoes I might have vented my frustration too. I'd have bankrupted us long ago by buying up everything on P.C. Hooftstraat.* And something else has happened.'

---

* The main shopping street.

'What?'

'Toni has left her husband. The man who never went to the chemo treatments because he couldn't cope with it. The husband she'd stopped talking to. That made me think. We've been through so much together, so we can deal with this too. It's happened, and we have to move on.'

I nod, as happy as a child whose mother has just told him they're going to be friends again.

'Come here, you bastard,' she says with a smile and runs her fingers through my hair. 'Forgiving is a part of love, too.'*

* Wrample from 'Wat is dan liefde' by André Hazes ('n Vriend, 1980).

However much money they spend, however much they urge,
I'd never think of leaving Mokum, you can laugh here,
it's all good fun, I can't imagine, where I'd rather be . . .

Danny de Munk, from 'Mjjn stad' (*Danny de Munk*, 1984)

Thirty-four

I was afraid this might happen.

I've asked Carmen three times this week whether she wouldn't rather go and stay with Anne on the day we're moving house. Then I'd be able to get the removal men to move all the stuff from Amstelveenseweg to Johannes Ver-hulststraat, set up the bedroom and the sitting-room, and in the evening Carmen would be able to move into a largely tidy new house. She wouldn't hear of it.

The removal men come in a quarter of an hour and Carmen is as sick as a dog. Not that I'd expected differently; Carmen's body is only present on a perfunctory basis at any time before midday. As long as she's asleep, or lying still, it's fine, but as soon as she strains herself, her body protests in an unusually effective way against this waste of energy, and throws everything she's consumed over the past few hours right back up again. She's already thrown up into the toilet three times in the past hour.

I wait until the removal men come, tell them the coffee's boiled and the applejacks in the back there can go on the table, and I'm just going to move my wife and a puke-bucket on my own. I help Carmen get dressed, walk her to the car, dash back upstairs, grab a pillow, a duvet and a bucket from the bedroom, throw everything into the Opal Astra from Budget Rent-A-Car and drive as carefully as possible, avoiding sharp bends and abrupt movements, to Johannes Verhulst-straat. There I first run upstairs with the duvet and the pillow to the bedroom, praise Our Lord and the waterbed shop for delivering in time, hurry back down to the car and then go back upstairs with Carmen in a lower gear. I help her undress and slip her into the soft waterbed. There she lies: a scrap of humanity, less than fifty kilos, pale as death, smiling in a big waterbed in an even bigger bedroom, completely empty apart from a puke-bucket.

'So while you get on with moving house, I'm going to sleep here comfortably in our new house,' she says with a giggle.

I burst out laughing. How I'm going to miss her sense of humour.

How ugly you are close up ...

Huub Hangop, from 'How ugly you are close up'
(*The Very Worst of Huub Hangop*, 1993)

Thirty-five

Our au pair has arrived. As ordered, from the Czech Republic, on the bus.

Carmen and I found her on the website of World Wide Au Pair a few months ago. At that time we didn't expect Carmen would actually see the au pair, but thanks to the LV chemo, that's what's happening. Carmen says she's glad to have seen her.

The other thing Carmen is glad about is that the au pair is even more ugly than she looked in her photograph. Christ, what sort of monstrosity have we brought into our house!

▶ **Our au pair** looks like a cross between a singer in a Goth rock band and a Furby with a piercing through its bottom lip. But Luna's wild about Furbys, so she's happy. So's Carmen. She cheerfully emails all her girlfriends to tell them she's absolutely certain I'm never going to make a pass at the au pair. And Handyman Rick, who's adding the last finishing touches to the house, texts me to ask for extra danger money, because of the increased risk of falling downstairs in the event of an unexpected encounter with the au pair.

It doesn't all go smoothly. In the time it took to explain to the au pair what she has to get from the supermarket, and what it's called in Dutch, and writing it out for her, and then explaining it all over again, I could have been to the shop and back three times. And when she finally gets it into her head what 'half a pound of mince' means, she refuses to buy it. She can't bring herself to walk through the meat section of Albert Heijn. The au pair's a vegan, and won't buy or cook anything an animal suffered or died to produce.

And she won't cycle, either. I thought there might be some religious or philosophical reason for that, but when I once urged her to try it, I'd seen enough. Pure horror. I'm still taking Luna to the crèche myself.

Finally, apart from the language barrier, her innate clumsiness and ugliness, and our objective difference of opinion concerning culinary preparations, there is one other problem. We discover very quickly our au pair isn't exactly a joy to be around. Every question is followed by an aggrieved sigh, like I'd just asked her to swallow her piercing. The child's as miserable as Kurt Cobain. (I sympathize – I mean, if you've spent your teenage years at school standing at the side while all your friends were necking with the cute boys, it's hardly going to give you a cheerful disposition.)

So what she does – albeit with a sigh – is the ironing, cleaning, sweeping and hoovering, and I've given her responsibility for the dishwasher, the washing-machine, the tumble-drier and the rubbish bags, otherwise I'd be back at square one, wasting nearly as much time as I did before she came, but with an extra problem in the house.

But quite honestly the arrival of the au pair has made me more flexible than I was before. At the weekend she takes on one of my morning shifts, and in the evening, when Carmen's in a coma after two sleeping tablets, she's at home to look after Luna. And then I can go to the late-night shop, finish something off at MIU or have sex with Rose.

Always look on the bright side of life . . .

Monty Python, from 'Always Look on the Bright Side of Life'
(*Life of Brian*, 1979)

Thirty-six

Another advantage to the depressing presence of our au pair
is that I become prouder of Carmen with each passing day.
She compares so favourably with her.

Carmen can't add any days to her life, so she adds life to
the days. Our au pair doesn't even know what living is. She
never enjoys doing anything. Never.

On days when she's feeling a little better, Carmen is always
filled with the love of life. This week, for example, she's been
looking forward to dinner with Anne and Thomas this evening. I haven't. So it doesn't suit me too badly that Carmen
feels absolutely wretched today.

But she wants to go anyway. In this particular case I'd be
happy to have a wife who'd rather stay at home when she
isn't feeling so great. But as far as I can tell Carmen will still
want to go out when she's long dead and buried.

I haven't talked to Thomas since my double flip with the
Chevy. When I get out of the Opel Astra, I barely dare to
look at him. Carmen walks ahead of me into the sitting-room.
Thomas pulls me aside.

'Nothing about carnival, OK?' he whispers nervously.

I look at him as innocently as possible.

'That – that stuff with Maud.' He utters her name as though he's talking about a cockroach, but his expression betrays the fact he still has the pictures of that night in his head. A smile even appears on his face. I make a movement with my hand as though to lock my mouth and swallow the key. Thomas does a nudge-nudge-wink-wink twinkle at me. So you see, the advantages of infidelity are under-estimated. It can, for example, make you more tolerant of it.

Anne and Thomas have done everything they can to make things nice for us. Carmen *and* me. Not with words, not with touch, like Frank, but in their own way. By not talking about the accident and the Opel Astra. By means of the bottle of vodka and a bottle of lime juice Thomas has bought specially for me. By going completely wild in the kitchen, as Anne has done for us today. She wants to spoil us this evening, she says. Carmen doesn't mention the fact she's been throwing up all day, and eats with us.

After the starter she goes to the toilet. Up comes the starter.

After the main course she goes to the toilet and throws that up, too.

After dessert she goes to the toilet and throws up the dessert.

'Thanks for this evening, boys and girls,' I say. Anne gives me three kisses and a wink. Thomas slaps me hard on the shoulder.

Carmen is pale, but her eyes are gleaming.

'Thanks so much, darlings. I've enjoyed this evening.'

Thomas suddenly hugs her, and for a moment I think he's never going to let her go.

As we're driving away, I see Thomas is holding Anne tightly, and wiping a tear from his eyes with his free hand.

Thirty-seven

The first member of the Mouflon group to die is Toni.

Carmen is completely distraught. Three weeks ago, Toni had heard there was no point in going on with the chemo. And now she's dead.

Toni hadn't seen her ex-husband since their divorce. He'll be able to see her one more time, in her coffin.

'At least they won't be able to have a row,' grins Carmen.

She says she wants to go to the funeral. When I hear when it is, I go crazy. Next Tuesday. That's Luna's and my birthday. Our third birthday in a row in the sign of cancer. And the last one, that much is certain. And Carmen wants to go to a *funeral*? It's like going to a preview of your own burial.

'Don't you think it might – it might be a bit hard for you?'

'Couldn't we celebrate your birthdays on Sunday? No one's coming on Tuesday. And it's only a couple of hours.'

I try not to let it show, but Carmen sees I'm not happy about it.

'I don't think it would be fair on Toni not to go.'

'But it would be fair on Luna and me?' I can't help it, it just slips out.

■

276

On Sunday the house is full. Friends of mine, family, little friends from Luna's crèche. Carmen's mother gives a start when she comes in, I notice. It's three weeks since she last saw her daughter. With her fat belly Carmen looks like an underfed pregnant woman. We stand and chatter in the kitchen. Luna walks in proudly with her new princess dress and angel wings. Carmen squats down to have a good look.

'How lovely,' she says enthusiastically to Luna, loses her balance and falls over, taking Luna with her.

Luna is scared and starts crying.

'Careful!' I shout, startled. 'You know you have no strength in your legs now, damn it all, Carm!'

Carmen feels humiliated by her own fall and my reaction, and starts crying too. The party hasn't got off to a great start.

■

'Are you doing anything nice on your birthday on Tuesday?' asks Anne, taking a bite of her orange birthday cake.

'Carmen is. She's going to Toni's funeral, the woman from her discussion group.'

'The funeral's on Tuesday?'

'Yes.'

Anne frowns.

■

The evening after the party Carmen says she's not going to go to the funeral on Tuesday. 'Anne brought it up. I'm going to put out a nice bunch of flowers for Toni. I like that. I think Toni would understand.'

'I'm absolutely sure Toni would understand.'

Happy birthday to you,
happy birthday to you,
happy birthday dear Danny and Luna,
happy birthday to you ...

Thirty-eight

And Carmen sings along, well aware that, while there may be many happy returns, she isn't going to see any of them. I can tell by everything she does she's decided to make up for the plan to go to Toni's funeral. Luna and I get breakfast in bed. Carmen made it for us and asked the au pair to take it upstairs. Luna, beaming, eats a croissant with peanut butter and coconut cake, I have one and some bread, and Carmen reluctantly gulps down six spoonfuls of Kellogg's Fruit 'n Fibre.

Things aren't easy today. Everything makes me emotional. When Frank texts me to say he's happy to have me as a friend, and he wants it to stay that way for many years. When Anne texts that she's happy Carmen and I are celebrating the birthdays together in spite of all that's happened. And when Carmen gives me an enlargement of a series of nude photographs I took of her when we first met.

After breakfast I see Carmen is tired and feeling unwell.

'You should lie down for an hour or two,' I say.

'Don't you think that's antisocial?' she asks hesitantly.

I shake my head. 'Lie down and sleep for a bit. I might go into town for half an hour later on. I got a record token from Maud on Sunday.'

I play with my little sunshine for an hour or so and then ask the au pair if she'd make pancakes with Luna. Her clumsiness has by now assumed mythical proportions, so I make her cross her heart to take care Luna doesn't fall off her stool by the kitchen sink.

'Trust me,' she says. Hmm. I know our au pair by now, and it creeps the hell out of me when she says things like that. But I can hardly spend the whole day making sure the cow doesn't hurt my daughter.

I run upstairs for a moment. Carmen has put a bucket down beside her bed. I look in and see it's not there for nothing. The Fruit 'n Fibre she managed to get down this morning was in vain.

I cycle like mad to the CD shop on Van Baerlestraat. In less than a quarter of an hour I've exchanged my record token for a Coldplay CD, and thus bought my alibi.

After that I cycle to Rose. She's wrapped herself in red lace like a Christmas present.

What was that?,
That was your life, mate.
Oh – that was quick – can I get another one?

Fawlty Towers (1976)*

Thirty-nine

I get hopelessly bored in the waiting-room outside Roden-bach's office. I've finished the football magazine I found in a rack by the entrance. I start reading Carmen's file. The nurse who's just emptied Carmen's belly gave it to us, with the request that we pass it on to Dr Rodenbach. Carmen's belly has been drained sixteen times since November, I read. I add up the numbers.

'Do you know how many litres of that fluid they've taken out of your belly?'

'No idea.'

'Just over seventy-one litres.'

'Hahaha – that's more than I weighed before they started doing the punctures!'

Carmen weighs forty-seven kilos now. You can see her getting thinner by the day. Six months ago she weighed almost seventy. Because of the lack of fat, she's been cold all the time for the last few weeks. The thermostat in the sitting-room is set at twenty-four degrees all day. The waterbed is

---

*   John Cleese philosophizing.

four degrees higher than the recommended temperature. Thank God we've got a waterbed. Any ordinary mattress would be too hard. There's nothing but skin between her bones and the mattress, no fat now.

We haven't got a good feeling about the discussion we're about to have with Rodenbach. The punctures, which dropped to once every two weeks at the start of the LV treatment, are now happening every few days. And they're getting more and more unpleasant. It looks like Carmen's organs have turned to mush, and they hurt more and more after each puncture. The last one was terrible. Even with a morphine injection Carmen threw up with the pain. I think I've been left with a lasting trauma by the image of my wife with her head over a vomit basin, while a tube from her belly slowly fills a bucket with litres of cloudy yellow fluid.

■

'Take a seat,' says Rodenbach amiably.

We've seen him about six times in the meantime, since we moved to the Antoni van Leeuwenhoek. There's a sense of mutual respect. He knows we don't whine and whinge, as his other patients do, and we know he doesn't trick or swindle us, as our previous doctors generally did.

Rodenbach is about to give us a new certainty.

'The tumour markers are going up again. The LV treatments have stopped doing their work.'

'And – what – and what does that mean?' I stammer, though I know what he's going to say.

'I'm afraid we're really going to have to give up the fight now.'

So that's it. End of exercise.

Carmen is being abandoned. Three weeks later Toni was dead.

Carmen sits looking at me, a hand over her mouth. I hold her other hand tight and look at her.

'Shall we go?' I ask cautiously.

She nods.

We arrange to meet up again at Rodenbach's office in three weeks' time. A bit hopeful, that, since by then Carmen might no longer be with us, and Rodenbach's role will be over. The only thing he can still do for Carmen is to put his signature to the letters in which he instructs the chemist to supply morphine, kytril, codeine, prednisone and temazepam. Pain management.

I start the car and put on the CD. De Dijk are wrong.

It won't sort itself out.

Part Three

CARMEN

I'd tell all my friends but they'd never believe me
they'd think that I have finally lost it completely ...

Radiohead, from 'Subterranean Homesick Alien'
(*OK Computer*, 1997)

One

I've called Nora. The day after Rodenbach's news.

Only Rose knows about it. I haven't said a word about it at home. Carmen would think I was idiotic for refusing to discuss my problems with a psychologist, as she has suggested so many times, when I'm happy to talk to someone like Nora.

Even I don't know exactly why I called her. I think it was something to do with the car accident. The fact I emerged without so much as a scratch, while the whole side of the Chevy was a complete wreck, is at least as miraculous as Marco's goal against Russia in '88.

Frank and Maud don't know I'm going to see Nora today, either. I got Tasha to say in the office diary that I was taking the afternoon off. She looked at me quizzically, winked and made a shagging motion with her hands. I didn't react.

The spiritual adviser's office is in a sixties terraced house in Buitenveldert. Heart thumping, I ring the bell.

Nora's an unremarkable, slender woman with black hair. She leads me upstairs to her consulting-room, and asks if I'd like some tea. I would. She goes out of the room. I take a quiet look around the place. Painted stones, arranged in a very feng shui sort of way. Smoking sticks that smell like something I remember from a holiday in India. Music that's probably high up the Himalayan top ten. Flyers for the 'Explaining Dreams' workshop Nora's giving next week.

The view of a block of gallery apartments from Nora's consulting-room strikes a dissonant chord with the unworldly whole. Say what you like about gallery apartments, but at least they aren't off with the fairies. The view puts me rather at ease. It reminds me of Breda-Noord.

Nora gives me a friendly smile when she comes back in with a tray. It looks like normal tea.

'You needed to come here,' she says. All at once I have a sense of déjà vu. My conversations with the psychotherapist, almost two years ago! Where have I ended up all over again? It's *Monty Python*, episode two.

'Let's go right back to the beginning, shall we?' she says, when she sees my suspicious expression. She tells me that from my name and date of birth, which I gave her when I rang her up, she got messages for me from another world. And those messages are in a letter she's now going to read out. I avoid telling her I don't believe a word of this kind of airy-fairy nonsense. Nora picks up the letter and starts to read.

The man for whom you are receiving this letter has a high level of energy, but he must control that energy throughout this period. He must make choices now. All wanting leads to chaos, he has noticed.

This insight is good. Let it come and penetrate. It is good.

Much will be asked of him in the time to come. Now he can no longer govern events in any other way. He must be present for his responsibilities. He can no longer flee them.

It will be as it will be. He can do it, even if he thinks he can't.

Tell him to trust his intuition. To take guidance from his heart's energy. That will help him, that will give him strength.

He can do it. Tell him to be confident. Much help is around him from this sphere.

In love . . .

You don't say. So much utter cobblers.

Nora calmly puts the letter down and waits for a moment. 'Do you recognize anything in that?'

'Hm, what can I say? It could refer to anything . . .'

'Do you think so?' she smiles. 'And the chaos described in the letter?'

OK, there might be something in that.

'Hmph. It's one of those horoscope tricks. Doesn't everybody find themselves in situations you could call chaotic? Have you ever been to the sales at IKEA?'

She bursts out laughing. 'I think the letter means something a bit more chaotic than that, don't you?'

I decide to give her a chance. 'A while ago I had a bump in my car that you might call chaotic.'

'A crash?'

I nod.

She nods back. 'Do you know we humans are protected by powers of which we have no knowledge?' – *Oh, Christ, here we go* – 'That crash was a sign your protection was running out.'* – *Hm. I'm not sure I'm happy about this. I mean, even if you don't believe in God or fate or whoever's in charge of these things, hearing your protection's run out is still pretty extreme.*

'But you're here because someone's seriously ill, aren't you?' – *Shock.*

'Erm – yeah. My wife . . .'

'What's your wife's name?'

'Carmen.'

'Carmen is ready to die.'

A chill runs down my spine – Dr Rodenbach telling me Carmen hasn't long to live is one thing, but a stranger in a sixties terraced house in Buitenveldert . . .

'You don't need to be afraid. She isn't. It's good.'

I swallow. Although I still don't believe a word she's saying, Nora has touched me. 'I feel there's still so much I've got to talk to her about . . .' I hear myself saying.

'You'll have the chance to do that' – *this Nora woman doesn't really have connections with higher – er – spheres, does she?* – 'Be sure and spend as much time with her as you can over the next little while' – *yup, off we go again. I think I could have worked that out on my own, in so far as I can work out anything lately. You know what, let's give her a shock. These esoteric types aren't so good at coping with that . . .*

'I've been having an affair for more than a year.' *1–0 to Danny! That sounded pretty challenging. So over to you . . .*

Nora is calm personified. She gestures to me to continue. For a moment I don't know what to say. Or if I should say anything at all. I know in my heart why I came. Just get to the point and ask her.

---

*   Wrample from *The Bridge Across Forever*, Richard Bach (1984).

'Carmen doesn't know about it. Do I have to tell her while I still can?'

Nora waits for a moment. 'She does know. She's known for ages' – *What?* – 'If she asks, you must tell her the truth' – *brrr* – 'but she isn't going to ask' – *sounds OK by me* – 'she's always known what you were like. Better than you did yourself. Lately she's come to terms with it' – *I like this Nora* – 'What's the name of the woman you're having the affair with?'

'Rose . . .'

'It wasn't in vain that you met Rose while Carmen was ill,' she says in a quiet voice. 'It was necessary.' *You see! Yes, Nora's bang on the money. I'm going to give her the benefit of the doubt. All that cynical stuff doesn't get you anywhere in the end.*

'Is Carmen actually happy with me? I've never been faithful, and I'm pretty much of a – a hedonist.'

'Without your ability to make light of life she wouldn't have been able to bear her illness,' she suddenly says sharply. 'Don't feel guilty. She's very happy with you. And you don't need to be ashamed of your weaknesses' – *Should I give her Thomas's mobile number?* – 'Carmen is ready now, but you aren't' – *I hope not.* 'Deep down inside, she's already forgiven you' – *she says that very firmly* – 'but you've still got to support her. Put everything else aside, and care for her with all the love you have inside you' – *Me as Florence Nightingale? I really can't* – 'Leave the housekeeping to other people. Is that possible?'

'Erm – we've got an au pair at home. She looks after my daughter and does the housework. If I ask her really nicely.'

'Good. Don't worry, just let her get on with all the work that has nothing to do with Carmen. And what's your daughter's name?'

'Luna. She's just turned three. On the same day as my birthday,' I say so proudly it makes me blush.

'That explains a lot. You and your daughter have a much stronger bond than you think' – *Yikes, you're getting soppy now, Nora love* – 'When your wife is no longer there, you won't want your au pair around' – *does she know my au pair?* – 'you'll want to look after your daughter yourself' – *Forget it. Who's going to take care of her when I have to go to work and the crèche is shut? Or – more to the point – if I want to go out?* – 'You'll become a different person' – *oh, that's enough, now!* – 'and your wife will support you in that. Even if she isn't there any more' – *as Carmen the Friendly Ghost, I suppose? Try to be nice, you old ghoul!*

Nora sees my worried face and laughs. 'Believe me on this,' she says, 'Carmen and you have known each other far longer than you think. She loves you. Deeply' – *I can't help feeling moved, and gulp down another lump in my throat* – 'You are soul-mates. For ever.'

Silence. I blink my eyes.

'Does Carmen know you're here?'

'No. She's far too sober for this kind of – vague stuff.'

'Tell her. It'll do her good.'

'I'm not sure . . .' I say hesitantly. 'She might find it ridiculous, and then she'll get cross. It seems like we've completely grown out of each other, and lately she's been getting really annoyed with everything I do.'

Nora shakes her head violently. 'I'll tell you again: Carmen loves you deeply. She doesn't want to be supported by anyone else' – *boom* – 'I'd go right home now. It's going to happen faster than you think' – BOOM – 'Be sure to be there when it happens' – **BOOM** – 'She'll be very grateful for it. And so will you. Now you've got the chance to give your wife back what you've had from her for all those years...'

■

When I'm in the car, it rumbles through my head: 'Now you've got the chance to give your wife back what you've had from her for all those years...'

I adjust my rear-view mirror and look at myself. To my surprise, I see a broad smile. And I feel incredibly happy. 'Now you've got the chance to give your wife back what you've had from her for all those years...' With an energy that would make Edgar Davids* jealous.

Thanks to Nora and her prompters, whoever they may be.

---

* The Molotov cocktail among footballers.

I was unrecognizable to myself,
I saw my reflection in the mirror,
didn't know my own face,
I can feel myself fading away,
and my clothes don't fit me no more . . .

Bruce Springsteen, from 'Streets of Philadelphia'
(music from the film *Philadelphia*, 1993)

Two

I switch my phone back on and see I've got a voicemail. It's Carmen. Would I call her? I can hear she's not well.

'Danny, I can't stop throwing up,' she says, sobbing. 'I'm so scared . . .'

'I'll be right there.'

Four minutes and fifty-one seconds later I run up the two flights of stairs to the bedroom in our house. Carmen is sitting over a bucket, trying to be sick.

I go and sit next to her and stroke her short, grey, red-dyed hair.

'I'm so glad you're here,' she says. Her voice sounds hollow through the bucket, which her head's halfway down. 'I've been feeling ill all morning. But nothing's coming out any more.'

Suddenly she retches and a little stream of vomit actually does come out of her mouth. I can see it's bile. No food. It's hard for food to come out if there isn't any in there in the first place.

Dr Bakker, our family doctor, who arrives an hour or so later, prescribes a liquid food preparation, two tins of primperan and a tin of kytril to counteract the vomiting. When Carmen's asleep, I go to the chemist's on Cornelis Schuytstraat to collect it all.

On the way I ring Rose. She's relieved things went well with Nora. I say Carmen doesn't look too great, and I probably won't be seeing her again for a while. I cancel our date for this coming Friday. Rose is cool about it. She wishes me a lot of strength, and says she'll keep a candle burning for Carmen, on a little box in her sitting-room. For the woman she's never met, but who she knows so much about by now. It's like she's known her for years.

Carmen's mother comes in the evening.

All four of us go and sit on the terrace of the King Arthur. Carmen's mother is wearing a thin silk blouse. Luna and I are in T-shirts. The evening sun is wonderful. It's even warm.

> ▶ The terrace of the **King Arthur** is in the middle of our posh reservation, where Cornelis Schuytstraat crosses Johannes Verhulststraat. The male clientele are more than averagely irritating (lawyers from the offices on De Lairessestraat and English businessmen staying at the Hilton who have managed to get a break from their wives and children), and you wouldn't come here for the women, either (local fossils). But the sun shines a good hour longer there than it does on the terrace in districts like De Pijp or Oud-West. Our neighbourhood is so swanky even the hours of sunlight seem to be properly regulated.

Carmen is in a wheelchair, wrapped up in a thick jacket and wearing a pair of sunglasses.

'It's a bit chilly, isn't it?' she asks just as we get our drinks.

'I think so too,' I lie.

'Yes, it isn't quite as warm as it looks,' agrees Carmen's mother.

Five minutes later we're back at home.

The evening sun can't warm up skin and bone.

You're packing a suitcase for a place none of us has been,
a place that has to be believed to be seen . . .

U2, from 'Walk On' (*All that You Can't Leave Behind*, 2000)

Three

'I hope it's all over soon,' says Carmen's mother and starts
crying, with her hands over her eyes. I put my arm around
her and pull her to me.

A mother who's losing her daughter. Her daughter, who
she's seen lying on her bed, terribly ill from her chemotherapy. Her daughter who, weeping, showed her the
spot where her breast used to be, and where now there
was nothing but a stitch like a zip fastener. Her daughter,
whose suffering she hopes will soon be over. They ought
to pass a law that mothers should never see their children
suffer.

She takes my hand and gives me a kiss. 'We'll get each
other through this, won't we?'

I nod. Frank sits in silence, watching the scene. Things are
going badly, which is why Frank's here. It's a hard and fast
rule. Anne's here too. I notice her warm embrace makes me
feel good, just as it did two years ago when she stood on the
step with Thomas on Amstelveenseweg.

'I'll go and see Carmen,' I say and go upstairs.

Carmen is just emerging from a nap. She sees me coming
into the bedroom and smiles. 'Hi, treasure,' she whispers.

'How are you?' I ask, going and sitting on her bed. I hold her hand tightly. My God, her hand is thin.

'I can't see the point any longer, Dan – if it goes on like this, I hope it'll all be over quickly . . .' She looks at my hand, which strokes hers. I see she wants to say something, but she's keeping it in.

'What's up?' I ask. I already know what she means, but I hold my tongue. I want her to start talking herself.

'I'd like to know what the rules are if I – if I want to put an end to things. And what you think about it.'

'You mean euthanasia?'

'Yes,' she says, relieved, glad I've called a spade a spade.

'Shall I call Dr Bakker and ask how it works?'

She nods. I take her in my arms. She feels more fragile than a newborn baby.

'I'll go and phone him. Is there anything else I can do for you?'

'I'd like some people to come over tomorrow.'

'Just say the word. Who?'

'Thomas and Anne. Maud. Frank.'

'Anne's here already, so's Frank.'

'Great! Send them up for a moment.'

'Fine. Do you want something to eat in the meantime?'

'I suppose I have to, don't I?'

'From today onwards you don't have to do anything at all.'

Just let me go my own way . . .

Ramses Shaffy, from 'Let me' (*Dag en nacht*, 1978)

Four

Since Luna discovered what cuddling is, the three of us have done a group cuddle every morning.

I ask Frank, who slept here last night, as did Carmen's mother, to take a photograph of our group cuddle this morning. I hold my beaming little ray of sunshine (3), radiant with health, and my stick-thin but still beaming wife (36) in my arms. Carmen is wearing a pair of silk pyjamas, Luna some white ones with little bears. They're both smiling broadly. I see Frank can hardly hold the camera still.

We have breakfast with Frank and Carmen's mother on Carmen's bed. At lunchtime Maud's there too. The moment she comes in she holds Carmen tightly and starts weeping violently. Anne and Thomas come in too. Even our au pair has, on her own initiative, made herself a little nest next to Carmen's bed. Carmen enjoys the huddle. She doesn't eat anything herself. She seems to have lost a bit more weight. I'd say she weighs about forty-two kilograms.

Meanwhile Dr Bakker turns up. I called him yesterday, and he explained to me precisely how euthanasia works. Carmen has to write a letter setting out the conditions under which she would like the euthanasia to take place. She has to sign it. Then she has a conversation first with him, and then with a different, independent doctor. The two doctors then agree this is 'a hopeless situation involving inhuman suffering'. And there is no compulsion or pressure from the family or anyone else. From that moment onwards Carmen herself can decide when she wants to die.

At least if everything goes according to plan. Our doctor rings to say he's done his back in, and is it really necessary for him to come today for the conversation with Carmen. I tell him it is.

Panting heavily, he comes into the bedroom, on the second floor of our house. He tells Carmen about his back. Concerned, she asks if it's giving him a lot of pain, and whether he wouldn't rather have come tomorrow.

'Painkillers don't help,' he says. 'What about you? Are you in a lot of pain?'

'More and more, yes – since yesterday my back's been hurting too,' she says to my surprise. She hadn't mentioned it to me.

He examines the spot Carmen indicates.

'I assume it must be spreading again.'

'Yeah,' says Carmen drily.

'I'll prescribe some morphine pills. Dan told me you wanted to get everything in order for when it really gets too much for you?'

Carmen nods. The doctor tells her he's sending another colleague over to sort out the legal aspect of the euthanasia.

'Fine,' says Carmen.

The second doctor comes late in the afternoon. He's a rather formal type. I ask if I should leave the room. I've no idea how something like this works. Perhaps it's like on *Mr and Mrs*, where you weren't allowed to hear what sort of answers your wife gave, and had to wait in the corner with a pair of headphones on.

I'm allowed to stay. Carmen says how much she really wants to make her own decision about whether and when she'll put an end to her illness. It's like she's discussing a job application. Like she has to sell herself. The doctor signs the form, without asking too many other questions. Carmen thanks him. She's happy, I notice. As if she's just been given the keys to her new car.

'You're really quite cheerful, aren't you?' I ask in surprise.

'Yes. Now I have a choice again. I can decide what happens to my life.'

What you don't know you can feel it somehow . . .

U2, from 'Beautiful Day' (*All that You Can't Leave Behind*, 2000)

Five

As well as Carmen's mother and Frank, Maud has decided to bivouac in our house to supply spiritual and organizational support, for as long as Carmen stays alive. Frank and Maud are to sleep together in one bed in one of the spare rooms. Carmen chuckles over this when Frank's out of the room, and tries to persuade Maud to give him a good time tonight. 'You just go and sit on top of him when he's asleep, and then start shrieking: *and now we're going to shag, you lazy sod!*' They explode with laughter. Carmen's cheerful again today.

'Shall we all eat together again this evening?' she asks hopefully.

'Don't you think the smell of all that hot food might make you feel sick?'

'Sure, but then something might finally come out.'

Our au pair does the cooking. Carmen doesn't eat, and the others barely touch theirs. The food smells like Carmen's bucket. Rice with something green and yellow. I recognize the yellow stuff as sweetcorn, but the green could be just about anything. Carmen watches us eating, every now and again darting a glance at each other and each other's plate, and goes off into paroxysms of laughter. So our au pair does have a function after all, as Carmen's unintentional deathbed jester.

After supper I stay with Carmen. Everyone else goes downstairs.

'Danny . . . I've got to . . . I need to take a crap.'

'Shall I go out?'

The home-care unit brought a sort of shitting-chair today. It looks just like a camping chair with a toilet seat where you would normally sit. Under the toilet seat there's a bucket.

'Erm . . . just wait a moment . . . I don't know if I can stand up all by myself.'

Very slowly Carmen tries to get out of bed. When she's nearly standing, she falls back, and starts crying.

'I have no strength in my legs,' she sobs.

'Come over here,' I say.

I put the shitting-chair closer to the bed and support her under her shoulders. She pulls down her pyjama trousers and her panties by herself. I let her fall slowly on to the seat.

'There now – Granny's sitting down,' she says.

When she's finished, she hesitates.

'Shall I wipe your bum?' I ask.

She nods, and can barely bring herself to look at me.

'I'm scared of falling . . .'

'Just support yourself on me. At least I get to touch your bum again, and there's nothing you can do about it,' I say with a wink.

She laughs through her tears. Her face is turned towards me, her arms around my neck. 'My dear friend . . .' she whispers. With one arm I hold her tightly under her arms, and with the other I wipe her bottom. After that my knees start going. Carmen drapes her arms around my neck, barely supporting herself on her legs. With my free hand I pull up the pyjama trousers and fasten them over her bottom.

'Are there any things you'd like me not to do when you're no longer with us?' I ask as I lay her back down in bed, breathless with tension.

'No.'

'Would you like me to wait for a while before I have sex again?'

'No,' she smiles. 'Just do what you feel like doing. Although – I hope you don't do it with Sharon again. She's pretty much the symbol of your infidelity. Was she the first one you were unfaithful with?'

'No – that must have been one of my exes. I think Merel. Or Emma. But Sharon was the first one you found out about.'

We both laugh.

'Yeah, but there are plenty of others to start something with. You just wait, they'll be all over you. You're free, you've got your own business, a beautiful house and an adorable daughter. You're a pretty good catch. I've already told Anne, Frank and my mother not to be surprised if you have a new wife more quickly than they think. That's just the way you are.'

'Oh?' I say, slightly startled.

'Hey, it doesn't matter. I hope you'll be happy again soon. With a new wife. And you need someone who can cope with you, and won't let herself be bossed around.'

'Anything else?'

'She'll have to be horny as fuck.'

I burst out laughing again.

'But you'll have to do something about your infidelity, Danny.'

'Be monogamous . . .'

'No, hardly anyone can do that for their whole lifetime.

You certainly can't. But you must never again make a woman feel she's a complete idiot. That you're shagging half of Amsterdam and Breda, and she's the only one who doesn't know about it. Take care *no one* knows.'

'Like you with Pim . . .'

'Exactly. Keep it to yourself. I don't think anyone is emotionally capable of seeing infidelity as something unconnected with love. I wish I'd been able to do that—'

I look guiltily at the floor. I hesitate for a moment, but then decide to ask the question that's been weighing on me. I ask it indirectly.

'Are there still things you want me to tell you? Things you've never dared to ask?'

She smiles again. 'No. You don't need to feel guilty. I know all I want to know.'

'Do you really?'

'Yes. It's fine.'

I feel myself growing smaller in comparison to this woman. I smile and then go to the toilet, empty the shit-pail and the puke-bucket and wash them both out.

When I come back, she watches me putting the shit-pail back in the shitting-chair. 'You've done so much for me since I've been ill,' she says, touched, 'and now on top of everything else you have to deal with all my horrible pee and poo . . .'

I think about what Nora said. *Now you've got the chance to give your wife back what you've had from her for all those years.*

I hesitate for a second. 'Yesterday I went to see someone I haven't dared say anything to you about . . .'

'Really? Tell me?' she asks curiously.

Embarrassed, I tell her about Nora and what it's done for me.

Carmen listens attentively as I read out the letter I got from Nora. I see she's touched.

'I think it's great you went there, and I'm so happy it's done you good. I think it's lovely . . .'

'Really? But do you believe in that kind of thing?' I ask in surprise.

'I don't know what I believe in, but what Nora's told you isn't nonsense. Increasingly I feel it isn't just a matter of chance I'm dying. It feels like I'm ready.'

'Do you believe we'll be together in some way when you aren't here any more?'

'Yes,' she says very firmly. 'I'll be there for you and for Luna.'

'I believe that too,' I say, 'but you sometimes hear that people believe in God or the afterlife just because their lives are over. As a kind of self-protection . . .'

'No,' she says resolutely, 'it's more than that. It's stronger. I just feel I'll still be there. It's like feeling you love someone. You just know. Just like I knew it was nonsense last year in Club Med, when you thought you didn't love me any more. It's as if I've always loved you, even before I met you . . .' By now I've gone to lie beside her on the bed.

'In spite of my selfish streak?'

'You always make sure you're OK,' she laughs, 'and true enough, that hasn't always been great for me. You remember that time two years ago when you dragged me along to the Vondelpark on Koninginnedag?' she asks.

'I did that for me, first and foremost,' I grin.

'That doesn't matter. It was symbolic. I've often thought of that moment when I was completely finished and couldn't see the point of anything.'

'And if you'd known before what I was like with women,' I ask. 'Would you have married me?'

She looks at me, smiles her smile I know so well, with her upper lip raised slightly on one side.

'Yes. Of course.'

We hold each other's hand tightly, passionately, without saying another word. We lie like that for several minutes. I see she's closed her eyes. A little later she's asleep.

I go downstairs, where Maud, Frank and Carmen's mother are drinking rosé. I'm beaming from ear to ear.

'You look happy,' says Maud.

'Yes,' I say brightly. 'It was fantastic.'

Hi, Goddess – I'm tired, I'm emotional, but I feel valuable. Dan goes Florence Nightingale. Told Carmen about Nora. She was glad. Me too. X.

The two of us here together,
this might be the moment . . .

Tröckener Kecks, from 'Nu of nooit'
(*Eén op één miljoen*, 1987)

Six

In the morning Luna is lying next to me in bed. Carmen is on the other side of me, sound asleep. I whisper to Luna that it might be nice to go to the spare room, because Frank and Maud are in there. She jumps up, wildly enthusiastic.

'Sssshhht!' I whisper in alarm. 'Mama still has to sleep!'

'Oh, yeah,' she says quietly, with her hand over her mouth.

I go into the room where Frank and Maud are sleeping. Frank is still asleep. Maud is lying reading, wearing a long T-shirt. It doesn't look like she's had a wild night. Shame. Carmen would have been pleased. Maud waves at Luna, who leaps excitedly on top of her.

I go back downstairs, and creep into bed beside Carmen. She's still asleep. I give her a loving look, gently take her hand and hold it tightly, as quietly as I can. Her breathing is heavy. Slow, with irregular pauses. Is it my imagination, or are the pauses getting longer? If she were to die now, in her sleep, it would actually be lovely. She looks peaceful. Suddenly it occurs to me I have absolutely no experience of death. What happens? When does the body decide to stop breathing, to stop the heartbeat? Does it happen very slowly? Do you see it coming? Does anything else happen just before? And do you have to call a doctor straight away, or do you just have to let it happen? I have no idea of the etiquette of dying, or rather *letting someone die*. I just have to trust my feeling, and my feeling tells me Carmen is so peaceful right now she could pass away as far as I'm concerned.

The slow breathing goes on for ten minutes. And then Carmen starts breathing normally again. Just as she did when she was alive. That's OK too.

Let's just make another nice day out of it.

I have become comfortably numb . . .

Pink Floyd, from 'Comfortably Numb' (*The Wall*, 1979)

Seven

When Carmen wakes up I ask her if she wants anything to eat.

'Yes. Half a morphine pill.'

'Are you in pain again?'

She nods. 'Terrible pain. My back.'

'Then I'll give you a whole one.'

'Are we supposed to do that?'

'What else? Scared it's going to kill you?'

She bursts out laughing. 'If only . . .'

All of a sudden her face grows taut. 'Isn't it time to tell Luna I soon won't be here?'

'I've already prepared her for that a little bit this morning.'

'And what did she say?'

'That' – gulp – 'it was OK if it meant you aren't in pain any more and you don't have to be sick.'

Together we cry over our little ray of sunshine.

'Feeling a bit better?' I ask after a while. She nods. 'Shall I read out the emails you've got?' She nods again. Like a real star, she replies to her fans. Like a real secretary I type in the answers Carmen dictates. In all her replies she says how happy she is now. 'You've written a lovely piece in your diary for Luna, too,' I say. 'I want to read it at the funeral service in the church.'

'Oh? What was it?'

I take Carmen's diary to Luna, open it at the page where I've stuck a yellow Post-it note, and start reading.

I really hope I'll leave something behind with people, and they'll tell you about it later. In fact I think, and not just now I'm sick, that if you want something in life you've got to go ahead and do it. You have to enjoy every day, because you don't know all the things that are going to happen later on. Now that sounds like an awful cliché, but it's the only way I can think of putting it.

Once when I was an au pair in London we used to go out a lot to pubs and restaurants. I remember that at one point I had one pair of shoes with holes in the soles. I had no money to get them mended. At least, if it was a choice between new soles on my shoes or a nice evening out with my mates, I opted for the latter. I thought to myself: I'll be happier if I go out and do something nice with other people than if I stay at home on my own with new soles on my shoes.

After that I travelled around the world. I hear about lots of people who wish they'd done the same, but never got round to it. Luna, there are often a hundred reasons not to do something, but just one reason to do it should be enough. It would be very sad if you regretted things you haven't done, because in the end you can only learn from all the things you do.

'There's something in that, if I say it myself,' she says, blushing.

After that I finish off the suitcase full of souvenirs of Carmen I've made for Luna. I read out a few of the letters friends, family and colleagues have written to our daughter.

Ramon writes that he only met Carmen once or twice, at parties in the agency where Papa and he worked at the time, so he can't say all that much about Mama's character, but he does have very precise memories of Carmen. 'I still remember how proud Papa was of her, when he introduced me to her. And how jealous I was of him. Luna, I'm not going to beat around the bush, I'm going to say exactly what I feel: your Mama was a gorgeous woman. I'll tell Papa you're not to read this until you're old enough, but your mother had ti – erm, breasts that turned everyone's heads. So. At least you know that. X, Ramon, Papa's amigo.'

Carmen laughs out loud. 'How nice of him to write that . . .'

I read the mails that have come in yesterday and today. As I read them aloud, Carmen dozes off every now and again. Sometimes she comes back all of a sudden.

'Danny, have you had our wedding photograph enlarged?'

'What?'

'Our wedding photograph. Very big. On the mantelpiece.'

'Ah, no . . .'

'I was afraid of that.' She smiles. 'Good stuff, this morphine.'

Silence.

'What did you say, Danny?'

'Nothing, darling – really, nothing.'

She sighs. 'I'm tired – I'm going to sleep for a bit. Are you all going to be eating up here again?'

> The morphine still makes Carmen
> hallucinate sometimes, but she still
> enjoys everything. I'm proud and happy
> for her. X.

Then we'll drink for seven days,
then we'll drink, such a thirst,
there's enough for everyone,
so let's drink together,
tap the barrel,
then we'll drink together, such a thirst,
then we'll eat, for seven days, then we'll eat ...

Bots, from 'Zeven dagen lang' (*Voor God en Vaderland*, 1976)

Eight

The shopkeepers on Cornelis Schuytstraat are rubbing their hands over Carmen's final send-off. It's like army catering. Van Nugteren, the posh greengrocer, is raking it in with trays of sun-dried tomatoes, grapes and vegetable salad. Nan, the delicatessen supermarket, can barely carry in our daily quantities of milk, pepper pâté, roast beef and steak tartare (bought by the au pair, under protest), farmhouse cheese, egg salad and bread rolls for breakfast and lunch chez Dan & Carmen & Luna & Maud & Frank & Carmen's mother & Co. The pharmacy on Cornelis Schuytstraat thinks we're going to set up our own pharmacy, or our own cycling team. Every day someone comes to collect a new prescription for Ms Carmen van Diepen. They have to sort out the prednisone, kytril, paracetamol with codeine, temazepam, primperan, vitamin drinks, morphine and lemon-flavoured cotton wool sticks to make the taste of vomit in Carmen's mouth a bit more bearable. Pasteuning, the off-licence, ask with a laugh if we're having a party, when I ring them up to order another two cases of rosé. We get through at least four bottles a night. And that's not counting the afternoon. Every time I come downstairs, there are new people sitting in the garden, the sitting-room and the kitchen. And they all want feeding.* A deathbed like that is certainly very sociable, but it does cost a fortune. Now I understand where the phrase 'fatally expensive' comes from.

'Money doesn't make you happy, but you can have one hell of a lot of fun with it,' says Carmen. She enjoys the fact we're an open house. Everybody wants to see Carmen again as much as they possibly can. No one wants to miss a thing. It's a bit like an event like Pinkpop, Dance Valley, the Parade, Carnival or the Breda Jazz Festival. Intoxicating. You'd almost hope a deathbed like this came round again every year.

The deathbed scene has been going on for a week now, but Carmen's feeling great. Even better than she did at the start of the week. The morphine gets her quite painlessly through the day. 'And you get to see loads of stuff, with all those hallucinations,' she points out. Even the vomiting doesn't bother her any more. She's got just as used to it as to blowing her nose.

'So shall I postpone the potion from the chemist's for a few days?' the doctor asks.

'Yes. Just call it injury time,' I say.

'Or extra time with sudden death!' Carmen adds with a laugh.

Bakker looks at us a little strangely, but also comes to the

---

*   Wrample from Wim Sonneveld, 'De Jongens' (*Conferences*, 1970).

conclusion that euthanasia in this pool of fun* might be a little on the early side.

Carmen asks if I want to set up a visitors' roster for the next few days. Apart from a few repeat visits from parents and her best girlfriends, she really wants to see her colleagues from Advertising Brokers, a few friends from her middle school years, and the women from the Mouflon. I phone everyone and come up with a pretty tight schedule. While the girls from Advertising Brokers are upstairs, I hear explosions of laughter every now and again. After an hour and a half I go upstairs to tell them the meet and greet is over. The star has to rest. An hour later the Mouflon women are standing on the doorstep (or at least the ones who are still alive), and this afternoon the undertaker's dropping by, too.

---

*   Wrample from Henk Elsink, *Harm met de harp* (1961).

I never say die and I never take myself too seriously…

Fun Lovin' Criminals, from 'The Fun Lovin' Criminals'
(*Come Find Yourself*, 1996)

Nine

The undertaker sat down beside Carmen's bed. She wanted to discuss her 'farewell party', so I found one in the Yellow Pages and called him over.

We show him the layout and text for the invitations.

'Just look at that,' the man says in astonishment, 'you've already got the layout done for the mourning cards.'

'The invitations,' Carmen corrects him.

'Erm – yes, quite. The invitations.'

We tell him we want Carmen to be laid out at home. And we want to have a service in the Obrechtkerk, which is just around the corner from us. So as long as Luna and I are living here, we'll be reminded of Carmen by 'Mama's church bells' every half-hour. We make it clear we ourselves, along with our parents and friends, want to do the service. We show him Carmen's CD, which has been ready for months, and tell him which songs we want to hear in the church. He says he'll find out if they've got a sound system in there. I say it doesn't matter, we'll sort everything out ourselves.

We tell him Carmen wants to be buried in Zorgvlied, and we want to go on to De Mirandapaviljoen for a drink afterwards.

'And a bite to eat,' says Carmen. 'Brownies, scones, waffles, bagels with salmon and cream cheese and Häagen-Dazs ice-cream. Macadamia Nut Brittle.'

'You don't need to write anything down,' I say when I see he's got his pen out. 'Two of our friends are already sorting out the food.'

The man likes the way we're going about things.

'Might I be able to help you choose a coffin, or had you got that sorted out already, too?' he asks with amusement.

'Let's have a look at what you've got,' says Carmen.

We choose a simple, white coffin. 'My blue Replay dress will match it nicely,' says Carmen. She looks at me. 'At least if you think it'll look pretty.'

I say I think it suits her very well. I can't quite bring myself to say the word 'pretty'.

'And the car to go to the church?' asks the undertaker.

'White. Nothing too showy.'

'Fine.'

'Now – I can't really say "see you again", can I?' says Carmen.

The man laughs sheepishly and goes.

'It would have been funny if he'd said "break a leg",' observes Carmen once he's out the door.

■

That evening we all eat by Carmen's bed again. The usual pot of green fodder the au pair has been ladling up for us for a week now was starting to lose its appeal. This evening I told the mob at our house I would kill for a rissole, chips with peanut butter and mayo or a great big tub of Chinese food. Lots of people seemed to agree. So I've given the au pair the evening off.

315

Maud and Frank go to the local oriental takeaway and come back with loads of sticky morsels. It's been days since we ate anything that wasn't green or yellow, and the babi pangang and ku lu yuk are joyfully devoured in the bedroom. The toast of the party, as Carmen calls herself, makes do with two cartons of yogurt.

Within a few minutes she feels sick. She does her best to throw up, but it doesn't work. She sticks a finger down her throat and retches, but nothing comes out.

'Christ almighty, why won't it come?' she curses.

All of a sudden out it all comes, including that morning's little bit of Fruit 'n Fibre. Like in a cartoon. As Carmen throws up, I kiss her on the top of her head. I give her tissues. Everybody's quiet. After one final stream of vomit her voice can be heard through the bucket: 'Christ, it's like the grave in here! Has somebody died or something?'

There's silence for a moment. And then everyone bursts out laughing.

> Though nothing will keep us together,
> we could steal time, just for one day,
> I, I will be king, and you, you will be queen,
> we can be heroes, just for one day . . .

David Bowie, from 'Heroes' (*Heroes*, 1977)

Ten

'Then I'll wear that new Diesel jacket over the dress,' says Carmen, when she wakes up in the morning. 'But I'm not quite sure which shoes to wear with it. Probably my Pumas.'

I have no idea which ones she means. Over the last few months she's come home every week with all kinds of new shoes, boots and clothes.

'What about you? Are you going to buy anything new?'

'Yeah. I'm not quite sure yet. I recently saw some kind of sand-coloured suit in a shop, I could wear it to work as well. Or a shiny cream suit by Joop I saw on P.C. Hooftstraat. But I could only wear it to parties.'

'Do that,' says Carmen enthusiastically. 'I'd rather you associated me with parties than work, afterwards.'

I laugh, touched, and hug her. She smells. Carmen hasn't had a bath for a week.

'I'm going to spoil you. You're going to have a bath.'

'Danny, no, it'll never work . . .'

'Just trust me,' I say and go to the bathroom. I fill the bath and put in her favourite bath-oil. I take the softest towel I can find in the cupboard and prepare two facecloths, a clean pair of panties and a clean pair of pyjamas. To spare her thin buttocks, I put three double-folded towels on the bottom of the bath. After that I go back to the bedroom.

'Now lift your arse for a moment.' I take off her pyjama trousers and give a start. She's got thinner again over the past few days. Her bottom has disappeared, and the little V above the cleft of her buttocks, which I always found so sexy, has gone.

I take off her pyjama jacket and recoil. You could count her ribs with your bare eyes. Her remaining breast is an empty D cup. She is shivering with cold. I quickly throw a dressing-gown over her shoulders. Then I lift her into the wheelchair and push her to the bathroom. I put the wheelchair parallel to the bath. She's scared.

'Don't worry. I won't let you fall in.'

I take off my dungarees and socks, put one foot in the bath and the other next to it. When I know for sure I'm stable, I lift her up and tell her she only has to put one leg into the bath, and it doesn't have to take her weight. Then the other leg. I bend my knees and ask Carmen to do the same. A moment later she's lying in the warm water. Her eyes fill with tears of pleasure. I dip the facecloth in the warm water, rub it with soap and start to wash her.

'Oooohh – that's wonderful,' she says, her eyes closed. Desperately tired, inwardly contented. I let the facecloth slide over her thin body. From her feet I move to her legs. Via her crotch to her belly. I wash her one, shrunken breast and then, taking a deep breath, move to the right. And then, for the very first time, I touch the place where her breast once was. My facecloth passes over it as though it was the most normal place in the world. She opens her eyes and says to me gently, 'Come here . . .'

I lean my head towards her. She kisses me on the mouth.

'I love you,' she whispers.

When I've finished washing her, I dry her off, performing the same exercise in reverse. In the bedroom, I put her in the clean pyjamas. Within two minutes she's asleep.

In the toilet I tap in a text.

> **I'm in a complete state, Rose. I'd love to hear from you soon. X. ?**

She rings straight away. I tell her what I've just done, and burst into tears. Rose comforts me and says that these weeks, after the event, will look like a present for my whole life. And that Frank called her this afternoon and gave her a detailed report on how things were going here. Rose says she's proud of me.

When I've hung up, I go to the bedroom and kiss my sleeping Carmen gently on the top of her head. With a blissful smile, I fall asleep.

Baby, is there no chance,
I can take you for a last dance . . .

The Troggs, from 'With a Girl Like You'
(*With a Girl Like You*, 1968)

Eleven

'Dan?'

'Yes?' I say sleepily. I notice the light's on. I look at the clock. It's a quarter past one in the morning. Everyone in the house is asleep.

'I'm hungry—'

'What would you like?'

'Erm – poffertjes.'

'Give us a minute, then.'

A little later we're sitting on the bed eating little puffy pancakes in the middle of the night.

'I think I'll wear the Gucci trainers rather than the Pumas.'

'Hm?'

'In the cupboard. With my blue dress.'

It's a moment before I get what she's saying. Then I burst out laughing. I can't stop. Carmen gets hysterical too.

'Stop, stop, I'll pee in my pants – ' she says, sobbing with laughter. Her sphincter isn't working as well as it might.

'Shall I put on some music?' I ask, when I've stopped laughing. 'Your own CD? Could you cope?'

She nods. We sing along with the songs, through the

320

pancakes. Track six is the opening dance from our wedding. 'Shall we dance?' I ask.

'Lunatic!'

I lift her up. Her feet just touch the ground. She hangs in my arms, and I turn her round, rocking gently. We're dancing more slowly than we did at our wedding, but we're dancing. Me in my underpants, Carmen in her silk pyjamas. I gently sing the lyrics in her ear.

I want to spend my life with a girl like you – And do all the things that you want me to – I tell by the way you dress that you're so real fine – And by the way you talk that you're just my kind – Till that time has come and we might live as one – Can I dance with you . . .*

When the song is over, I give her a French kiss. It's more intimate than sex.

I wake up half an hour later. The poffertjes are coming back up.

'I'm fine,' she says from the bucket. 'They were really delicious.'

She takes a tissue and wipes her mouth. 'So. I'm going back to sleep. Night night.'

---

* From 'With a Girl Like You' by The Troggs (1968).

Waiting for that day . . .

George Michael, from 'Waiting for that Day'
(*Listen Without Prejudice*, 1990)

Twelve

The eighth and ninth days of Carmen's deathbed scene come and go. Every now and again she cries. When the pain in her back gets too much for a while. When she has to cough, and notices she's losing a little urine. When she's a bit lost because of the morphine, which she needs more and more to keep the pain down. Much of the day she's as dazed as an Italian coffee-shop tourist.

The other thing that makes her cry is Luna, whom she's been able to love and enjoy for only three years. 'If only she was a brat,' she laughs through her tears when she's been watching a *Sesame Street* video with Luna next to her on the bed.

In the bedroom in the evening, when the rest of the gang downstairs are drinking rosé, we sometimes cry together. When we drag up memories of the holidays we've had, about our friends, about the beautiful moments we've enjoyed. But more often we laugh.

Every morning Carmen excitedly asks what our plans are for the day. Who's coming to see her today. By now she's seen everyone she wanted to see. I've just counted them, and in nine days thirty-six people have been by her bedside. Some of them came once, others we couldn't keep away.

Every now and again friends, both male and female, come downstairs in tears.

'She said she felt so sorry for us for having to put up with such misery,' sobs Anne, when she's been with Carmen for an hour or so. I go upstairs to see if Carmen is equally emotional. When I walk into the bedroom, she's sitting on the edge of the bed smoking a cigarette. Her thin legs are swinging back and forth, the hand holding the cigarette trembling so much she can barely bring it to her mouth. Her grin covers the whole of her face. As though nothing's wrong. Mentally, she's been the strongest of all of us over the past few days.

The days pass according to the same pattern. We all have lunch and dinner together upstairs, Carmen spews merrily away, the au pair sighs and moans as she does the housework, Maud, Frank and Carmen's mother receive the guests and play with Luna, and I lift Carmen on to and off the potty a few times a day, and take the buckets of stool and vomit to the toilet.

Her liver has now clearly given up the ghost: her stools are grey, her urine dark brown. Carmen's eyes are as yellow as a Post-it note. Her eyes are set deep in their sockets. Today I collected the photographs I took of Carmen with everyone who's come to visit this week. I don't think anyone's going to want them afterwards. In practically all the pictures, particularly the ones taken over the last two days, Carmen looks dreadful. She looks like she weighs less than forty kilograms. I think she actually does.

When I've been to the toilet to empty the puke-bucket for the umpteenth time that day, I hear her shouting.

'Dan! Oh, be quick – I'm busting for a pee all of a sudden . . .' The TENA Lady I bought for her yesterday might work for coughing urine and laughing urine, but it won't stand up to a proper stream. I run to her. 'Stay in bed. I'll put the potty underneath you.'

'No – I can't keep it in any more,' she cries in panic, 'Oh – it's almost coming, Danny . . .'

I quickly grab a few towels from the cupboard, pull down Carmen's pyjama trousers, shove a double-folded towel under her buttocks and press another one against her crotch. She drenches it with her pee. So here I am. With a towel pressed against her pussy. Her pussy I was always so wild about. Her pussy I've licked hundreds of times. That I've stuck my cock into, my fingers, my tongue, everything you can imagine. Her pussy in which I came time after time after time the first night I went out with her. Her pussy, which she held open for me with both hands to make me even hornier than I was already. Her pussy that she yelled at me in encouragement to fuck harder and harder. That pussy which I'm now dabbing dry with a big towel because my dear darling can't hold in her pee any more. Carmen weeps with shame.

'It doesn't matter, my love,' I whisper. I hold her tight and kiss her all over. My little scrap of fantastic humanity.

When I've washed her crotch and her thighs, I go and lie next to her and stroke her face. She's miserable. 'You can't cope with this either, Danny, can you? I'm scared I'm going to have to lie here like this for weeks, and it's going to get worse and worse,' she sobs. 'I don't know if I want to go on . . .'

A slight shock runs through me. For a moment I wonder how to say it. 'Darling, I've always been able to think about this with you, but in the end it has to be your decision. I'm happy to be able to look after you, and I want to do that for many weeks to come. But if you don't want to go on, then I understand that too. I'm OK with whatever you decide.'

She nods. 'Thank heavens. I've seen all the people I wanted to see, and done what I wanted to do. I've said all that I wanted to say. I want to stop. Tomorrow.'

'Are you absolutely sure?'

'Yes.'

'Then I'll go and call the doctor right now.'

I've lived a life that's full,
I travelled each and every highway . . .

Frank Sinatra, from 'My Way' (*My Way*, 1969)

Thirteen

Our family doctor walks slowly up the stairs in front of me. He pointedly rubs his back. I refuse to ask. I endure the lamentations of our au pair because it's so nice to be able to grumble about them with Frank, Maud and Carmen's mother, but a doctor shouldn't complain. Certainly not when my wife's morphined up to the eyeballs and is going to die tomorrow.

'How's your back?' Carmen asks when he comes into the room.

Before he can answer, I dart him a cross look.

'Oh, it's fine, thank you. But you're not doing so well, are you?' he asks Carmen hastily.

'No. The pain's worse than it was yesterday, and there are whole stretches when I can't remember anything at all. I don't want to go on. I want to stop tomorrow,' she says firmly.

Bakker studies her closely. 'Fine. I'll tell you what will happen. Tomorrow I'll bring a potion with me. You have to drink it. After that, you'll be gone within thirty seconds. You won't feel a thing.'

'Sounds great,' says Carmen.

The doctor laughs. 'Do you want anybody to be there when it happens?'

'Just Danny,' says Carmen without hesitation.

I beam with pride, as though she's just invited me to watch the Champions League Final from her VIP box.

'Well,' the doctor concludes, 'then I'll give you a call tomorrow morning to hear if you're sticking with your decision, and you'll see me again tomorrow towards the end of the day.'

I'm already growing nervous about the moment when I hear the doorbell ring late tomorrow afternoon. As though the hangman's at the door.

Downstairs I tell them that Carmen has opted for euthanasia, and it's going to happen tomorrow. Everybody's relieved. Now it's certain. Frank, Maud and Carmen's mother go and busy themselves with the room where Carmen's going to be laid out. Anne takes Luna into town to find sunflower clasps for Luna's hair. I take my laptop into the garden to write the loveliest speech I can manage around Carmen's letter to Luna.

At the end of the afternoon I go to the bedroom.

'I've got my address ready . . .'

'Can I hear it?' she says, eyes gleaming.

'Yes.' I start reading. She listens, with her eyes closed.

– You wanted to give people something, you wrote to Luna. You wanted them to enjoy every day. To enjoy your funeral. To enjoy the rest of their lives. To enjoy love, friendship, beautiful clothes, little things, decadent things. Enjoyment is an art of living. And you were a professional expert in the art of living.

'And then I'll read the text you wrote for Luna.'

I look at Carmen. She wipes her tears away.

'You're my hero . . .' she whispers.

Carmen has decided to say goodbye
tomorrow evening. I'm going to be there.
Will you keep Tuesday evening free for
me? I'll need you. X.

When you're chewing on life's gristle,
don't grumble, give a whistle,
life's a laugh and death's a joke, it's true…

Monty Python, from 'Always Look on the Bright Side of Life'
(*Life of Brian*, 1979)

Fourteen

I lie awake that night. Because of something I don't dare tell anyone. I'm not sure I can cope with my first *live* experience of death. I've seen a few dead people. Two in coffins and one in the street, but luckily that one was under a car, so I couldn't see him properly. So he doesn't actually count.

The two in coffins were an aunt of mine – and I wasn't especially scared of her because she looked terrifying enough when she was alive – and my grandmother, who I couldn't stand. That's not to say I was particularly comfortable about those corpses. No, I'm not a great fan of death. And seeing someone die *live* isn't exactly my idea of a party.

Now, I find this anxiety of mine pretty embarrassing. Carmen isn't scared, and she's the one who's going to be putting death *into practice*. I'm just going to be watching. For the first time in my life I'm going to be seeing someone die and, on top of everything, it's going to be my wife. I mean, when you're playing football you start the season by playing Klokkentorense Boys or somebody, don't you? Why can't I be broken in lightly by watching someone I don't care about kicking the bucket? A passer-by in the street, say, or someone having a heart attack in the stand at an Ajax game? Why does it have to be Carmen I'm going to see die tomorrow?

And another thing: am I going to have to phone the funeral director tomorrow, to say we'd like to confirm the booking for the dressing of the body, ideally after – and, if possible, soon after – Carmen's planned death? Shall we say around seven in the evening? With a margin of an hour or so either way, if that's possible, or is that difficult to plan? Do you book something like that in advance? Or maybe I'll ring him and discover that, of course, I should have called much sooner, they've got six corpses to deal with right now, and that our turn won't come until the end of the week at the earliest.

And then? Two hours after Carmen has died and been washed in our bed, am I supposed to lie down happily in the very same bed? Am I allowed to say I find that ever so slightly weird?

They don't tell you any of *that* on the euthanasia website.

And I know it aches, and your heart it breaks,
and you can only take so much, walk on, walk on . . .

U2, from 'Walk On' (*All That You Can't Leave Behind*, 2000)

Fifteen

Carmen wakes me up. It's half-past six in the morning. She's crying.

I take her in my arms and press her to me.

'This is my last day . . .'

'Would you rather go on?'

'No . . . but . . . it's just so strange . . . Would you do one more thing for me?'

'What?'

'Will you send away any extra visitors who come today? I find it so hard to do it myself . . . And I don't want to miss any time with Luna and you . . .'

Yesterday Carmen herself determined how much time she wants with everyone, who's to come together, and who's to come on his or her own. Like a rock star organizing interviews.

'And will you phone the doctor? Say we're going ahead.'

> Hi. It's going to be pretty intense today.
> Everyone here is miserable, but also
> relieved today's the day. Think about me a
> lot and light an extra candle for Carmen.
> X.

The first ones to go upstairs are Thomas and Anne. They sit with Carmen for about an hour. Then they come downstairs. Anne keeps her composure. Thomas asks me to come with him for a moment. We stand in the kitchen. His eyes are red. 'I miss her so terribly already.'

He throws an arm around me, takes my head in his big hands and kisses me on my forehead. For the first time since I've known him, the Bear of Maarssen kisses me.

'Danny, I, um – I have to say I've not always been, um – a good friend over the past year. I'm not much of a – a talker when it comes down to it. And – and maybe I've neglected you a little sometimes – Carmen told me about that woman, what was her name, Toni, from the Mouflon. How she and her husband got divorced. And about the chemo, and how you were the only ones who went along together. And how you carried her through all that time. And how happy you've made her over the past few weeks. I – I'm proud of you, man.'

He hugs me so firmly I'm worried I'm going to suffer the same injury as our doctor, but the moment's too beautiful to complain. We cry. Both of us. And then we burst out laughing.

'That's enough now, you big poof,' I blub, laughing.

'Yeah. You wanker.'

'Tosser.'

'Twat.'

With our arms around each other's shoulders we walk into the garden. Maud looks at us like she's seeing Louis van Gaal singing a duet with Johan Cruyff.

Frank has a big smile on his face as he comes downstairs. 'It was really nice. We had a good laugh.'

Maud comes back sobbing. 'It was wonderful. She looks really quite relieved.'

332

Most people don't come downstairs of their own accord, and I have to force them gently to bring the session to an end. Carmen lies there like a queen, enjoying all the lovely things people are saying to her, all the wonderful conversations. Soon we're over an hour and a half behind schedule. I haven't the heart to herd people out of the room, like a policeman, before they are ready. But neither am I too keen on the idea of being the closing entry in Carmen's book, and not having enough time with her.

'Is it OK if I call the doctor to say we're running late?' I ask.

'Yeah, do that. This is nice. And there's no hurry, is there?'

I call the doctor and ask if he could come at half-past seven rather than half-past five. 'She's enjoying herself too much at the moment.'

Carmen's mother is the last one before Luna and me. She's back in a quarter of an hour. I'm ready to catch her, but she isn't emotional. She looks happy.

'We'd said everything we had to say,' she says. 'All she said was "See you on Friday at my funeral."'

Never forget who you are, little star,
never forget where you come from, from love . . .

Madonna, from 'Little Star' (*Ray of Light*, 1998)

Sixteen

Luna spent this morning at the crèche. I didn't want her to have to face people in tears all day. On the way there I explained to her the doctors couldn't make Mama better any more. Luna reacted with a sober 'Oh'. I told her she'd be seeing Mama for the last time this afternoon. And after that Mama will die.

'Like Little Bird?' she asks.

'Yes,' I sobbed, 'just like Little Bird.'

'And like Elvis and Beavis?'

'Yes.' I laughed. 'Just like Elvis and Beavis.'

'But Mummy isn't going down the toilet. Not to fish heaven.'

'No. Mama is going to human heaven. And once she's there she'll be the loveliest angel there is.'

I've just picked her up. The assistants, whom I've kept informed about developments at the front for the past few weeks, said Luna proudly told the other children her mother was going to die this evening, and turn into an angel. Suddenly Luna was the most popular toddler in the group.

I have a knot in my stomach when I walk into the bedroom with Luna. Carmen starts crying the moment she sees us.

'Will you explain?' she asks me in a tremulous voice.

I nod.

'Luna, will you come and sit on my lap?' I ask. We sit down right next to Carmen's bed. Luna is very calm. She studies her Mama intensely. She doesn't look away, just stares at Carmen.

I begin.

'I told you Mama is very ill, and she's going to die today, didn't I?'

Luna nods.

'Later a doctor will come, and he'll bring a potion with him. Mama is going to drink the potion, and then she'll go to sleep. But it isn't real sleep, because you don't wake up again afterwards. Then she won't be in pain any more, she won't be ill.'

'And she won't have to throw up any more?'

'No. Then' – I have to stop for a moment, because I see Carmen's tears trickling down her cheeks – 'then she won't have to throw up any more.'

Meanwhile Carmen takes Luna's hand and starts stroking it.

'And then she'll die. Very peacefully.'

'And will Mama have to go in a box?'

'Yes. Then Mama will go in a box.'

'Like Snow White?'

'Yes. But even prettier,' I say, my face drenched with tears.

Luna looks at me and kisses me on the cheek. I go on.

'And we'll put that box in the sitting-room, with a glass cover on it. And Mama will have her prettiest dress on.'

'Which dress?' Luna asks, curious.

'The blue one,' says Carmen.

'Wait a minute, I'll go and get it,' I say.

I pick up the Replay dress that's been hanging against the wardrobe behind her bed for days.

'Nice, isn't it?' I ask.

Luna nods.

'And then we can look at Mama for a few more days, for as long as we like, but she won't be able to say anything back.'

Luna nods again. She seems to find the whole thing perfectly logical.

'And then when Mama has been lying in the sitting-room for a few days, we'll go to the church, with loads of friends of Mama's, to sing songs and tell lovely stories about Mama. And then we'll bury Mama. Just like Little Bird in the book, do you remember?'

I see she's a bit crestfallen.

'But isn't Mama going to heaven?'

Carmen laughs.

'Yes. But it's very hard to explain. Even grown-ups don't understand it exactly,' I say. 'I think Mama's body will be buried, but she'll get another body in heaven.'

'An angel's body!' cries Luna enthusiastically.

'Yes...' I say, biting my lip.

'I think it's a shame Mama's dying.'

'Me too, darling,' whispers Carmen, 'me too.'

'Won't I be able to see you any more?'

'No. Later, when you're very old, and you die too and turn into an angel as well, then I think we'll see each other again...' says Carmen.

'Oh...'

'That's why we've put loads of things of Mama's in that trunk over there. Later, when you're a bit bigger, you can read them and look at them.'

'And Papa will be able to tell you all about me. And later, perhaps you'll have a new Mama as well,' says Carmen.

Silence.

'What do you think?' I ask Carmen, because I don't know how else to ask if she's ready to say goodbye to her daughter.

'Let's just do it.' Carmen weeps.

She stretches out her arms. I put Luna on the ground. Now she's standing next to Carmen's bed.

'I love you, darling,' says Carmen.

'I love you,' says Luna, suddenly confused.

And then she starts kissing Carmen. Over her whole face. Everywhere. Like she's never done before. Luna kisses Carmen's cheek, her eyes, her forehead, her other cheek, her mouth – Luna wipes away a tear from Carmen's cheek. My heart aches, I'd give anything if I could change this, I'd . . . I'd . . .

There's nothing I can do about it.

Except to kneel down next to Carmen and Luna for our very last group cuddle.

Then I break away and walk towards the door with Luna.

Carmen nods.

'Bye, my own little darling,' she says again, intensely miserable.

Luna doesn't say anything. She waves at Carmen, with one hand in mine. And she blows a kiss at Carmen. Carmen holds her hand to her mouth, crying.

Luna and I walk out of the bedroom. Carmen will never see Luna again.

God, please let there be a heaven where they'll see each other again.

Please.

Please.

Please, God.

You go, I'll stay here, but I want to thank you,
for what you've done, farewell always comes too soon . . .

Tröckener Kecks, from 'Een dag, zo mooi'
(*Andere plaats, andere tijd*, 1992)

Seventeen

We've already said all we have to say to each other. But we have another hour and a half together before the doctor comes. Like when you're on holiday and you have to spend the last hour waiting for the bus to take you to the airport. I want to do a Carmen-style farewell. I go and get the video camera, switch it on and film the text Maud and Frank painted on the sitting-room wall this morning. I take off my dungarees and T-shirt and put on the blue shirt I set out ready this morning. The one that matches Carmen's dress. Then I take the cream suit out of the plastic Oger bag and put that on, too.

In the bedroom I go and stand by the bed and spread my arms.

'Look. Shopping is healthy,' I say.

Her eyes begin to twinkle. 'You've bought it!'

'For you. And?'

'It's gorgeous . . .' She's touched. She laughs and smiles at the same time. She gestures to me to turn round. 'It's really fantastic – it looks great on you. Will you always think of me when you're wearing it?'

'Always. At every party I go to.'

'Then I know for sure you'll be thinking of me loads,' she laughs.

I go and lie next to her, and hug her as best I can. For several minutes we don't say a word.

'I'm curious about the other side,' Carmen says suddenly. She says it like she's about to go to a film she's heard a lot about. 'I'm glad it's about to happen. And however much I miss you and Luna, I'm glad I'm not in your shoes. Left alone with Luna, without you – I wouldn't have the strength. I wouldn't want to swap with you . . .'

'Nor I with you . . .'

'Pretty lucky, then, aren't we?' She laughs.

We talk, as we have done so often over the last few weeks, about us. Why we fell in love with each other, what we value in each other, what we've learned from each other, all the things we've done together. We're happy we've been us. Fuck all the rows, all the problems, fuck the cancer, fuck the evening of the car accident, fuck Pim, fuck Sharon and fuck all the women I've screwed, apart from Rose. And Maud.

'Shall we take off our wedding rings?' I ask cautiously.

'Yes.' We hold each other's hands tightly and repeat the ritual from our wedding day. Just the other way round. I put the rings in a silver jewellery box and put it in the trunk of souvenirs for Luna.

Carmen looks at the ring on my other ring finger.

'Can I put it on you again?' she asks, embarrassed.

I take the ring she gave me six months ago off my finger and give it to Carmen. She tries to read the words she had engraved on the inside of the ring. She can't do it.

'*To my great love. xxx Carmen,*' I read out loud.

'Oh, yes,' she says, looking contentedly at the ring.

She tries to shove it on to my finger, but hasn't the strength. We do it together.

'Will you keep it on?'

'Always.'

'Good,' she says gently.

Silence.

'I've got something to cheer you up,' I say.

I pick up the video camera. Over the past few days I've put the whole house on video. The house we bought together – the only part of which, for the last eleven days, aside from a quarter of an hour bathing, Carmen has seen is the bedroom. My voice on the tape provides a commentary:

> Hi Carmen. It's been a while, so you mightn't recognize it: this is our garden. Here you can see the new parasol under which, as usual, Frank, Maud and your mother are getting pissed from eleven in the morning onwards, while their best friend and daughter lies fatally ill upstairs in bed – *Laughter* – Perhaps you could manage to be polite enough to raise a toast to Carmen? – *They raise their glasses, cheering* – You'll note that Maud is barely capable of lifting her glass, and your mother has drunk so much she can hardly talk – *Bluster* . . .

Carmen laughs.

> . . . Now we're coming into the hall, and just look: hastily hung by Handyman Rick, the chandelier you bought weeks ago, but which he was too lazy to put up. We can see – *I go upstairs* – the magnificent photographs we bought in Ireland, finally on the wall, where you didn't

think they'd look nice and I did – I thought, let's take advantage of the fact you can't get out of bed . . .

Carmen laughs loudly.

. . . which brings us to the sitting-room. Anne and Thomas are sitting in here, eating a croquette, oh, correction, Thomas has two, I can see, presumably to fill up after the vegetarian mouse-food our au pair's been shovelling out for him – '*Hi Carmen!!!*' *they bellow into the camera with their mouths full* – We can clearly see the neighbourhood has gone downhill since our friends have been coming here regularly. Eating with your mouth shut is still normal practice in Maarssen. And then we have the nude photograph of you I got for my birthday, which seems to give even Frank the horn . . .

Carmen laughs and shakes her head.

. . . and finally – *the camera pans to the other part of the L-shaped room, we see an empty space, with flower-vases around the side, half of it's still empty* – you see the space of honour where – *the voice on the video-tape stalls for a moment and becomes a little softer* – you'll be laid out.

Carmen sobs and grips my hand, I ask if she wants me to stop the tape, and she shakes her head.

. . . Here we see a photograph of you, me and Luna that we took just before you went bald for the second time. I hung it up here in the sitting-room yesterday . . .

Carmen nods contentedly and says gently, 'Nice spot.'

. . . and then last but not least – *the camera pans from one wall over the table by the window, where the vases stand ready to be filled, to the other wall* – a text Frank and Maud painted on the wall at my request this afternoon, and which will always remind me of you as long as Luna and I live in this house – *the camera zooms out and shows two words sprayed the full length of the wall, in massive capitals, in silver paint; the voice falls silent as the camera settles on the two words and stays there* . . .

'Carpe Diem,' whispers Carmen, looking motionlessly at the screen on the camera. She nods and looks at me tenderly.
'Fantastic. Even the house is ready.'
The bell rings.

No alarms, no surprises, silence . . .

Radiohead, from 'No Surprises' (*OK Computer*, 1997)

Eighteen

The doctor comes upstairs with a case in his hand. He's in a good mood, and cheerfully shakes hands with both of us.

'So,' he says, and goes and sits on a chair beside our bed.

'Is your back at all better?' Carmen asks.

He begins a lengthy account about where the pain is in his back and how bad it is before it passes and what a nuisance it all is. Carmen listens politely. This time I let him get on with it. It breaks the tension a bit.

'But it's not about me,' he says, changing the subject, 'young lady – This form of cancer at such a young age is very rare. You've been terribly unlucky . . .'

'Yes. Perhaps . . .' says Carmen, looking at me.

We don't believe in bad luck any more. Bad luck doesn't exist. Luck doesn't exist. Believing in luck, in chance, is an insult to life. What's happened has happened. We'll never find out why. Perhaps in an hour Carmen will know. I could almost be jealous.

'Shall I get the things ready?' asks Dr Bakker.

We nod. He takes a little bottle from his bag.

'Have you got a big glass for me, Daniel?'

I dash down the stairs to the glass cabinet and look at the glasses. Now – yes, what sort of glass would you use for

344

something like this? I pick up a long-drink glass. 'DON'T FORGET TO THROW THE GLASS AWAY AFTER-WARDS,' I repeat to myself over and over again. Before you know it, someone else will drink out of it this evening and I'll have two funerals to organize. Bakker carefully empties the bottle into the glass. It's half full.

'It looks like water,' says Carmen.

'It tastes of aniseed. You have to drink it slowly, in one go.'

Carmen nods.

'And then in about ten seconds you'll notice you're grow-ing drowsy. So you'll have to say goodbye to each other before you drink it. Because sometimes it all happens very quickly.'

'OK.'

'Are you ready, Carmen?' the doctor asks solemnly.

'Completely,' replies Carmen with a smile.

'Then you'd better say your goodbyes.'

I lie on my side next to Carmen and put my head next to hers, looking into her eyes. We are both a bit giggly and nervous. We whisper.

'I'm glad I was your wife,' she whispers. 'I'm happy now.'

'No one who hasn't been to our house would ever believe that . . .'

'But it's true. Thank you for everything, Danny. I love you. For ever.'

I sob. 'I'll always love you, Carm . . .'

The doctor sits with his arms folded, staring out the window.

'Enjoy the rest of your life,' she says gently, and strokes my cheek.

'I will do. And I'll take good care of your daughter.'

345

'Bye, great love of mine . . .'

'Bye, lovey . . .'

We kiss each other and then Carmen tells the doctor she's ready.

'Daniel, will you help me sit Carmen upright for a moment and put a few pillows behind her back? It makes drinking easier.'

We help Carmen up. It doesn't take a lot of strength.

The doctor hands her the glass.

Carmen looks at me once more. She smiles. I take her hand.

'Here we go, then,' says Carmen. She puts the glass to her mouth and starts drinking.

While the doctor watches with great concentration, and says calmly, 'Drink it down . . . drink it down . . . drink it down . . .', for the millionth time in the past two years I find I'm incredibly proud of my wife's courage.

The glass is empty.

'It doesn't even taste too bad,' Carmen jokes, 'A bit like ouzo.'

'That's right!' says Dr Bakker, taking the pillows away from behind her back.

Carmen lies down again. She looks at me once again. Contented, calm, loving.

'Mmmm – this feels good,' she says after a few seconds, as though she's lying in a warm bath. Her eyes are closed.

Bakker looks at me and winks. Oh, he means well.

I keep stroking Carmen's hand. Bakker is holding Carmen's other wrist. He looks at his watch.

'Look, she's gone now,' he says gently, his eyes now fixed on Carmen.

I look at Carmen. My Carmen. She isn't moving any more.

'No, I'm still here,' says Carmen suddenly, very softly, and she opens her eyes for a moment.

I don't give a start, I just smile.

She doesn't say anything after that. Her breathing is slowing. So is her pulse, says the doctor.

'She'll be gone in a minute,' he says.

A minute passes. Carmen's breath stalls every now and again. 'Don't be startled,' says the doctor. 'She can't feel anything now.'

Two minutes pass. Carmen is still breathing, every now and again.

'Come on, girl, give up now,' says the doctor.

Another minute passes.

'She's very strong, isn't she! My, my.'

I'm proud of Carmen again, though I'm not actually sure you can be proud of your wife's body for not giving up when the body's boss, Carmen herself, has already stopped.

A short time passes again. Carmen breathes shallowly. She's started rasping a bit.

'It looks scarier than it is,' says the doctor.

I don't think it's scary at all. I just think it's terrible for her mother down in the garden, doubtless wondering what in heaven's name is going on. Has Carmen changed her mind?

Five minutes later – the doctor has been talking about the legal aspects of active and passive euthanasia, about assisted suicide and other terminal technicalities, and I've been answering vaguely, never taking my eyes off Carmen – he suggests giving her an intravenous injection.

'Will she feel anything?'

'No, nothing at all.'

'And her body will give up then?'

'Yes. Then she'll pass on straight away.'

'Do it then.'

Bakker looks in his bag. He takes out a syringe, fills it up with the same colourless fluid and puts it on the bedside table. Then he goes in search of a decent vein. Which he doesn't find. All of a sudden the problems with the tube during the chemo treatment shoot through me. Carmen's veins are apparently a long way under her skin. Bakker ties off Carmen's arm and looks and looks. Nada.

'Could you move aside for a moment?' he asks, and creeps round to the other side of Carmen on the waterbed, holding the syringe in one hand and supporting his full weight with the other. It looks to me like a death-defying stunt, and I don't know whether to watch anxiously or burst out laughing. If he loses his balance, he's going to fall on the euthanasia needle. Hoist with his own syringe, you might say. And I'll be sitting here with a dead doctor and Carmen's nearly dead body. Try explaining that one to the police.

Bakker can't find a vein in Carmen's other arm, either. He tries a few times, but without success. The needle can't find a vein. I can't help finding it a little bit comical. Her body is so used to enjoying life it refuses to give in.

'It'll have to be the groin, then,' says Bakker. Twenty-five minutes have passed since she drank the potion.

'Done it!' says Bakker enthusiastically.

Fifteen seconds later Carmen has stopped breathing.

I stroke her hand, kiss her forehead and feel a tear sliding down my cheek.

'Bye, my darling Carmie . . .' I whisper.

The doctor's stopped listening. He's phoning another

doctor who will have to come and verify that the euthanasia happened as it should have from the technical and legal points of view.

I go to the garden and tell them Carmen has passed away. Everyone reacts with resignation. Relieved, without daring to say so.

Frank and Maud just nod.

Thomas stares in front of him. Anne holds his hand tightly.

Luna is cheerful, and giggles as she pinches Carmen's mother's nose.

Her mother, her daughter, their friend, my wife is dead.

Love, so what is love?

André Hazes, from 'Wat is dan liefde?' (*'n Vriend*, 1980)

Epilogue

We all look at The Artist Formerly Known As Carmen.*

Well, what can you say? It doesn't look like the person Carmen was. Carmen has disappeared – God knows where to – and she's carelessly left her body behind. Whatever way you look at it – when the mortician's assistants get brazenly to work with their tight-fitting gloves, we quickly leave the room – this is a corpse. Dead as a doornail.

But it's also a good thing Carmen's dead; if she'd seen the guys who are now – erm – preparing her body, she'd have had a heart attack. When I saw them coming into the hall downstairs, walking almost soundlessly behind their boss, their hands folded piously in front of their stomachs, shivers ran down my spine. They shook hands with Carmen's mother and me and whispered professional condolences. One of them was straight out of a *Lucky Luke* cartoon – hollow cheeks, a shaved head and the posture and expression of a vulture. Bent low, angling for his chance to get to work. His colleague looks like the fat guy in the Addams Family. He's biologically bald, and flabby, and he could hardly keep from licking his lips at

---

*   From TAFKAP, The Artist Formerly Known As Prince.

the prospect of starting work on Carmen's body. Oh well, at least they've turned a hobby into a profession.

As the undertaker stands in the Carpe Diem section of our sitting-room, explaining the cooling system that Carmen's coffin and body will be standing on, I see the vulture going up the stairs. I catch a glimpse of the stretcher he and the fat man are carrying. I don't want to see that. I quickly go into the garden.

Finally Carmen's mother and I are allowed in to look. We take a deep sigh and go into the sitting-room. I'm about to see my wife's body in a coffin.

It's not a disappointment. Her bright blue Replay dress, with her Diesel bomber jacket, really suits her. Tomorrow Anne will put her make-up on, she promised. We're assuming Carmen's body isn't as vain as Carmen was herself.

Anne and Thomas say goodbye and go to Maarssen. Carmen's mother goes to bed. Frank, Maud and I open another bottle of wine. We talk about all the things we have to sort out in the next few days. The funeral is on Friday.

'Have you called everybody?' I ask.

'Yes, family, friends, colleagues: everybody.'

'Good,' I say, looking at my glass.

'Does Rose know?' Frank asks.

'Not yet,' I say, shaking my head, 'I'll just send her a text.'

Frank nods.

'I want to ask you all something,' I say, looking Maud and Frank closely in the eyes. 'I want an honest answer.'

They nod.

'I'm wondering about asking Rose to come to the funeral.'

They're both silent for a moment.

'Do it,' says Frank.

Maud waits for a moment and then nods.

'Yes. I think that would be OK.'

■

I go to bed at half-past eleven. I'm a bit startled when I come into the bedroom. My eyes go quite naturally to the place in the bed where Carmen lay for eleven days. It's empty. I take my clothes off and get into bed. Carmen's mother has already cleaned the room and thrown away the old sheets. Even so, I don't go and sleep in the middle, but on my own side.

Then I get out my phone.

> **Carmen died peacefully at a quarter past eight tonight. I was there. I feel reasonably OK right now. I'll call you tomorrow. Will you keep Friday free for the funeral?**

After that I pick up the television remote control. I look up teletext to see what the weather's going to be like in the morning. Twenty-one degrees, sunny. Mmmm. Tomorrow I'll be able to go on my own and read a paper and drink a cappuccino on the terrace of Het Blauwe Theehuis.

As I'm setting the remote control down on the bedside table, I see a pair of white trainers with a green, red and green stripe in the corner of the room. I laugh and shake my head. The Guccis she was never entirely sure about. Tomorrow I'll call the undertaker and tell him to put them on her. On the other hand, that's just silly. I get out of bed, put on a dressing-gown and pick up the trainers. Very quietly, so as

353

not to wake Luna, I go downstairs. With the trainers in my hand I go and open, quite nervously, the door to the sitting-room, where the cooling system under Carmen's coffin emits a quiet hum.

You're so vain, I bet you think this book is about you, don't you, don't you, you're so vain ...

After Carly Simon, 'You're So Vain' (*No Secrets*, 1972)

Acknowledgements

It isn't impossible there might be doctors, surgeons, psychotherapists and other kinds of healer who recognize themselves in particular characters, events or meetings. Not all of them are going to be delighted. I comfort myself with the thought that a novel is, by definition, a work of fiction.

The other characters are the fruit of my interpretation and the combination of existing people. Combination was entirely necessary, my editor said when she read the original version of my manuscript. About four hundred densely written A4 pages with a hopelessly large number of superfluous and badly developed characters (with all the names to remember it sometimes read like a family saga by the novelist Louis Couperus, although – fortunately – much nicer and – sadly – less well written), interminable descriptions of countless hospital visits, extensive adolescent-style sex scenes and, most importantly, a lot of incomprehensible philosophy stuff about the meaning of life.

The hospitals, hotels, restaurants, pubs and clubs and other locations all really exist.

Thanks

Brenda, Don, Kurt and Naat for their mercilessly critical reading of the original manuscript.

Bart H, Bart V, Engin, Eric H, Eric L, Geert, Hugo, Jan, Marco, Mars, Sieb, Sikko and Yonneke for the efforts they put into the manuscript, music, website, design, game and presentation.

Janneke and Joost for confidence.

André, Bono, Brett, Bruce, F-Side, Hans, Huub H, Huub vd L, Jan, Johan, Michael, Milan, Ramses, Rick, Ronald, Sándor, Thom and other heroes I've wrampled, for inspiration.

Juut for your consent and your strength.

Naat for everything you do for me, and everything you let me do.

Eva for I-want-to-give-you-a-kiss-quickly-Papa while I'm writing.

PS

To give to Cancer Research UK, go to
http://www.cancerresearchuk.org/donate